# PROMISE

## LEIGH MORGAN

*Sometimes, when life gives you lemons.*
*You just gotta tell it...fuck off.*

# CONTENTS

# PROMISE PLAYLIST



- Chapter 1: I Can Do It With a Broken Heart - Taylor Swift
- Chapter 1: Wings - Jackson Dean
- Chapter 6: Lighter - Galantis, David Guetta, 5 Seconds of Summer
- Chapter 7: Tearin' up My Heart - *NSYNC
- Chapter 7: Ghost - Josiah and the Bonnevilles
- Chapter 7: Austin (Boots Stop Workin') - Dasha
- Chapter 8: All The Small Things - blink-182
- Chapter 9: The One That You Call - Mackenzie Mackay
- Chapter 9: Heaven - Beyoncé
- Chapter 10: Beggin' - Måneskin
- Chapter 11: Little Life - Cordelia
- Chapter 11: The Answer to Our Life - Backstreet Boys
- Chapter 12: cut my hair - Tate McRae
- Chapter 12: Burn The House Down - AJR
- Chapter 13: Hold Me Now - Thompson Twins

- Chapter 13: All Of The Girls You Loved Before - Taylor Swift
- Chapter 15: SNAP - Rosa Linn
- Chapter 16: I'll Be There - Walk off the Earth
- Chapter 17: My Greatest Fear - Benson Boone
- Chapter 18: What Happens Now? - Dasha
- Chapter 19: DARKSIDE - Neoni
- Chapter 21: Sweet Moment - Mackenzie Mackay
- Chapter 24: Pray - Jessie Murph
- Chapter 25: Magic - Will Linley
- Chapter 27: A Bar Song (Tipsy) - Shaboozey
- Chapter 27: You're the One That I Want - Dylan Rockoff, Caroline Kole
- Chapter 29: Sweet and Dark - Miles Hardt
- Chapter 34: Three Little Birds - Bob Marley & The Wailers
- Chapter 35: Never Let Go - Blake Rose
- Chapter 36: If We Have Each Other - Alec Benjamin
- Chapter 39: Call my name - GRAHAM, Henrik
- Chapter 40: Walls Could Talk - Halsey
- Chapter 42: Before You Leave Me - Alex Warren
- Chapter 45: Afterglow - Taylor Swift
- Chapter 46: Save You a Seat - Alex Warren
- Chapter 47: high water - Tori Kelly
- Chapter 48: Dangerous Hands - Austin Giorgio
- Chapter 50: 10-90 - Muscadine Bloodline

# INTRODUCTION & TRIGGER WARNINGS

This book did not start out how it ended. I let the characters grow into whatever they needed to be. Along the way Ella and Cillian find themselves as well as each other. Walking through their individual trauma allowed them to walk together. I hope their story gives you, the reader, the power to find love. Even in the dark moments, there is light.

Trigger Warnings:

- Mention of miscarriage (not in detail)
- Depictions of grief and loss of a spouse
- Mention of child abuse (not in detail)
- Unrealistic description of a man's...thing

# PROMISE

______

Leigh Morgan

# ONE
# BEGIN AGAIN
## ELLA



"ARE WE THERE YET?"

The colorful blur of cars and highway signs whiz past us and I blink my eyes to clear the memories. Leaning against the headrest, I'm amazed that I haven't crashed while I've been zoned out. I push my fingers into the soft tissue of my eyes and rub them back into focus. I quickly glance in the rearview mirror at Rone. Stuffed between his bags, blankets, and the endless amount of toys and stuffed animals I begged him to leave behind, my son looks up at me with bored eyes.

"Almost, I promise. Not much longer," I say.

The home I recently purchased in the rolling hills of Spring Hill, Tennessee isn't too far from our old home in Huntsville, Alabama, but driving still makes me uneasy. It's been just shy of a year since the night that our lives were flipped upside down—literally. I wanted nothing more than to stay in our home, to keep everything as normal as I could for Rone. But who the fuck am I kidding? Nothing will ever be normal for us again. I figured new surroundings might help us feel like we were moving forward with this new chapter in our lives.

I can work from anywhere; my job as a writer has always given me the freedom to set up shop wherever I needed. The pool during the summer while Rone and James swam, the park while Rone and James rode bikes, the backyard while I watched James push Rone in the swing. My eyes fill with tears and I promptly wipe them away, checking in the mirror again to make sure Rone hasn't noticed.

Cars pass us, but I keep the car on cruise control, happy to take my time in the slow lane. I pull off the 396, and after a few wrong turns through the cozy, small downtown, the car dash lights up with an incoming call from my sister.

"Hey," I say, hoping that she doesn't pick up on my nerves.

"Hi, babe. I saw you just pulled into town. How is it? How's my nephew?"

"Hi, Auntie!" Rone calls out excitedly from the back. He and my sister, Olivia, have always had a special bond. We've been relying on her more than ever this past year. After everything happened, she moved in with us. She took care of Rone when I couldn't get out of bed and took care of me when I couldn't take care of myself. She and her boyfriend of three years had just broken up, and we were all just, well, broken. So, it worked out.

I'm the oldest of the two of us. My parents had us young, and now that we are grown and can take care of ourselves, our parents spend their time traveling the world. Living the life they missed out on while raising kids when they were practically kids, themselves. They flew in from Thailand when Olivia called them from the hospital and didn't leave my side for close to two months. Once I felt like I could function without my mother following me into the bathroom every time I had to pee, I strongly encouraged them to continue their travels. Now, they are in Italy–no–Greece, maybe? They'll check in eventually, but it's been months and I'm desperate to find a way to move on and have some space of our own. The looks of pity and hesitation as to what to say to me was getting old. I never wanted to be alone; I love having people around me, feeding off their energy. But after everything that my son and I have been through this past year, all I want is to be left alone.

There isn't a time I remember not having James by my side. We met in high school and were inseparable ever since. Being on my own used to terrify me. All the things I relied on for him to take care of flash through my mind while I do my best to focus on the road in front of me. I can cry about all of that later, now is not the time. *I am not afraid.* I repeat the words my therapist and I have worked on during our sessions. Gripping the steering wheel tightly in my hands, I slowly ground myself. *One, two, three. Three, two, one.* I count each breath, pushing my lungs to expand and hold before pushing the air out and doing it over again. I focus on the music playing through the car, finding the energy to create stability in the moment.

"I'm just pulling up now, plenty of daylight left to get settled and order some pizza!" I reply to Olivia.

Rone bounces in the back, giving me a thumbs up of approval.

"I can't believe you bought this place without seeing it in person! What if it's haunted?" Olivia asks over the phone.

I notice how Rone's eyes widen from the backseat and I give him a shake of my head. "Stop!" I reply. "Ghosts aren't real. Besides, the pictures looked gorgeous and the town looked adorable. It'll be great!" *It'll be great. It'll be great.* I feel like the more I say it, the more it loses its appeal.

"I have no doubt it will be a fresh start. Well, FaceTime me when you get your pizza. I'll order some, too, and we can eat together," Olivia says.

"I love you," I say.

"Love you both." Olivia's cheerful voice makes me smile.

Honestly, the last thing I wanted to do after everything happened was go look at houses. All I'd be able to picture is how half of my future would be missing. The town looked small and friendly, plus this house popped up in my price range. The pictures were beautiful; big windows, hard wood floors, and a gorgeous kitchen. It has recently been remodeled, but the lot and the garden alone would have sold me. The drive is lined with big trees that bend over the car and cast a muted glow down on us as we drive through. A long, green lawn stretches from the main road up to the house. Just when we reach the end of the drive, a gorgeous farmhouse that looks like it was made from my Pinterest board comes into view. A soft, wood door peeks out from under the front archway. Large, front windows look into the front living room on one side of the front door and another gives a view into the office space. I can see the early blooms of roses and large lavender bushes under the front of the windows, just waiting for the spring rain and summer sun to turn them into a kaleidoscope of bright colors.

Putting the car in park, Rone wastes no time unbuckling and hops out to stretch his legs. While he looks around, my heart pumps a little faster, working its way up my throat as I wait for his reaction. He's been so strong through it all, I worry I'm going to ruin his life now that I'm doing this parenting thing all on my own. He and I have never been as close as he was to James. Their bond used to make my heart burst with happiness, but now it just fills me with dread. They've been inseparable since the moment he was born. I remember laying there in the hospital bed, staring at them sleeping together in the chair next to me. James didn't wear a shirt for three days straight so he could hold Rone on his chest, skin-to-skin. Multiple times I caught the nurses stealing a glance, but I couldn't blame them.

On many occasions I catch myself thinking, *"Why me? I wish it was James that was here."*

"This is all ours..." Rone's sweet voice breaks me out of my memories. I turn to see him looking up at me with wide eyes.

Bending down so we're eye-to-eye, I reach out and wrap his little hand in mine. "Yeah, bud. What do you think?" He nods slowly, taking another look around the yard.

"Dad would have loved it," he says with conviction. I can't argue with him there–James had a way of making every situation feel like an adventure.

"I think so, too, but the real question is, do *you* love it?"

He meets my eyes and then leans around me to look at the front of the house with the stone archway on the side that leads to the garden.

"Yeah, I think I do." My eyes bulge a bit and I have to swallow my excitement. I don't ever want him to think that we moved away to forget his dad. There is nowhere we could run that would ever erase the memory of what our family used to be or what we had hoped it would be.

"We'll be ok," I reassure him, and really, myself. Again, I find myself wishing that just saying it would make me feel better, but it seems that the more I lie to him and myself, the sicker I feel.

"Promise?" His chocolate brown eyes are swimming in unshed tears as I wrap him in my arms.

I pull him tightly to my chest. "I promise." Reaching into my pocket, I pull out the key to the house. "Here, take the key and go pick out the best room." That seems to do the trick, for the moment, at least. Rone grabs the small brass key from my palm and races towards the door.

I stand up and take a look around. If my heart wasn't still shattered into pieces, I might be able to smile at the sound of life moving on around me. The birds sing in the towering trees above me and the sun shines down, warming my face. Too bad my soul is frozen. I put my head down, slam my car door with a little more force than necessary, and push all my emotions, thoughts, and memories deep down.

I move towards the shaded stone archway that will lead me to the garden, praying that the further I walk, the further I'll leave everything behind. My boots crunch on the gravel as I follow the straight path to the gated off area that is surprisingly not overgrown in weeds. The house has been vacant for a few months, so I thought for sure that things would need to be trimmed down or cleaned up a bit. But the garden is beautiful. Massive rose bushes outline the enclosed garden. Not quite in full bloom, but the buds are popping through. The arbor has thick vines climbing up and down each side. I walk closer to see what it is. Wisteria, maybe Clematis. Whatever it is, I can't wait to watch it take life. Gardening has always brought me joy. No matter where we lived, I always found a way to grow something. I find peace in getting my hands dirty, planting something, and tending to it as it starts to grow. The irony is not lost on me that life has come to a standstill. At the same time, I still can't wait to watch it continue on. I take a seat on the metal bench that sits facing the raised planter boxes, finally taking a moment for myself.

———

*"Have I told you that you're beautiful today?" James looks over at me with an adoring look on his face.*

*"I'm literally a three hundred pound whale, Jamie. How can you even think that!" I gesture down to my pregnant belly, giving him a view of my swollen fingers.*

*"You are not! And even if you were a five hundred pound whale, it wouldn't matter to me. You'll always be the most beautiful thing in the world."*

*"Promise?" I whisper as I lean over the center console of our truck to hug his arm.*

*"Promise." He leans in and kisses my temple.*

———

Dropping my head into my hands, my body shakes with silent sobs. *James, please help us.* I'm not sure if I think it or whisper it aloud. Just as the memory fades and his smiling face slips away, I have the distinct feeling that someone is staring at me. A cold shiver works its way between my shoulders and down my spine. I stand abruptly and spin around. Although nothing is staring back at me, I can still feel a cold, eerie presence surrounding me. And not just a feeling, but a very clear aura of something.

Or someone.

"You shouldn't be here," a haunting whisper slides over my shoulder.

Despite the chill that runs through my body, I can make out the childlike lilt in the feminine voice. I whip around and again, nothing. Turning toward the house, I catch a glimpse of Rone playing with his airplane around the living room through the big windows. He stops when he notices me, the biggest smile on his face. He waves before taking off down the hall.

The chill creeps closer, a slippery feeling like holding a snake as it wraps itself around your skin. The whisper slithers across my skin, goosebumps popping up in its path.

"Why are you here? You shouldn't be here."

I should be terrified. Deep down, I know that I am. For a split second I want to run, grab Rone, and leave. But just as I'm about to sprint over the gravel to the front of the house, something else takes over. A feeling of pure rage and anger pulses under the surface. After everything I've been through, *I AM NOT AFRAID.* Maybe my therapist is right and I need to get on some meds. *Regulate,* she says. Nothing wrong with managing your depression, anxiety, fear, the list goes on and on. Maybe it's just my subconscious finally realizing that I am the one in charge of our lives now. I don't have a spouse to lean on, to stand up for me, to fight my battles. It's just me. I'm on my own.

Whirling around, I yell into the empty space around me. "Who the *fuck* do you think you are to tell me where I can and cannot be?" The old me would never taunt a presence I could not see, but the new me? Oh, the new me has lost everything. I'm not going to be scared another day in my life. I'm here, I'm staying.

There is no cold chill, no haunting reply, only a deep laugh that ripples across the gravel towards me. I turn around in the direction it came from, now facing the trees at the back of the property. The voice is different from the cold whisper from before. *I am not afraid. I am not afraid.* Nodding slowly, I inhale and exhale. *One, two, three. I am Ella Carter and I am NOT afraid.*

Over and over again I say this to myself until I am once again firm and unshakable.

A rich voice speaks closer to me now. "I know who you are, Ella Carter." Clearly a man by the tone, but who it belongs to is a mystery. It slides over me like honey, the cold feeling that surrounded me before has now been replaced by his voice, calming me. In a weird way, the heat from him so close to me thaws the ice around my heart for the briefest moment. The thought of someone seeing through my false front of confidence comforts me in a way I can't explain. When was the last time it felt like someone saw *me*? Of course, Olivia and my parents, but not in the way that your person sees you. The way that *James* saw me.

"If this is some kind of joke, small town initiation kind of thing, I get it. Ha-ha." I clap slowly. "You win. Now, come out and let's shake hands or whatever. You can tell me when trash day is and we can drink some sweet tea or whatever shit it is we need to do to move past this."

Again, the laugh wraps around me, clinging to me like the thick humid air.

# TWO
# HOME

CILLIAN

HER REDDISH BROWN HAIR FALLS AROUND HER ROUND FACE AS SHE calls out to me. Her taunting should anger me; I shouldn't be egging her on. But something about the fire that I saw ignite in her eyes feeds my energy, something tells me she needs this. A release. One I'm happy to give her. It's been years since I've had a good verbal spar and I'm anxious to see how far I can push her. I know she can't see me, yet somehow it feels like she does.

"LEAVE!" the twins scream out. Their voices are terrifying, catching me off guard and making me jump back. The twins are only eleven, but unlike most girls their age, they aren't running around with their friends and enjoying the youthful innocence that was stolen away from them. The hand they were dealt left them cold and emotionless. I find myself more scared of them than I'd care to admit. Ella pales, her resolve melting away. I should be proud of the girls–we don't need anyone here. This is ours. But seeing her seek refuge on the same bench that I so often come to did something to my heart. Her deep, blue eyes widen in fear as I watch the sisters make their way closer to her. Instantly, I take a step forward and their eyes snap towards me. I put out my hands, nodding at them to walk away. They look at me, their shocked expression quickly masked over by anger and annoyance. We had an agreement: we would handle the new owners together.

I heard the real estate agent on the phone last week confirming the sale. Ella Carter was set to arrive today and we've been waiting. This property, The Rose Manor, has been in my family for over one hundred years. The last living descendant, my slimy cousin, Peter, passed away earlier this year, leaving no option other than to sell. What I didn't expect when Ella stepped out of her car, followed by a little boy, was the twist of warmth that flowed through me. My heart has been hardened for so long that I almost didn't recognize the pain that had it crack a little when she knelt down and pulled her son to her. I kept looking for another car to pull up with her husband, ready to settle into their new home. But when I saw the boy's eyes fill with tears as he whispered something about his dad, I knew that something was off. The odd feeling only grew as I watched her sit on *my* bench and cry into her hands. Was she abused? On the run from an abusive spouse? Both of the ideas send a weird sensation of anger and possessiveness washing over me. Then she whispered an almost silent plea, *"James, please help us."* And I knew, *I knew* she wasn't on the run, but trying to run *back* to something.

The sound of Ella's heavy breathing and her knees hitting the ground pulls me back to the moment playing out before me. The twins have retreated and I'm left alone with this woman who is slowly sinking to the ground. Before I can stop myself, I'm moving to her, crouching in front of her. When I reach my hand out to brush the strands of fallen hair from her face, I stop suddenly, mere inches from her skin. I'm afraid of reaching out and touching something I know I won't feel. My heart beats wildly in my chest, so loud I'm sure she can hear it. Gasping, she jerks her head up, one hand cupping the cheek I was so close to touching. It's as if she can feel me near her, like she can feel the warmth of my hand so close to her. She looks around and I look between her eyes and my outstretched hand. I'm just as shocked as she is. The last living person I tried to interact with never acknowledged my presence, never *felt* me.

"What is happening?" Her soft voice is directed more to herself than me.

The sudden urge to tell her everything, anything, is so strong I have to clamp my mouth shut. The force of it causes pain to radiate through my jaw.

"You're where you are supposed to be. Please don't be afraid." *What the fuck? That is not what I meant to say.* The words spill out without my permission. I tilt my head back and close my eyes, trying to figure out what about this woman has caused a decade of planning to go to shit in less than ten minutes.

"I'm hearing voices now?" Sitting back on her heels, she throws her hands in the air. "Great, I've definitely lost my mind." She lets out a crazed laugh.

A slow smirk crosses my face as I gaze down at her. She stands slowly and I rise with her.

"We won't hurt you. You're safe here." *Again, what the fuck am I saying to her.* She stares into the garden, wiping the tears from her cheeks. I expect her to ask questions, demand answers for what has just transpired. However, she surprises me when she says, "All I want is to feel at home." More tears spill down her cheeks, making me clench my fists so hard my bones scream out in pain. The urge to reach out and wipe her tears away is so overwhelming it's hard for me to breathe. "I just want to find peace." She turns to leave, after a few steps up the path, she stops and looks back in my direction. I watch her and wait, but she just stares back at the space around me with something that looks like hope in her eyes.

"You will, I promise." is all I whisper before turning to walk off down the path.

## THREE
# THE STORM

### ELLA

THE FOLLOWING WEEK IS FILLED WITH MOVING TRUCKS, NEW furniture, and confusing as fuck IKEA instructions. I sold a lot of what we had in our old home—new things felt like a new start. The walls now have a coat of fresh paint while our newly hung family pictures smile down at us from their new spots. They are a daily reminder of the life we left behind, oddly though, it feels like home here. I thought that seeing James smiling at me every day when I walked down the steps would send me into a spiral of depression, but without fail I smile every time. The memories replayed like an episode of a favorite TV show. You know each line and scene, but it makes you feel safe, comfortable. Rone met new friends down the street and has adjusted better than I expected. He's out playing while a spring thunderstorm is rumbling in the distance. I can smell the moisture in the air as it rolls closer.

I toss down the tools in my hand and roll my shoulders back, cracking my neck and stretching my back. I groan at the stiffness that has settled into my body. I'm too old to sit on the floor for hours. My phone pings with a text from Madi,

> Ty is wondering if Rone would like to stay for pizza and a movie?

Smiling, I type out my response.

> Oh I'd love that and so would he. I'm currently cursing the Swed who designed this nightstand.

> We'll keep him for a while then. Let me know if you want me to send Michael down with his tools!

I wasn't expecting to make friends so quickly, but when the doorbell rang the morning after we moved in with Madi standing on the porch with a basket full of chocolate muffins and her bright smile, I knew I needed her in my life. I feel like I've known her longer than the week we've been here. She keeps telling me we are kindred spirits. Lord knows I need all the help I can get if I'm going to be raising Rone the way James and I had always planned.

I go back to my instructions, trying and failing to make it through another step. Sighing in defeat, I stand and head down the staircase to the kitchen. I open the door and let the cool air rush out, easing the exhaustion that has taken a hold of me this past week. I grab a drink from the fridge and settle into the breakfast nook by the big windows off to the side. I rest my cheek in my palm and watch the storm roll in. Lightning lights up the sky, illuminating the garden outside the window and the tree line in the distance. Thunder rattles the window and I sink deeper into the cushioned seat, pulling my knees up to my chest. Although I've kept myself busy with all the things that come with filling a new house, not to mention trying to find some summer camps for Rone to attend, any down time I have seems to grant permission for my mind to drift back to the promise made to me in my garden by someone I couldn't see. Couldn't see, but could *very much* feel. My skin tingles at the memory of his voice and the heat of him surrounding me.

"*You will, I promise.*" Did I imagine that? I mean, of course I did. There is no such thing as ghosts and sure as hell not ghosts who have conversations with me in *my garden*. Thunder shakes the window so violently I'm surprised the glass doesn't shatter right across my table. And then, just like a scratched CD, the scene from that night skips over and over through my mind as I cradle my head in my hands and bury my fingers in my hair.

*Inhale, exhale. Keep breathing, the memory will pass.*

———

*"So where are you taking me, love?" I ask James as he turns the car onto the freeway.*

*"Hmmm…I don't want to ruin the surprise. You deserve a night out. This pregnancy hasn't been easy and I'm not wasting a night of babysitting. You'll have to wait and see." I love this man. We were married for years before we got pregnant with Rone and we thought we'd be able to give him a sibling sooner, but it just didn't happen as quickly as we hoped. This pregnancy was a surprise, one we waited a long time for.*

*"Do you remember when we were pregnant with Rone?"*

*"How could I forget? Everything was so new and exciting. And of course, so terrifying. But man, he's so big now." The smile on his face is infectious and I can see six years of memories play in his eyes.*

*"Are you nervous, excited, and terrified for another baby?" I ask playfully, poking him in the ribs.*

*"Are you kidding? I'm a pro now. Nothing to be afraid of." A smile eases across his handsome face.*

*"It's a girl this time…does that change how you feel?" His face stills and he gives me a terrified look.*

*"IT'S A GIRL!? Why wouldn't you tell me, this changes everything!"*

*"Ha-ha, very funny," I mock laugh*

*"Of course I'm terrified, but we've got each other, we'll be fine!"*

*He glances over his shoulder to check his blind spot and starts to merge into the left lane. Just as he crosses the line, a car swerves from the other lane to avoid a crash on the side of the road. The back of the car slams into the front of our hood, making our car go into a spin.*

*"Fuck, Ella!!" James screams as he tries to maneuver our car to straighten out. We spin for what feels like hours, the scenery that was so peaceful just moments before blurring around me. Finally, we skid to a stop facing the opposite direction. I look over at James as I'm grabbing onto the handle on the roof.*

*"Shit that was wild. You ok, ba..." The words fade when there is a deafening crash of metal and shattered glass. Pain radiates through my belly and flying glass stings my cheeks.*

*"Ella! Ella!" James' voice sounds like it's coming from the end of a tunnel. I open my eyes and try to orient myself. I'm dangling upside down, held in by my seat belt. I turn my head towards his voice and see him trying to get his seat belt undone. When it finally snaps free, he falls with a thud, to what now is the roof of the car.*

*"What happened?" I rasp. Looking down at the roof below me, I see a growing pool of blood with accompanying drops of red falling in front of my face. I look towards my belly and pain shoots up my spine. I gasp, trying to ease the pressure of the belt off my stomach.*

*"Ella! I can't find my phone." His eyes are filled with terror when he looks up at me. "Babe, you're bleeding!" His voice is scared, but he's trying to hide it.*

*"I hurt, James," I whisper.*

*"I know, love. I'm going to call 911, just hang on."*

*"James, I'm gonna pass out." My vision goes blurry as I try to open my eyes and turn back towards him.*

*"Hang on, baby, you're going to be ok. I promise!" His words soothe me and my eyes drift closed. Screeching tires and blaring horns jerk me awake, just in time to see another car smash into us, sending us into another spiral. The world goes black, but I still hear his words in my ear.*

.  .  .

*"Hang on, baby, you're going to be ok. I promise!"*

———

A bang on the floor above me snaps me back to reality. I rub my eyes and twist my wedding ring around my finger. Another flash of lightning cracks outside and just as the thunder shakes the window, followed by another bang above me. I drop my head against the wall. "Shit!" I really don't have time for this. Time, energy, fucks even. I set my drink down on the table and head towards the stairs, slowly taking them up to my room.

As I walk, I take in the house. Honestly, the pictures didn't do it justice. The moment I dropped my bags on the floor in the master bedroom, I almost cried with joy. The room is large enough that I've got my king bed right in the middle of the wall. Even with the huge bed, I still have room off to the side under the wall of windows to have a couple of plush sitting chairs and a small coffee table in between. The first time I stepped into the attached bathroom, I think I fell in love. Like literally, I could have kissed the floor. A double vanity made of the most beautiful, soft white granite sits under a mirror spanning the entire length of the wall. On the other side of the room is a shower enclosed in glass on three sides, the back wall covered in the most gorgeous, deep blue tiles. There are two shower heads dropping down from the ceiling and a steam vent that I haven't been able to try out yet. Behind the shower is a massive tub, large enough for two people, that I can already see myself soaking in for hours reading my way through my endless to be read list. Above the bath is a large window that overlooks the backyard. Lush green grass stretches back towards a large grove of tall trees that line the back of the property. It's like it was made for me. I'm grateful at least one thing is working in my favor these days.

As I push open the door and let my toes sink into the deep, soft carpet, I come to a dead stop. My nightstand that has given me hell for the better part of the day is completely finished and sitting upright next to my bed. All my books are stacked neatly on top and the hanging lamp above has been turned on, casting my room in a warm glow that contradicts the dark clouds gathering outside the window. I stand there with my mouth hanging open, eyes wide. I'm losing my mind. This is insane, I know I didn't do this. *I am not afraid.*

"You're not afraid of us?" The slippery cold feeling from before is back and I can feel my already tense body seize up even more.

"You should be." Before I couldn't make it out, but now I can physically feel *two* separate spirits or auras circling me. Just as the cold starts to make me shiver and the hair on my arms starts to rise, a deep voice growls from behind me, quiet, but demanding.

"Get out, both of you." I flinch as their parting chill whips angrily across my arm. That strange feeling of comfort and knowing eases the tension from before. I have to pull back from leaning into the warmth that now encircles me.

"Who are you?" I turn in a circle, finally asking the question that has been eating at me for the past week since I first felt his presence in the garden.

There is a beat of silence before he responds, "Are you sure you don't mean, thank you?"

I almost laugh out loud. "For what? Making me feel like I should have moved into an insane asylum?" I ask, my voice laced with sarcasm. His deep rumble of a laugh mirrors the thunder that crashes outside.

"Are you going to hurt my boy?" I don't care if this spirit murders me in my sleep. *Just please don't hurt Rone.*

"You think I would hurt your boy?" He sounds exasperated, like I've just insulted him.

"I don't know who or what you are. You could murder us.

You could, I don't know—" I trail off. "I just need to know if he's safe or not."

"I promise you, you both are safe."

I spin towards the sound of the voice. "Why do you keep saying that?"

I can feel him right in front of me. "Saying what?" he responds calmly. I'm tempted to reach out and lay my hands on him. But I hesitate, remembering being told something about not trying to touch spirits. I'm not ready to test that theory.

"It doesn't matter, please just tell me what you want from me..." My confidence melts away and exhaustion seeps into my voice.

# FOUR
## BURN ME

CILLIAN

"Please just tell me what you want from me..." she asks just above a whisper. This is the first time I'm letting myself think about this. *What do I want from her?* I look her up and down and my dick pushes up against my slacks. *What the fuck is happening to me?* Being stuck in the *in between*, as I've started to refer to it as, is confusing as shit. One moment, you're walking down the street and the next, you're waking up to the sound of trucks and movers loading all your things into moving vans and dumpsters.

The worst part is my idiot cousin had moved into the house. I chased him around, trying to talk to him, but he acted like he couldn't hear me. All my things had been replaced with furniture that looked so uncomfortable to sit on, it was no wonder he walked around like he had a stick up his ass. It wasn't until I ran into what was supposed to be *my office* to call my lawyer, that I saw the paper spread out on the desk.

***Spring Hill Tribune***

<u>*Hit and Run Accident Causes Tragic Death*</u>

*The small community of Spring Hill mourns the loss of one of our own this week. Our beloved Cillian Rose was hit and killed Sunday evening while walking home from helping at a neighbor's house. The Rose family has owned Rose Manor for over one hundred years. Cillian was the only son of Rita and Matthew Rose and will be missed by all in the community. He will be remembered for his infectious smile and willingness to help anyone and everyone at a moment's notice. His cousin, Peter Millan, has taken over the estate. Peter is the last living relative of the Rose family.*

I've lived that moment over and over for the past ten years. I was down the street helping my neighbor late into the evening. She had finally stopped talking long enough for me to say my goodbye. Finally, I made my way down her long driveway and turned onto the road, heading back to *my* house. I wasn't even looking at my phone. I had my head up, looking around, soaking in the beauty of this place I had called home since I was a kid. A smile crossed my face as I thought of the gorgeous farmhouse I had just had renovated. Every detail thought out, ready for the next chapter in my life. At twenty seven, I was ready to settle down. I'd lived out my frat boy days, spending enough time on Broadway to know what I wanted wasn't a quick one night thrill or a back alley blow job. I had a successful career, one that would allow me to take time off to be with a family. I was ready, and for the first time in my life, I was excited at the idea of settling down. Out of nowhere, headlights illuminated my face, blinding me. I knew they were going way too fast for the curve in the road. I didn't even have time to jump to the side before the car lost control and spun straight for me. I have vague memories of being bounced around in the back of a sterile ambulance. The lights were so blinding, I couldn't keep my eyes open. Anytime I'd try, I was pulled back into a fog.

I woke up in my room gasping for air, the nightmare was so

real. A slick sweat still covered my body and my mouth tasted sour, like I'd just woken from surgery. The sounds of scratching furniture over hardwood and shouts of voices I didn't recognize jolted me from sleep. I stumbled from my room only to find multiple people I didn't know, walking around *my* house, moving things around, and carrying out *my* things. I'd tried to grab one of them that was so obviously ignoring me, but my hand slipped through the air. I laughed, looking around for someone to jump out and yell *"Gotcha!"*, but it never happened.

———

"I can still feel you..." Her voice is breathy and has both my dick and eyes at full attention. *That's concerning.* At first, I wanted to get her out of my house so it could be mine again. Maybe I could finally find a way to move beyond after ten years of living a half-life. There is no one to give advice, no one to guide me through this process. I'm stuck and I'm so lost, in more ways than one. The twins have been my only company for years. Their story seems to be much more traumatizing than my own, but they have yet to tell me all the details. We made a deal that we would do what we could to get us all to the end of this miserable existence.

"I haven't left you," I whisper back, taking a step towards her before I realize what my feet are doing. "I'm not here to hurt you, I couldn't if I tried." God, something about her makes me want to cut my chest open and lay my heart at her feet. "What do you mean? Why are you in my house?" She's building her walls back up. Brick by brick, confidence and fake composure stack into place. But I see her. I see her pain. Once again, I'm finding it hard not to pour my heart out to her.

"Technically you are in *my house*. I live here. The Rose Manor has been in my family for a very long time." I circle her slowly, letting my eyes wander down her body. She is soft in all the right places; strong but curvy. I can tell without touching her that her skin would be soft under my touch. It takes more effort than I'd like to hold back from reaching out and running my fingers along it. Her hair is piled in a bun, loose pieces falling down and framing her face.

"You can't live here, you're a ghost," she says flatly.

"You can call me whatever you'd like, sweetheart, but it looks like we're in a standoff."

I make my way back around and stand in front of her again. She folds her arms across her chest and looks around the room, settling her gaze on the nightstand.

"Did you build my nightstand?" I'd heard her frustrated sighs and not so quiet curses as she sat on the floor for the better part of the day, trying to piece together the oddly shaped wood boards. When she finally gave up and went downstairs, I couldn't help but sit in her place to look at the paper instructions. I reached out to run my hand over the light wood. When I felt the smooth material under my hand, I couldn't help myself. Before I knew it, I had built the whole thing. I've always been good at putting things together. My job as an architect let me practically play Legos as an adult and get paid for it—very well.

Once it was finished, I noticed her stack of books on the floor next to her bed. I lifted the nightstand into place and stacked the books neatly on top. One of the titles caught my eye and I lifted it, turning to the page that was dogeared to mark her place. My eyes bugged out at the scene before me and I dropped the book like a teenager caught looking at porn. It made a distinct thump as it hit the carpet. Then, being the cluster fuck I am, when I bent to pick it up, the book on the top of the stack in my arm slid off and landed with another thud next to the first one on the carpet.

At this point, I could hear her moving up the stairs in the hall. As quickly and carefully as I could, I finished stacking the books neatly on the nightstand. Her footsteps hit the landing and as she padded across it, I had just made it to the other side of the room before she walked through the doorway. The look on her face was a mix of confusion and shock, but I didn't miss the sense of relief that seemed to wash over her for a split second. I could almost see her mind checking another thing off her list that she didn't need to do on her own.

"I could tell it was giving you a run for your money. Besides, I'm good with my hands." Her cheeks turn a rosy color and a smirk spreads across my face. I didn't mean it like that, but I don't make any move to correct the implication. *Does she like dirty talk?* I can do better than that if that's what she needs. *Stop.* Why am I thinking about this? Can I even have sex with a living person in my condition? Shit. This is not the distraction I need.

"Thank you. It's been a bitch putting all this together. James used to…" she trails off.

The cute rosy color that had flooded her cheeks disappears and her eyes mist over. The walls she so quickly built crumbled around her.

"Is James your husband?" I step closer, purposely trying to crowd into her space. The sudden need to be close to her is too strong. If she says yes, if she belongs to someone else, I know I'll need to walk away from her. The pull I have to her will be damn near impossible to break away from. A tingling deep down in some part of me that I've never paid attention to buzzes to life. *Endgame,* it whispers. I lean down so I can look into her eyes better. As if she can sense me closing in, she lifts her gaze and my stomach plummets. She not only looks in my direction, but I swear she stares into my soul. I should be terrified. I should end this now and make her leave. But something pulls me to her like the ocean during low tide, so I stand there, staring into her ocean blue eyes. A soft white circle lines her pupil, making it look like actual waves crashing against a shore. Dark lashes frame her almond shaped eyes, so blue and full of depth I can't look away.

She chews on her lip for a moment and my heart hammers against my chest. She shakes her head and the breath I've been holding comes out in one big rush. My mind slowly puts the pieces together; her whispered plea in the garden, the pictures in the hallway, crying in the shower. My eyes snap back to hers just as she confirms what I've just realized. "He's gone, they both are." *They? Who is they?* Then she shudders, her shoulders slump over as tears spill from her eyes. The dams break free and turn into rivers running down her pale cheeks. As if on instinct, I reach out my hand, not sure if I will feel her warmth or the cool air of nothingness like in the past. But at this moment, I don't care. Her crying in front of me is breaking my heart.

Most of the time I can touch objects and move them around. I would mess with Peter all the time, hoping he'd finally snap and move out. I never did anything too ominous, like carving crosses into the walls, but I definitely put in effort to scare the shit out of him. My personal favorite was standing behind him at his desk and pulling the chair out from under him when he went to take a seat. But more recently, when I reach for things, they slip through my grasp. Almost as if I'm the one slipping away.

I spent days reliving that moment in the garden when I swear she reacted to my outstretched hand. Still unsure if that was an odd coincidence, I don't expect it to happen again. This time, though, I'm met with a sudden jolt of electricity. A sharp zap that runs through me as if I touched a live wire. Her skin. I feel her skin. The warmth and soft curve of her cheek burns into me like the sun on a hot summer day. She gasps and quickly wipes at her face. I pull back and stare at the moisture coating my fingertips. *What the hell was that?* I've never had that kind of physical reaction before. We stand there, both unsure of what just happened. Her hand still rests on her cheek, holding the spot where we touched. The doorbell rings loudly, making us both step apart quickly. The buzzing I hadn't noticed around us until now fades as she walks past me and out the door, the moment lost to the door opening and little feet running through the entryway.

### FIVE
# GREEN EYES

ELLA

I STILL FEEL THE WARMTH OF HIS TOUCH ON MY CHEEK AS I HEAD down the stairs to meet Rone and Ty, followed by Madi and Michael. My mind races with unanswered questions about my sanity, the creepy cold that runs over my skin with the voices of two young girls, and especially the comfort and familiarity of the warm, male voice that seems to come to my rescue far too often. I rub my hands down my face and through my hair, trying to shake the feeling of his warmth and fingertips wiping my tears away.

"Hey, we tried calling, but didn't get through." Madi greets me with her bright smile that reaches her eyes. From the moment I met her, she's done nothing short of amaze me with her happy disposition and outlook on life. It's as if nothing can break her. I want to bottle a little bit of that up for myself.

"Oh, I'm so sorry! I must have left my phone in the kitchen." I wrap my arms around Rone as he runs up and gives a quick hug before taking off into the living room with Ty.

"How's the building coming? Anything I can help with?" Madi's husband, Michael, asks while carrying leftover pizza through the doorway to the kitchen. I quickly think through how to explain my sudden skill in furniture building without revealing that I am now friends with a handy ghost.

"I think I'm done for the night. I was able to finish my night-stand, but the rest can wait for another day. Thank you, though," I lie through my smile. Grabbing a slice of pizza, I settle onto a stool and watch the two across the massive, white, granite island.

"Anytime, I'm happy to help." Michael is kind, one that I could see James being quick friends with. A sharp stab of sadness radiates through me, as it does anytime I think about James and the life that he won't get to live or the people he will never meet.

"Actually, I wanted to ask you two something," I say around a bite. Chewing quickly, I cast a quick look over my shoulder into the living room at Rone and Ty.

"Everything ok?" Madi gives Michael a quick glance and looks back at me. I wave my hand dismissively.

"What do you guys know about this house? Its previous owners, I mean." I look at them expectantly, hoping that I don't give away how curious I am.

*Technically, you are in my house.* I can still feel his presence as he said those words. I rest my elbows on the counter and hold my chin in my palms, thumbs rubbing the spot on my face where his touch still burns my skin. My heart beats a little faster at the thought of him.

Madi and Michael let out relieved sighs as if they were expecting something much worse. They go on to tell me that the last owner who they knew, Peter Millan, passed away earlier in the year from a heart attack. He was only fifty-five and the last living relative of the Rose line. Before Peter, their childhood friend, Cillian, grew up here. When his parents passed away shortly after he graduated college, he ended up staying and kept the house in the family. He was the one who had the estate remodeled into its present glory. He even had the main frame adjusted to accommodate the massive windows that I love so much. The manor has been in the Rose family line since Madi or Michael can remember. It's been passed down from father to son since the land was purchased and the structure built.

Madi mentions that Cillian's mother, Rita, kept the garden full of the most amazing plants and flowers. Her eyes dance as she goes into detail about the bright colors of flowers, vividly explaining the lavender and rosemary smell that drifted through open windows in the summer breeze. She remembers visiting the house and garden when she was younger. I smile at the memories taking shape before me.

"Damn shame what happened to him. He took such good care of this place. Not that you won't, Ella," Michael stumbles over his words and I reach across the island, placing a hand over his. I can't imagine how hard it is to see someone else living in your best friend's childhood home. A house that felt so much like his own. "I don't mean...*shit*. I don't know what I'm saying." Michael shifts uncomfortably on his feet.

I pull my hand back and give him a smile. "I know what you mean, Michael. I plan to do just that. Lord knows I need something to keep my mind and hands busy." I give him the happiest smile I can muster. The garden is well taken care of, but once the weather turns, I plan to fill every open space with vegetables and herbs.

"What happened to him? Cillian, I mean." The name sounds so familiar to me. Like I've been saying it my whole life. I want to say it again, and again, just to feel it roll off my tongue.

Madi takes a peek at the boys playing in the other room and says, "Cillian was on his way home from helping Susan Miles. You know the grouchy lady down the road with all the cats?" *Oh, do I know Susan.* I tried to befriend my closest neighbor while out for a walk earlier this week. She wasted no time letting me know I shouldn't be in this house and I was not to pet her cats. *Noted.*

"He was really good with his hands, kind of a handyman in a sense" Madi continues, but her voice is drowned out by the memory of walking into my room and seeing the finished nightstand by my bed. The memory of his sexual implication runs back through my mind and I feel the heat creep up my neck. Could Cillian be the man behind the voice I've been hearing? If it's Peter that is still hanging around, I want nothing to do with him.

"People always called him for odd shit to help out with. Anyway, he was walking home that evening and a car hit him. He died on the way to the hospital. It was awful, I cried for weeks. Cillian had such a good heart. I always wanted to see where life would take him." She tucks a stray strand of her perfect blonde hair behind her ear.

Michael and Madi grew up in Spring Hill, and true to the small town stereotype, they know everyone. Michael gives her shoulders a hug and finishes the story.

"It's been ten years and we still see his face in people we pass. He was our best friend. We're glad you're here, though. This house didn't feel right with Peter in it." I nod my head. He sounds like a douche. Rest in peace, Peter.

After I send my friends on their way and get Rone settled in bed, I head back downstairs to lock up the house and turn the lights off. When I turn the corner to the kitchen, a mug sits in the middle of the island that wasn't there before. Half of me wants to crawl out of my skin, curl up and hide, pretending I'm imagining things. But something feels *comfortable*. Something feels *safe*.

I lift the mug and inhale the chamomile, instantly feeling the tension in my muscles relax. I reach for the honey in the pantry and give a decent squeeze before stirring my mug on my way up the stairs. I stop half way and turn around, facing the bottom level. Obviously, the home is gorgeous. That's why I purchased it. I've gawked over every detail numerous times since we stepped inside. But to be honest, I never would have guessed a man could design something so detailed. James was oblivious to little details and always gave me a hard time when I hyper focused on the small things. He'd roll his eyes when I'd bring up what color I should paint the accent wall in our baby's room for the tenth time, or if I should change the doorknobs to all match, on and on. James was beyond supportive in every avenue of life, but I knew that my fixation on those kinds of things drove him insane.

This home feels elegant, but cozy. Modern, but timeless. Even the banister hugging the sides of the staircase matches seamlessly to the window sills on the interior of each room. The soft wood pulls all the white walls and deep green accents together. I shouldn't want to know more about the man who drew out every inch of this house, but I can't help the curiosity that picks at my mind. I softly back down the steps and turn into my office, the large window looking out over the front drive. The lights on the front of the house cast the front lawn and gravel driveway in a soft glow. Opening Google, I type in *Rose Manor Spring Hill TN*. Clicking on the top article, I read a little about the history of Rose Manor.

*Built back before the Civil War, Rose Manor has been home to the prominent Rose family for over one hundred years. During the war, Martha Rose turned the manor into a field hospital for wounded soldiers on both sides. The Rose family soon came under attack by the local community for helping soldiers that they saw as traitors. However, Martha never turned away a soul in need. The estate has been passed down from father to son over the years.*

I go back to the main screen and type in *Cillian Rose*, sipping on my hot tea while the screen loads. I choke on the hot liquid when I'm met with stunning eyes the color of moss in the forest as a picture of Cillian stares back at me. His orthodontist deserves a gold fucking medal for how perfectly straight his teeth are. And his smile, *fuck*, his smile is heart stopping. He looks like he's laughing at something behind the camera. Even though I heard his laugh in the garden on my first day here, I find myself longing to hear it again. Begging to be the source of his laughter. His hair is so dark, almost black, and it falls just above his eyes, touching the bottom of his ears in soft waves. I clench my hand into a fist, fighting the urge to run my fingers across the screen. My heart rate increases, my breath quickens, and I'm basically drooling. Then, in an instant, I'm flooded with shame and guilt. The thought that any man besides James could make me feel anything is almost enough to make me sick to my stomach. I slam my chair back and leave the mug on the desk, hitting the light off with more force than it deserves on my way out the door.

# SIX
# LIKE WHAT YOU SEE?

## CILLIAN

THE WEIRD THING ABOUT BEING STUCK BETWEEN DIMENSIONS, IS things can be how they were when I was alive and also how they are in the moment. For example, my room turned into a guest room when Peter moved in. Some days, my room looks how I left it. Other days I wake up in a panic not knowing where I am. When I had the house remodeled years ago, I moved from the master bedroom into this room to allow the contractor to work on the master bathroom. But as soon as I had settled in here, I ended up liking it more and never went back.

It's not much smaller than the master. The window that over-looks the backyard lets in the perfect amount of light to work on my designs. I'm replaying the conversation with Ella over and over again. While she was helping Rone get ready for bed, I made my way down the stairs to the kitchen. I knew how stressed she must be; having a conversation with someone she couldn't see must be traumatizing. Hell, I'm traumatized and I'm dead. I've begun to catch on to her routine at this point. Every night after she gets Rone settled, she softly closes his door, throws her hair up, and heads down to the kitchen. The sweet, comforting smell of chamomile tea follows not long after. I thought making her a cup would help ease her confusion of being confronted by myself and the twins. What I didn't expect was the angry huffing of her breathing and stomping feet headed up the stairs.

I immediately feel like I'm twelve again and my mom will bust through the door to scold me for forgetting to take the trash out. But instead, she turns into her room and closes the door. I ease off the bed and slowly pull my door open. Looking across the wide hallway, I see Rone's door open a crack and hear the shower turn on in the master bath. I internally groan at the thought of Ella peeling off her clothes and stepping into the steaming shower, her body barely hidden by the fogged up glass doors. I knock my head against the doorframe, clenching and unclenching my fists a few times. I could sneak in…she'd never know. But something inside tells me that she would feel me watching. *Great idea, idiot. Perverted ghost would make an excellent headline.*

I decided that thinking with my dick is not the smartest decision. Needing to put some space between myself and the naked woman in the other room, I head down the stairs to see what upset her. I make my way around the downstairs, turning off a light here and there and double checking the doors are locked. When I circle back to the front door, that's when I see the glow of the computer in the office. In a few short strides, I cross the doorway and reach the back of the desk, grabbing the chair that has been haphazardly thrown against the bookcase. I shake the mouse to wake up the screen and almost scream when I see my face staring back at me. I put my hands over my mouth, not wanting to add any more ghost moaning and noises to the situation at hand. *She Googled me?* I get a warm feeling and realize I'm smiling so big my cheeks hurt. Shit, did I just get *butterflies?*

A neat stack of sticky notes and colorful pens next to the monitor catch my eye. I scribble a message and stick the note right over the image of my smiling face. Neatly tucking the chair and pen back to their rightful place, I grab her mug to take to the kitchen. After I wash it and place it on the drying rack, I head back up to my room.

Feeling lighter than I have in fucking forever.

## SEVEN

# COCKY

ELLA

EXHAUSTED AND CONFUSED, I FINALLY DRAG MYSELF TO BED. Dropping my head into the pillows, I blow out a deep breath and look up at the white ceiling. My mind is still reeling from all the information thrown at me this evening. I know I need to take time to figure out what is happening around me. Who is behind these voices I can hear? Why do some of them make me feel like I want to curl up in a ball and cry while the other makes me feel so *safe*? I wear myself out from trying to put the pieces together from what Michael and Madi told me in the kitchen and the picture of the man with green eyes I pulled up on my computer. Somewhere in the chaos I drift off with even more questions than when I collapsed into bed.

———

*The walk home from my high school isn't too far, maybe five blocks. But I tend to take my time, listening to whatever mixed CD my girlfriends and I put together. My headphones are big and always need to be put back in place after I jog across the crosswalk. I hate making the cars wait. I hate making anyone wait on me, to be honest. The Walkman skips as I run, so I stop on the other side of the street to start the song over. When the familiar intro of one of my favorite NSYNC songs starts up again, I begin to move forward. Before I can lift my head, I run face first into something rock solid and strong. My heel catches on the crack in the sidewalk and I feel the weightless feeling of falling through the air. I brace for impact just as two warm, soft palms reach out to hold me steady.*

*"Shit, sorry!" Those big hands reach up and tug my headphones out and place them down around my neck. "You ok?" I look up only to be met with deep coffee eyes that are framed by long, dark lashes. Clearing his throat roughly as our eyes meet, he pushes his blonde hair out of his eyes. I can't look away from his thick forearms that bulge as he folds his arms over his chest.*

*"Umm, I'm...what?" Did I forget how to talk? What the fuck is happening to me!*

*The annoyingly handsome face of this brick wall just smiles at me. I hate him. I hate what he is doing to my insides. They flip around like a dying fish while his eyes shine with amusement.*

*"Are. You. Ok?" He punctuates each word slowly, squinting his eyes at me like I may be concussed.*

*"I'm...Ella. I mean, yes, I'm Ella." I huff out a frustrated breather. "I'M FINE." I put out my hands to make my point, trying to focus on anything besides his lopsided smile and perfectly white teeth. A group of boys stand in a huddle up the street. They eye us, letting out whistles and catcalls. I feel my cheeks flame. He tears his eyes off my face and his smile slips.*

*"Well, Ella, I have to go. I'll see you around. By the way, Backstreet Boys are way better than NSYNC." He taps my headphones and takes off towards his friends. He looks back at me and waves. Stupidly, I raise my hand and then smack my forehead from embarrassment. I pick up the pace and head down the sidewalk, planning to cry in humiliation the second I close myself in my room. His smile is stuck in my mind, the lingering feeling of his hands on my arms.*

———

"Mom, wake up! It's summer camp day!"

"Rone, leave me alone. It's Sunday." I reach over to my newly built nightstand and grab my phone, pulling the charging cord from the portal. *Shit.* It is not Sunday, it's Monday. I peel my eyes open and am met with the mirror image of James. Hersey brown eyes and round face smile back at me. My heart melts at the fact he's so excited about summer camp, he doesn't linger on the fact that the bed I'm sleeping in is empty on the other side.

The first few months were obviously tough on him. How do you explain to a kid that is still learning to understand his own emotions that his daddy won't be coming home anymore? He was confused and would ask me daily when Dad would be back from work or why we weren't waiting for Dad to read our bedtime stories. As if my heart wasn't already pulverized, he always wanted to feel Paige kick, placing his small hands on my stomach and waiting patiently for a nudge that never came. Gentle reminders that Daddy and sister were gone and looking at photos of our past helped him reason with the loss. It was the hardest thing I had to do, but it made it a visual thing for him and made my arms a safe place where he could curl up and mourn in his own way.

Looking at photos is undeniably the most painful experience, but I never want to forget the looks captured on our faces during the memories caught on camera. Occasionally, he still has night-mares and he often reminds me that Daddy and sissy are in Heaven watching us. He has coped remarkably well to losing his dad and never meeting the sister he was so excited to share toys and stories with. Better than myself, that's for damn sure.

"Can I eat cereal before you take me to summer camp?" Before all of this, his energy used to bother me first thing in the morning. It drove me mad. I'm a night owl and tend to stay up late finishing my manuscripts. I am not a morning person. James was the early bird and often let me sleep in while he got Rone up and ready for school or sat on the couch eating cereal while watching cartoons together on Saturday mornings. My heart hurts, like little splinters burying themselves deeper with each painful memory of what used to be. I rub my chest, trying to ease the ache.

"Sure, baby. Let me shower while you eat and then we'll get in the car. Ok?"

Pumping his little arm in the air he shouts, "Yes!" He jumps off my bed and narrowly misses slamming his head into the door frame as he skids out into the hallway. I wince and close my eyes, saying a silent prayer that today will be the day James comes walking in the room and life goes on like it hasn't just hit a dead end. I shake the fog from my head and make my way into the bathroom for a quick shower. I hit play on my phone and *Ghost* by Josiah and the Bonnevilles fills the room. The lyrics are a sweet reminder of how James will always be with me, around me, and watching me. But I want more than just a presence, I want *him*. I let the shower and tears mix together until I'm able to pull myself from the misery of another morning of waking up and getting ready alone.

After dropping Rone off at camp, I decided to stop by the garden center in town. Today is a nice spring day and feels like the perfect chance to get started on the garden now that the fear of frost has passed. I sing along to the music blasting through the car when a call from my publisher sounds through the speakers.

"Hi, Mabel, how are you?" My publisher has been with me for years. She's always been a solid sounding board not just in my writing, but in my personal life as well.

"Hey, Ella, I'm doing well. How are you and Rone adjusting to Tennessee?" I nervously bite my bottom lip as I recount the happenings from the past couple weeks. She will definitely call my therapist if I confide in her about my very real conversations with a man I can't see.

"Ella, did I lose you?" I've lost something all right. My fucking sanity.

"No, sorry, I'm here. We're doing as well as can be expected. Just dropped Rone off at summer camp, hopefully he'll burn off his endless energy. I'm just headed to the garden center to grab some plants to fill the garden with." I know eventually I'll have to get back to my writing. I was closing in on my deadline before the accident and haven't been able to get my groove back, yet.

"Ahhh, I remember those days. What I wouldn't give to have that kind of energy back. I just wanted to check in and let you know that I've spoken with our team here at work and we've approved the pushback date for your latest book. That is, if you still feel like you'd like to continue, there is no pressure to rush back into things." Even though no one could push me back into the writing chair except for myself, it's still a relief to hear that I have more time without causing some major delays.

"I appreciate you all being there for me this past year. I know it wasn't in your plans, but I do feel like I'm getting to a point where I'll be able to jump back in. Will you please tell your team thank you for me and email me the details?" It's not a complete lie. There is no timeline on grief. Some days I feel like I need to sit down and escape through my writing. And now that we're settled, I feel like that time may be getting closer.

"Sure thing, I'll see you." We say our goodbyes and the call disconnects. I turn down the radio and roll my window down, letting the cool spring breeze float through my hair. Something about the wind on my face and the sun shining down is so liberating. I feel lighter, a bit of light leaking into my dead interior. And as so frequently happens when I start to feel like I'm taking some steps forward, guilt slams into me and forces me to take ten steps back. I know James would want me to be happy. He would hate that I'm here sad and lonely. But the guilt sits heavy just the same. How can I be happy when my life was shattered to pieces right before my eyes? I turn into the parking lot of the store and decide to buy the brightest flowers I can find. Maybe some color will trick my mind into believing we can be happy for longer than those rare, fleeting moments.

I spend the next few hours after getting back to the house out in the garden. The fresh black soil in the raised beds has been turned over. One of the large boxes is full of herbs; thyme, rose-mary, sage, lemon balm, basil, and mint. The heady smell of newly planted soil overwhelms the air as I walk out the gate to the metal bench, admiring the space. I look over the other boxes and am planning what else to plant when my phone pings from my pocket. Wiping the dirt from my hands, I fish my phone out and pull up the text from Mabel.

> Just emailed you the details for your next
> deadline. No rush at all, let me know if you have
> any questions.

Deciding I better take a look at the agreement before I get side tracked with another project and forget to respond, I head inside. Kicking my shoes off on the porch and tossing my dirty hat on the chair, I open the door and turn into the office. I pull out my chair from my desk and take a seat. Just as I look up to the monitor I remember my search history from the night before. As the screen lights up, it's then that I notice the sticky note placed carefully over the face of Cillian Rose now displayed on my screen. The same page I rushed away from so quickly last night. The note simply reads:

*Like what you see, sweetheart?*

I let out a deep breath. At least now I know it's actually Cillian that I'm talking to. That confirmation brings a little bit of peace to me. Happy that it's not Peter the douche, I let out a relieved sigh. However, it does little to ease my annoyance as I uncap a pen and angrily scribble a response. Smiling to myself in triumph, I look over the agreement from Mabel. Before I stand to leave, I place the sticky note back on the monitor.

# EIGHT
# MOON MEET OCEAN

CILLIAN

THAT MORNING I SAT OUTSIDE HER BEDROOM DOOR WITH MY HEART aching, listening as she pulled herself together before getting up for the day. I want to reach for her and tell her she'll be ok. Comfort her and tell her that she will survive this. The crack threatens to kill me all over again when I hear the song come over the speakers in the bathroom followed by quiet sobs. Her pain pulses through the house and I find myself in awe of the woman who a short while later breezes out of her door with dry eyes and a face of determination. She comes out of her room dressed in leggings I have no right to be jealous of and an over-sized Dolly Parton t-shirt. Her hair is up in its usual bun with little waves of caramel hair grazing her face as she skips down the stairs to get Rone ready for the day. She is gone for a couple hours and I find myself even more lost than usual, wondering what to do with myself.

Over the decade since my physical death, I've learned to let time move around me. I don't notice the hours ticking by like I did when I was living. Time doesn't seem to have a place when you don't have anything to look forward to. I slide out the back door and settle on the steps that lead down to the backyard that overlooks the trees lining the property line in the distance. A cool breeze rustles the leaves and they seem to glide in my direction. A chill I've become accustomed to washes over me and seeps into my bones. The twins stand before me and I know I owe them answers.

Before they even have a chance to question me, I rest my forearms on my knees and simply say, "I know how betrayed you both must feel, but I promise we'll still make it." If they feel any compassion towards me, it's buried under a cold exterior. "I just need to figure out what this all means." Black ink on the inside of my wrist catches my eye. I rub my thumb over my tattoo, *John 11:25*. When I walked into the tattoo shop with the verse in mind, I could never have imagined how significant it would be. I got it not long after I decided to get my life on track. I remembered what my married friends would say when I'd tell them about my wild, single escapades. They'd click their tongues at me and say, "You need Jesus." I consider my current situation. *How ironic.*

"She is a distraction." The chill in one of the twin's voices turns my blood cold and I have to swallow my emotions before I respond. I don't know their story, despite my efforts, and pushed it aside because they have been the only company I've had in a decade. Part of me feels like I owe them, but another part of me feels like there is something more that I need to do here before I can move on. I've tried to pry in their past, but have been met with dead ends and harsh reprimands. They don't want to relive whatever happened to them. I of all people understand how painful it is to look back on the ending of your life as you knew it. More than anyone, I know the feelings of confusion and frustration of being stuck in a place between living and dead. There is no closure, no real sense of peace. Just waking up day after day hoping that the next you just...cease to exist.

"Give me time." I look into their sad eyes and hope they realize that we have plenty of time to give. What's the rush if we don't even know where we are trying to get to? I used to believe there was a life after death, but if this is it, then count me out.

Before they can respond, gravel crunches under car tires pulling up the drive. When I turn my attention back to the sisters, they are walking off into the tree line. More times than I can count I've invited them into the house to stay, but they refuse each time, saying they feel more at home in the trees. I close my eyes and try to breathe through the emotions and questions swirling around in my mind. How desperately I wish I knew why Ella brings up these feelings. Why for the first time, in a very long time, I feel like something is worth living for again.

I spend the afternoon sitting on my bench watching Ella work in the garden. There is a blanket of calm that descends upon the grounds as she takes note of what needs to be trimmed and removed. A grin breaks out across my face when she turns on music and starts to sing along. She goes about filling one of the garden boxes with herbs and I let the fragrance drift over me, closing my eyes and leaning my head back as I feel the sun shining down on us from overhead. Soft laughter startles me and I whip my head in her direction. She stares at the speaker on the fence post as the iconic intro to *All The Small Things* by Blink-182 plays. She turns her head to the sky grinning as she says, "Nice one, James." She continues on planting and trimming while singing every line. As a child of the 90's, I can't help but quietly sing along, laughing to myself as I admire the woman before me, throwing her arms up and belting out the chorus. I can feel the heavy clouds that seem to follow her around part, letting the sun shine through. As the song fades out and her work for the day comes to an end, Ella steps through the gate and takes a seat on the bench next to me. I breathe her in, resisting the urge to wrap my arm around her shoulder and pull her to me. Gardenia and a hint of rose are covered by the earthy smell of freshly planted soil. The sun creates a halo around her as she looks down at her phone and for a while I let myself admire her. Being unseen has its perks. I let my eyes wander over the gentle slope of her nose, her full lips, and the soft curves of her neck. A light shine of sweat covers her skin and my mind begins to wander to what else that sweat is clinging to under her loose shirt and skin tight leggings. Before I can get carried away, her phone buzzes and she stands from the bench. I watch her head into the house before letting my head fall back, once again soaking in the warmth of the sun and the woman in my house.

Later that evening, I sit in the far corner of the kitchen nook and watch as Ella and Rone eat dinner at the island. She looks at Rone with so much love it makes my chest ache. She listens intently as he recounts every second of camp; the games they played, all the friends he made, the snacks they enjoyed under the shade of a huge oak tree, even telling her about his near miss of throwing up after rolling down the grassy hill one too many times. She lets him go on and on about his day, only speaking up to ask questions, encouraging him to slow down, or chew his food before he continues his stories. He kicks his legs back and forth, not a worry clouding his brown eyes. He must be the spitting image of his father. His curly sandy blonde hair is so different from Ella's straight, auburn-brown hair.

My heart bleeds as I picture the life that slipped by me. I'll never know what it's like to sit with my son or daughter and listen to them detail their day. Emotions swirl within me and before I can get caught up in a whirlwind of pain and pity, I sneak out of the kitchen and head for the stairs. But then I remember the note I left on Ella's computer. My stomach flips as I quickly glance to the kitchen before slipping into the open barn doors that lead into the office. I round the desk and look around for the note. Part of me has decided that I should take it down and toss it before she sees it. Another part worries if she did see my note that I've scared her off. Relief washes over me when I notice the note still stuck on the screen. I grab it, curling my fingers around the edges, about to crumple and toss in the trash. Then I notice the hurried handwriting below my message. *Her handwriting.*

*So what if I do?*

I sink into the chair, her words hit me straight in the gut. My mind has gone blank and I stare at her hastily written words. I'm thrown off the edge and plunged into the deep end. *This woman.* She has stepped into my world, into the one place I have ever called home, the one place I *planned* to ever call home. I'm at a loss at what to do now. She's pulled me in. I should fight back and put distance between the war she has caused in my mind and heart, but deep down I know I can't do that. I won't deny that having her so close terrifies me. I'm terrified of how I feel around her, terrified of what will happen if I stay, but even more terrified of what will happen if I go.

# NINE
## PUT YOUR HANDS ON MY WAIST

### ELLA

After Rone is bathed and in bed, I take my time cleaning up dinner, meticulously spraying the countertops and wiping them down. The silence wraps around me uncomfortably, so I open my phone and pull up my *Most Played* playlist. As my favorite songs fill the air, the music distracts me from my mind that is hell bent on reminding me of the pain that I've lived through this past year. I finish loading the dishwasher and put leftovers in the fridge. *The One That You Call* by Mackenzy Mackay starts to play and I let the music roll through me. I put the cleaning supplies away and place my hands on the countertop, dropping my head between my shoulders. I focus on the cold granite beneath my fingers, grounding myself while the music fills the kitchen.

When I start to sway to the beat, I feel *him*. The way my body reacts to his presence makes red flags pop up in my mind.

*He's not James!*

*Traitor!*

*You've lost your mind!*

But a small voice whispers back.

*Breathe.*

*Safe.*

*Live.*

I'm too stuck in the battle of voices in my head that the feeling against my waist takes me by surprise. I sensed him in the garden, felt his presence around me. But there was no mistaking the distinct feeling of his hands on my face when we stood in my bedroom that night. It wasn't just a whisper or blanket of warmth, it was *his* body on mine. And tonight, here in my kitchen with this song playing, I feel his arms wind around my stomach and pull me close. I close my eyes and let my head fall back against a strong shoulder.

Quieting the conflicting thoughts in my mind, I let my body relax. For just a few minutes, we move together in the dimly lit kitchen. For the first time in a long while, I don't feel as sad but a bit more hopeful, a little lighter. The warmth of his arms that I'm circled in soaks into my soul, picking up one piece of my broken heart off the floor and settling it back in place. The song fades into the next. The peace that he brings to my fragmented life still fills the room, but the feeling of arms around me pulls away, leaving a trail of goosebumps in their place.

I let my heart rate slow and allow my mind to drift to the future and the possibility of dancing around the kitchen late at night with someone besides my James. That feeling of shame and guilt that so often floods through me when I find myself picturing a happy future slowly begins to seep in, but this time it's not as overwhelming as it normally is. Taking this as my win for the evening, I shake off the complex emotions swirling around within me, turn the lights off, and head towards my room.

———

*Muffled voices and steady machine beeping pulls me from a groggy sleep. I try to open my eyes, but one of them is too heavy to open. My arms feel weighed down, my legs tingle like they've been asleep for days, and my blood is finally moving through again. Out of instinct, I reach for my belly, moving painfully slow. When my hands find the soft padding of my stomach, I can't stop the flood of tears that flow from my eyes. It's not firm. There are no kicks answering my prodding fingers. I lean my head back into the pillow and let the emotions break free as the memory comes back into focus.*

*Playful banter, dreams about the future.*

*Laughter, flirting with my husband.*

*Tires skidding, car horns, crushing metal.*

*Shattered glass slicing through my skin.*

*My seatbelt snapping tight across my chest and stomach.*

*James slipping beneath me as the car spins, watching him disappear through the broken window.*

*Red and white lights casting a kaleidoscope of shapes dancing across the interior of the destroyed car.*

*Paramedics and police officers yelling directions.*

*Gentle hands reaching for me, pulling me carefully out of the wreckage.*

*Pain pulling me under before I jolt back to consciousness.*

*In and out before I'm finally in the present.*

*Confused and in shock, laying in a cold white hospital room.*

*"Ella, honey. It's Mom, we're all here with you." My mom's soft voice is beside me and I turn towards her.*

*"James? Where is James?" There are so many questions, but the one I need the answer to the most is why James is not next to me. How badly did he get hurt and when can I see him?*

*"Oh, honey, I'm so sorry..." Her words fade and I know without hearing anything else that he is gone. I can feel it in my soul. My best friend, my heart, gone. My mouth opens and a sound I don't even recognize as my own screams out. All my pain, my dreams, my future, surrendering to the universe. Arms surround me as my mom and dad try to give me comfort. Sometime in the middle of it all, a nurse comes in and gives me something to help me relax and find sleep.*

*I wake the next day to a small, warm body curled up next to me. Tears threaten to break free again, but I can't summon the energy to produce any more after last night. Instead, I focus on turning my body, as painful as it is, and wrapping my small son in my arms. I kiss his hair, the same color as his dad's, and hold him tight as I drift into a dreamless sleep once more.*

*When I wake, Rone looks at my battered face. Fear is nowhere to be found like I had expected. I can't imagine how dreadful I must look, but he looks at me with such tenderness. His little hands reach out to brush against the cuts on my cheeks and my swollen eye. I reach up and hold his hand to my face, kissing his little palm and giving him the brightest smile I can summon from my broken heart.*

*"Mommy, I'm glad you are ok." Ok. Such a stupid fucking word. So sweet and innocent from his lips, but it hits me like a truck. I'm the furthest thing from ok, but for him I'll live my whole life being just ok if it makes him feel better.*

*"Hi, my Rone. I'm much better now that you are here." I hold him close and try to find the right words to tell him that our future will never be the same.*

*My parents come through the door with Olivia. She takes Rone's hand and leads him from the room, telling him she found the most delicious pancakes on the face of the planet. My parents take a seat on my bed and shortly after a doctor comes into the room, closing the door behind him. He confirms what I already knew, but needed to hear. James died on impact when the second car slammed into us. I do find a small piece of comfort knowing it was quick and a sick part of me wishes I could have gone with him. The doctor goes on to explain that due to the injuries I sustained in the crash, my daughter was lost in the accident as well. When the paramedics finally got me out of the mangled car, it was too late to save her. She had slipped away with James. As torn apart as I am that I will never get to meet her, that I'll never see her grow, I'm happy in the saddest way that she and James get to be together in the next life. Leaving Rone and I to live together in this life.*

---

I wake in a cold sweat, breathing hard and clutching my stomach. The memories of those few days after the accident have my stomach churning and my body weak. I stumble from bed and push through the bathroom door, dropping roughly to the cold floor and losing my dinner to the toilet. I sit back and rest my head against the wall, allowing my mind to complete its torture and flash back. James and I had a whole list of names we could never agree on. But with everything rushing around me, both slowly and quickly at the same time, the name Paige weighed on me. It felt right, I was going to be starting over without them, turning a new *page* as some would say. It's cheesy and ridiculous sounding now that I can look back with a clear mind, but I can't deny that it fits. I clean myself up and return to bed, hoping that the next few hours before sunrise will give me some peace.

# TEN
# BIG FUCKING MISTAKE

CILLIAN

I sat outside her door last night contemplating what my next move should be. I listened to her soft breathing turn quick and ragged. The door was left open a crack so she could hear if Rone called for her. Would it be so bad to slip inside if the door was left open? When she sat up in bed gasping for air and holding her stomach, I couldn't help myself. I pushed the door open just wide enough to step through sideways and held my breath when she jumped from bed and rushed past me, leaving a wake of her gardenia and rose smell in her path to the bathroom. I listened to her lose the food she had barely eaten at dinner and I was in physical pain from holding myself back. I wanted so badly to rush in to comfort her. Slowly, she made her way back to her bed and settled under the covers. I intended to leave after I knew she was asleep, but my feet wouldn't take me out the door. I stood in her doorway for what felt like hours, until my legs ached and my eyes stung with exhaustion. Finally, I settled into the soft armchair by the window just across from her bed, eyes stuck on the rise and fall of her soft breathing.

I rested my chin on my knuckles and let the quiet, peaceful hum of the ceiling fan relax my mind. But I couldn't stop replaying the memory of watching her in the kitchen earlier that night. She was so focused on her routine, cleaning up after the day. I was mesmerized as she moved around, putting things away and wiping the counter down. Then a song came on that made her slow down. I could tell in the way the energy shifted in the room that she was spiraling into dark memories. I tried like hell to stay away. But my eyes drifted down over the curves of her hips as she swayed to the beat. Pulled to her once again, I moved forward and wrapped my arms around her. For a brief moment she stilled, standing frozen between my chest and the edge of the counter. I could hear the thoughts bouncing around in her mind, but I didn't let go. I've never been able to reach out and touch another person before. Until *her*. For a solid minute, she stood there but I didn't let go. She can feel *me*, my touch. Not just the presence of me. She didn't pull away and finally gave herself to the ease that fell over us as we moved back and forth together. I've danced with plenty of women over the years, can even say I thought I'd been in love once or twice. But it always felt as if I was missing a piece to my puzzle. It always felt like I was settling. We weren't even dancing, just swaying to the beat and finding an odd comfort in one another. Holding her felt like I'd been doing it all my life. It felt natural. It felt *right*.

A sudden burst of water wakes me from my chair, immediately looking to the bed which is now empty. It's then that I realize the sound is coming from the bathroom, Ella is awake and taking her morning shower. I lean back in the chair and try to think of my great grandma Marie, or the time I walked into the women's bathroom and saw that old lady putting her wig on backwards. Anything to ease the growing pressure between my legs. I groan and slide my hand past the button of my pants and into my briefs. I grab the head of my dick and try to calm the erection that is quickly becoming painful. Against my better judgment, I stand from the chair and walk across the room, straight through the open bathroom door.

Steam is spilling out from the glass walls of the shower, the smell of her body wash intoxicating. My mind is still trying to justify why I invaded her space. If I'm just a ghost, she'll never see me, so what is the harm in watching her shower? I give in to the pull of the woman who is veiled from view by the cloud of mist and sweltering humidity. I lean against the counter and face the shower. *Big* fucking mistake. The steam parts and my mouth drops. Water runs over her hair and down the rivets in her back, flowing over her perfectly round ass. Soap suds cling to her thighs and calves as they wash down her body and across the tile floor of the shower. She has her back turned towards me as I slowly but firmly stroke my length. I could come here and now just watching her run her hands over her body. And then…she turns. Her body is a goddamn dream come true.

I heard her on the phone the other day telling her sister how she needs to go back to the gym and get in shape. But *fuck me*. If this is her out of shape, consider it my new fetish. What I wouldn't do to sink my fingers into the soft skin of her hips and pull her over me. Her hair reaches just to the point of her rosy, pink nipples. Her eyes close as she tips her head back to rinse the soap out. I don't realize I've just come all over my hand until I squeeze a little too hard and hiss at the sudden shock of pain. I look back up at Ella just as she turns back around, taking that as my que to leave. I clean up the best I can and wash my hands, hoping the spray of the shower drowns out the sound of the water running at the sink. Before I leave, I take one last look in the mirror, which has fogged over completely. A vexatious thought comes to mind. I reach one finger out and drag it slowly across the glass.

# ELEVEN
# I LIKE WHAT I SEE

ELLA

Something about water running over me, the sound of it raining on the tile floor, makes me want to stay in the shower all day long. I step out and grab my towel, wrapping it around my body and tucking it into itself. Dropping my head down to the floor, I twist my hair up in another towel and about fall over when I stand back up and notice words written in the fading condensation on the mirror.

*I like what I see.*

I blink a few times, wiping drops of water off my face and do a double take, leaning across the sink to take a closer look at the words.

In the books I read, I scream at the women doing just what I am. Run, scream, get away. Do anything but stand there. But I'm captivated by his presence. I want more, I want to be wanted again. And something about imagining him watching me as I shower has me pressing my thighs together to ease the excitement that settles in my lower belly. He saw me naked and still thinks I'm attractive? I haven't given much thought and care to my physical wellbeing in the past year. I've learned there is no timeline for grief and recovery after losing someone you love, so I haven't pressured myself into working out or following a super healthy eating plan. I made sure to go through therapy after losing Paige and James. I knew I couldn't help Rone if I wasn't dealing with my trauma in a healthy way. I still meet with my therapist once a month, but lately I've been feeling like I need to get back to taking better care of my physical health.

As if the timing couldn't be better planned, there is a knock on the door just as I'm stepping out of my room. I usher Rone back to his room to finish getting dressed for camp, quickly throw on a pair of leggings and big shirt, and head down to answer the front door.

"Ella Carter?" the delivery worker asks. I can hardly contain my excitement that the home gym I ordered is finally here.

"Yes, let me show you where it will be set up." After showing the delivery crew to the garage and the space I've cleaned up for the equipment, I load Rone in the car and head towards camp. He talks my ear off about how excited he is for his friends to come over this weekend for a sleepover. He lists off all the snacks he wants to buy, movies they want to watch, and games to play. It brings a smile to my face hearing him get excited about these kinds of things. *Little Life* by Cordelia starts to play through the speakers and I turn up the volume, letting the warm breeze tangle with the lyrics and fill the air.

When I pull back up to the house, the delivery guys have wrapped up their work and are waiting for me to sign the papers. After walking me through how the system works and signing all the forms, I send them on their way. I decide to get some work done on my manuscript for a couple hours. Settling into my office chair, I bring the computer to life, opening the last draft I have saved. I reread the last few chapters to refresh my memory.

The main characters have just met for the first time and I'm struggling to find the perfect words to describe their instant chemistry. She is annoyed at how easily he fits into her life and he can't seem to stay away. My gaze drifts to the big window overlooking the front and my memories pull me back to my own love story...

———

*"Ella! Hey, Ella!" It's been a couple days since I've seen James on my walk home from school. I've got my headphones on this time listening to Backstreet Boys blasting in my ears. I don't hear him yelling at me until I'm almost tackled by a massive body.*

*"Umm, ouch!" I practically yell as I right myself and smooth out my skirt. My Walkman has fallen out of my hands and is now laying in two pieces on the sidewalk. My eyes start to mist over and I angrily look up at the boy standing before me. His eyes are wide and he looks at me through obnoxiously long, dark eyelashes. His sandy blonde hair falls over them as he looks between me and the broken Walkman. He leans down and grabs the bottom piece of the CD player, looking up at me with a grin on his face. I want to kiss him and slap him at the same time. Gingerly, he pulls the Backstreet Boys CD out and stands to face me.*

*"I told you they were better." He points to the CD in his hand. "Sorry, I didn't mean to tackle you. I've been yelling at you from across the street for two blocks! I was crossing over to you, but that damn car almost ran me over." He turns and flips off the car speeding off down the street. "I had to sprint the rest of the way over so I didn't get hit." I can feel the heat in my cheeks as he grins at me still holding my scratched CD.*

*Rolling my eyes, I look him square in the eyes and dryly say, "They are so not better than NSYNC, but I decided to give them a chance." We start walking in a comfortable companionship, bickering back and forth about music. When we've walked another few blocks he stops and points up the street.*

*"I'm this way. How far away are you?"*

*"Only over on the next street. Thanks for walking with me, I'm*

sure you had better things to do than talk about boy bands for the last ten minutes." I look up at him and instantly regret it. He is even more handsome than I remember. His eyes are such a rich, chocolate brown I want to pull him down and lick them. Gross, Ella, pull yourself together.

"I can promise you, Ella, there is no one else I'd rather spend my time with." When I say that butterflies erupt in my belly, that would be a huge understatement. I honestly think I could have melted. Not knowing what to say, I awkwardly turn and walk backwards as I wave him off.

"See you tomorrow, cute girl!" He gives me a heart stopping smile and jogs away up his street.

———

A pair of birds rest on the lip of the birdfeeder I hung outside the office window. I watch them flit around for a minute before I turn back to the screen. The yellow note on the desk catches my eye. I hold it in my hand, reading and rereading the correspondence written on the small square.

*Like what you see, sweetheart?*
*So what if I do?*

Shaking my head, I can't even begin to rationalize what is happening. I decide that denial is the best option. So I place the note in my drawer and do my best to forget about the green eyed, sexy as hell ghost roaming around my house. I turn my attention back to the chapters I need to get done. The love story pours quickly from my fingertips as I think fondly about the first week meeting James. Glancing at the clock, I notice I've been writing for about three hours straight. My eyes are dry and my body is restless. I click save and stand to stretch. I climb the stairs two at a time up to my room and change for my workout, not about to waste any free time I have left before I need to pick up Rone.

# TWELVE
# SLOW MOTION STRIP SHOW

### CILLIAN

A LOUD THUD DRAWS MY ATTENTION TO THE GARAGE. I NOTICED A crew arrived earlier, but haven't had a moment to see what they were setting up. Another thud and then loud music plays through the doorway, leading to the garage. *Cut My Hair* by Tate McRae blasts through the open door. I angle it open a little more so I can see what is going on. Ella is dressed in biker shorts and a loose, long sleeve warm up cover. She is watching the coach on the screen, mirroring their movements as she's guided through a warm up. Just like when she was in the kitchen last night and in the shower earlier today, I can't stay away. I settle onto an old stool in the corner and take in the view before me. Starting at the floor, I let my gaze slide higher and higher up her long legs. I've always been into women with curves—twig girls have never quite done it for me. Ella is thick in all the right places. Her thighs look like she's spent years working on building them to be strong. Even though I know it's been a while since she's put in time at the gym, her body looks like it hasn't lost the strength and definition she has clearly devoted time to in the past. I'm proud of her for taking this step to take care of herself again.

I feel like a teenager again, staring at the body moving in front of me. Emotions swirl in my mind and other parts of my body so strong, they are hard to shove down and ignore. Fuck, I want her. Ten years ago if I walked by her on the street, there isn't much I wouldn't have done even to just know her name. In a weird way, I'm thankful for the position I'm in where I can sit back and enjoy her without her knowing. I notice her phone next to me is open to her playlist. Glancing up at her to make sure she's still focused on the program in front of her, I scroll through her selections. An obscene amount of girly music is saved, but I'm surprised to find a few of my favorites as well. There are a few Backstreet Boys tracks that make me smile. I've always thought N-SYNC was better, but I won't hold that against her. Then I find one of my old gym go-tos, letting my finger hover for a split second before dropping it to hit play. *Burn The House Down* by AJR starts to play. She doesn't turn around, not surprised at all by the song that loudly blasts through the new home gym.

I'm nodding up and down to the beat when she sets down the weight and turns around to grab a drink from her water bottle, which I didn't notice is right by my feet. She stops just before me, *and fuck me,* grabs the hem of her cover up and pulls it over her head in a slow motion strip show. Just for me. I have to bite my knuckle to keep from leaping off the stool and doing something that I'm sure will land me on a paranormal ghost hunter show. Her chest is covered in the lightest shine of sweat as a couple drops run together and cascade down the valley between her breasts. She's breathing so heavily that her chest is threatening to spill over the top of her sports bra. Then, in what I'm sure will be my ending, I watch her kneel down before me. I forget where I am, who I am—I forget everything. I just stare at this gorgeous woman on her knees between my legs. My dick seems to forget we aren't real and grows harder at the sight of the woman kneeling before me. I swear if I wasn't already dead, I'd die from the lack of oxygen I'm getting in at the moment. She grabs the water bottle from the floor, wraps her full lips around the straw, hollowing out her cheeks as she sucks more and more and…*fuck me*. For the second time today, I've just blown my load all over my pants. She stands and walks away, not a clue in the world as to what just happened in front of her. I watch her go back to her workout and I slowly rise from my seat. I run a hand through my unruly hair and down my face, shaking her from my head before retreating back inside the house.

# THIRTEEN
# WHAT GIRLS?

### ELLA

As I'm walking down the front steps, my phone buzzes. I drop down to the last step and fish my phone out of the bottom of my bag. Madi's name flashes on the screen.

"Hi, Madi. What's up?"

"Hey, I meant to call earlier, but I got caught up in the day. Ty is wondering if Rone would like to sleep over tonight. Is that ok with you?"

"Oh, sure, I guess so." I want nothing more than for him to have a fun night with a friend, but I haven't spent a night alone in years. It brings me comfort hearing his little footsteps and being able to peek in his room, seeing his blonde head asleep on his pillow.

"Are you sure? If you don't want to be alone, I can come over for a bit tonight." The thought is appealing, but I'm also exhausted and entertaining sounds like a chore right now.

"You are too good to me, I'll be ok. I'm sure Rone will be ecstatic to spend the night. I'll pick him up from camp and drop him off with his things!"

"Sounds great, we'll be ready." We say our goodbyes and I run back inside to pack a bag for Rone. As we're driving from camp to Madi's house, he talks my ear off about his day. When we pull up to their house, Ty is skipping down the steps to meet us and the two of them take off into the house. Madi meets me outside and grabs the bag from my arms.

"Thank you so much for letting him spend the night, he loves spending time with Ty. It's helped him transition so much more than you know. Are you still planning on sending Ty over this weekend for the big sleepover?" I may be taking on more than I should, but having my house full of wild six-year-olds sounds like the perfect distraction.

"We've planned a night out while Ty's at your place, so yes! We are planning on it." Her smile is contagious and I give her a tight hug before waving and getting back in my car to head home.

That evening I lock up the house and settle onto the couch with a bowl of popcorn, scrolling through the endless possibilities of movies and TV shows. Madi sent over a picture of Ty and Rone, tucked inside a fort the size of their living room. Packed with pillows and stuffed animals, I have to zoom in just to see their smiling faces somewhere wedged between. I smile and save the picture to my photo album. Giving up on the search for a show to watch, I make my way back into the kitchen and pull open the freezer. The cool air skates over my skin and I reach in to grab a box of frozen Junior Mints. When I get situated back in the cushions and pull the blanket over my legs, I notice that *10 Things I Hate About You* is cued up and ready to play. It's honestly one of the best movies ever made and may be in my top five all-time favorites.

Half way into the movie, I've abandoned my snacks on the floor and pull the blanket up over my shoulders. My eyes grow heavy and I let myself sink into the couch, feeling a warm embrace tug me close. I savor the feeling of being held as I drift off into a comfortable sleep as *Hold Me Now* by Thompson Twins plays on the TV.

At some point I feel like I'm floating, being carried upward. After a short while, I'm laid down into the comfort of my bed.

The soft glow of the lamp is clicked off and the room is plunged into darkness before my eyes adjust to the moonlight streaming through the half open blinds. The warmth that surrounded me on the couch slides out from around me and instinctively I reach out, trying to hold it to me.

"Stay," I whisper as sleep pulls me under once again. My dreams drift years back to the routine of a tall, handsome boy walking me home from school every day. Our walks became the highlight of my day and I dreaded the weekends when I wouldn't see him. About a month after he almost knocked me over and broke my Walkman, he was waiting for me outside of our high school. He quickly shoved away from his friends and jogged over to me, falling into step like we'd been walking side by side our whole lives.

---

*"Hey, cute girl, I have something for you." He effortlessly shrugs his backpack to his front and digs around for a moment before pulling out a square box wrapped in Christmas wrapping paper. "Sorry about the paper, that's all I could find without asking my mom." He smiles sheepishly at me and for the first time in his life, James Carter is embarrassed. I could let him off easily, but that's not my nature. So I blink up at him through my lashes.*

*"Are you embarrassed of me, James?" I give him my biggest, sweetest smile.*

*He scoffs and runs a broad hand through his hair.*

*"Me? Embarrassed? No, of course not. I mean, why would I be?" His shrug stings and my smile drops. I turn my attention back to the gift. I don't know what I was expecting, it's not like we're dating. Why would I even think that he's told his mom about me?*

*"Shit! No, that came out wrong. Ella, stop, please." I hadn't even noticed I'd started walking until he grabs my arm gently, turning me back around to face him.*

*"I'm not embarrassed to talk to my mom about you, honestly." He*

shifts from foot to foot, trying to find the right words to say. "I kind of already have. I'm not embarrassed to be seen with you at all." Letting out a deep breath, he says the words that will forever be burned in my mind as the moment I fell for James Carter: "I'm just going to lay it out there. Being with you is the only place I want to be." He runs his hands across his face before he continues, "I'm embarrassed that I hardly know you and I can't stop thinking about you." I must be in shock. I can't unjumble my brain to make sense of what he just said. I open and close my mouth a few times, trying and failing to force anything out of it.

"You don't have to lie, James. It's ok, I shouldn't have teased you." I try to muster a smile and reach for the clumsy bow on the package. As the wrapping paper falls away, I'm staring at a brand new Walkman. Blue, my favorite color. Looking up at him, he gives me a shy smile, running that obnoxiously sexy hand through his hair again. Reaching down, he grabs my free hand with both of his.

I stare at our hands, swimming in the feeling of his body touching mine. "I want you to tease me. I want to be around you. I just, ahh, I just want **you**, Ella." His confession catches me off guard and I let out a laugh.

"You…you want me? This isn't funny, James. Please tell me you're joking." My eyes volley back and forth between his. I'm standing here dumb struck. Literally the hottest boy in our high school just admitted he wants me and I am too stunned to even see straight. I'm laughing at him, for crying out loud. His face turns serious so quickly and the sarcasm dies on my tongue. Any sign of his earlier embarrassment is gone in an instant. Tugging me into him, he wraps both arms around my back, my hands still clutching the gift between us. He pulls me into him and my arms rest against his firm chest. "Ella, I like you. I'm not joking or trying to be funny. I'm serious, I promise you. I'm so serious." I close my eyes and whisper, "I don't know what to say right now. How can you like me?" I look around the front lawn of our high school, students talking and falling into groups as they filter to the parking lot. I can't help but notice multiple pairs of eyes flick over to us, envy seeping from them and flooding me with a sense of jealousy.

*"Don't you see all these girls around us?" I throw an arm out, gesturing to the girls blatantly gawking at him. "They are staring at you like they want you all to themselves. I can't compete with that." His arms tighten around my waist and he doesn't look away once when he tilts my chin to look at him.*

*"What girls, Ella? All I see is you." His eyes shine with conviction. "Please go out with me, please be mine."*

———

I used to roll my eyes when people would say *and the rest is history,* like their story didn't have anything else worth telling. But that's the only way I can describe what it was like between James and I after that afternoon. Our love story would take a lifetime to tell; no simple words would do it justice. The way he looked at me felt like the way the sun peeks out from behind the clouds on that first spring day. The feeling of rolling your window down at the same time the perfect song plays through the stereo, as all the worries and drama of the day drift away with the breeze. He was it for me. He was everything. He was my endgame.

After that moment on the front lawn of our high school, nobody could tear us apart. Our parents were supportive of us going on dates, but didn't hide their concern when our curfews were missed because we couldn't stop making out in the car that was parked on the street outside my house. Once they caught on that we were serious and not a quick hook up in the backseat, they lightened up a bit. My parents loved James and his parents couldn't get enough of having me around. As an only child, his parents loved the company of another kid in the house and around the dinner table. We'd sneak out of class to make out in the stairwell, risking getting caught because being apart didn't feel right to either of us. He was a senior and I was a junior. To say I was terrified of him graduating at the end of the year was an understatement. But James only had eyes for me. I never felt like he was slipping away or looking for anything more than just *me*.

After he graduated he went to A&M University, living at home with his parents to save money. I saw him just about as often as we did when we went to school together. When his class schedule allowed, James would wait for me outside our high school and we'd walk home together. It wasn't until one day that year, he walked me to my house. We ended up making out on the couch, not anything out of the norm. However, this time, something felt deeper. I'd never been with anyone sexually before and the thought of the first time being with James made my head spin with need. The kisses grew hungrier and hands wandered further. Before long, he scooped me up and walked me to my room, bumping into door frames and knocking over furniture because he never once broke our kiss. When we finally stumbled into my room, he set me on the edge of my bed and reached over his head with one arm, pulling his shirt off in an effortlessly sexy way. Even though I'd seen him without his shirt many times, this was different. I swear in the year he'd been in college, he's grown from a handsome boy into a sexy man. And I wanted it *all*.

———

*"You're looking at me like you want me to finally fuck you, cute girl." He's never talked dirty to me before. All I could do was sit there and stare at this gorgeous body in front of me. My head was a nest of inter-twined words and thoughts. If I reached for one and pulled, I knew I'd just end up more twisted than I started. So instead of talking, I reached both hands to the bottom of my shirt and pulled it slowly over my head. My hair dropped down, brushing the top of my bra and I slowly drew my hands up my stomach to the clasp in between my breasts, unhooking one hook at a time. His eyes zeroed in on the motion, his breathing becoming quicker. His tongue runs over his lips, teeth*

*grazing his bottom one as his eyes bounce between my eyes and my chest. I glance at the clock on my nightstand.*

*"My parents won't be home until late tonight."*

*I didn't have to say anymore to confirm what we both knew was about to happen. He lunged at me and I laughed out loud as we rolled back onto my bed. He pulled back just enough to stare at my pebbled nipples. Looking back to my eyes, he didn't look away as he stuck his tongue out and slid his body between my legs. My eyes closed when his tongue drifted down my chest and his long, thick fingers pulled the fabric of my bra completely away before pulling one of my peaked breasts into his mouth. I moaned and moved my body against him, silently asking for more. He grinned and moved his mouth to the other side, his hands finding the waistband of my jeans and running his fingertips just below the top. I dragged my hands through his gorgeous hair, nails scraping against his scalp. I pulled the strands softly and then harder when he groaned against my skin. When he looked up at me, he stole more than the air from my body. When he smiled at me and told me I'm the most beautiful thing he'd ever seen, the tears that had been building in my eyes from the feel of him all over me finally spilled down my cheeks. I was happy he didn't notice my tear soaked face. If he did, he didn't say anything. He just slid even further down my body and slowly undid the button on my pants, pulling the zipper down and pushing the jeans down my legs.*

*"Fuck, Ella. You're so fucking hot it's not fair." He rolled onto his back and grabbed his crotch with one hand and ran his other down his face. Without him on top of me, I was suddenly cold and felt exposed. I wasn't ready to let that moment pass. I wanted him, he wanted me, and that's all I cared about. I struggled to pull my jeans the rest of the way off my legs and stood at the end of the bed in nothing but my cotton thong. His chocolate eyes melted as he peeked at me through the hand still covering his face as I stepped between his legs. I pushed them apart further until my thighs were rubbing up against his center. I put my hand over the one on his lap and slowly rubbed it up and down. He groaned again and his eyes rolled back in his head. I tucked both thumbs*

*under the thin strap of my thong and took my time rolling it down my legs, never looking away from his face. His eyes turned dark moving with my hands, his tongue peeked out to wet his lips as he drank in every inch of my bare skin. I sank to my knees in front of him, grabbing the top of his sweats and silently encouraging him to give me control. My core throbbed when he lifted both hands above his head and raised his hips in confirmation. I wasted no time rolling the sweats down his hips and over the tent in his briefs. I massaged his muscular thighs as I dragged the fabric painfully slow down his legs and off his feet. I stood and moved my legs over him so I was straddling his lap. His arms came back down over his body to grip my hips. I rubbed myself on him slowly, dropping my head back at the sensation building in my core. I was dripping on him, leaving behind a wet trail on his briefs as I dragged myself forward and back, over and over until I felt like I was about to fall.*

*In an instant, he sat up and wrapped his huge arms around my body and rolled us so I was now under him. His briefs were off in a heartbeat and there we were, left naked in each other's arms, heavy breathing filling my room.*

*"Is this what you want, Ella? Because I'm yours. I want you so bad." I'd only seen James vulnerable a couple of times. That afternoon standing in the courtyard when he asked me to be his, another time when he kissed me in front of all his friends, and now. Everything felt so right. I couldn't think of a more perfect moment than the one I was basking in. I never wanted this to end. I never wanted to know the feeling of looking up into anyone else's eyes but his.*

*"I feel the same way. I love you, James." The confession fell from my lips and his parted in surprise. He leaned in and kissed me so tenderly and with so much damn emotion that more tears fell down my face. I felt like my chest was going to burst with the amount of love I had for him.*

*His forehead fell to mine and the smile I had quickly become obsessed with filled his face.*

*"Damn, baby. I've wanted to tell you for so long, but just couldn't find the right moment. I love you, too. Forever and ever." His eyes mist over and I reached up to pull him to me for a soft kiss.*

"Promise?"

"I promise." In that moment our worlds collided, lips locked together in a kiss that couldn't last long enough. Every part of our bodies wanted to meld together until we were physically one. His words came out as a whisper before he reached for his pants on the floor and pulled out a condom. I looked up into his eyes and he read the question on my face before I could ask.

"I wasn't expecting anything, but I just wanted to be prepared for when we were both ready." I was glad one of us was prepared, because at that moment, I wouldn't have had the sense to stop and ask what we would do about protection. To be honest, I don't think I would have cared. I wanted all of him, forever. Nothing between us, ever.

I looked up at him nervously, worrying my lip between my teeth. "Can I do it?" Without any hesitation, he ripped the foil between his teeth and handed me the package. That act alone had me pulsing with need. I pulled the condom out and reached between us to roll it on him. He sucked in a breath and pulled his bottom lip between his teeth, dropping his forehead to mine. As soon as I removed my hands he reached between us and ran his fingers through me. I swear I died and went to heaven. If sex felt anything like this first touch, I will come undone in record time. He stroked me back and forth until I was writhing on the bed.

"More, baby, I need more." I felt his smile on my skin as he kissed up and down my neck, leaving me panting and damn near begging. He moved his hand to his dick and rubbed the head against my entrance, coating it in my arousal before slowly edging the tip in. The stretch was deliciously painful and I rocked back and forth, allowing myself time to adjust. Reading me like a book, he moved slowly. When I was ready for more of him, he eased another inch in. Slowly, inch by inch, he pushed in, the pleasure overtaking any pain as my body pulled him in. Stretching me. Ruining me. Once he bottomed out, I pulled his hair, tugging hard; memorizing what he liked. His eyes rolled down to stare into mine. He was just about drooling and I reached up to wipe his lips before I sucked them into my mouth. Wrapping my legs around his hips, I pulled him roughly into me. He moaned into my mouth and I gasped at the friction building between us.

"Give it to me, James. I won't break." That did it. He pulled himself almost all the way out of me, so slow it was agonizing. Just as I was about to complain, he winked at me, fucking winked at me, pulled his hips back, and in one swift motion, slammed back into me. White heat zapped through me and I screamed out at the quick pain that turned into a storm of lust. Over and over he pulled almost completely out and then smacked back against my pelvis. In and out, in and out, the movement built my orgasm like a spring. Coil by coil, tighter and tighter. Our breathing became frantic, hands searching for more skin to mark, lips locked in a possessive kiss. My orgasm grew and grew until I was again just on the edge of falling as our sweaty bodies rhythmically moved together.

"Come for me, Ella. I'm almost there." His voice was deep and raspy. Stars flashed in my eyes. My lungs were devoid of oxygen as I toppled over the edge and felt him pulse inside me as he chased his own climax. As we came down from the most exquisite high I'm convinced I'll ever have in my life, he rolled us so I was once again laying on top of him. We laid on one another for what felt like hours, exchanging lazy smiles and tender kisses. I listened to his heart beat slow back down, my head against his chest. His thick fingers worked through the tangles in my hair. And in that moment, I knew I'd never love anyone the way that I loved this man.

———

# FOURTEEN
## THIS KIND OF AUTHOR

### CILLIAN

SITTING IN MY SPOT AT THE KITCHEN NOOK, I WATCH ELLA TYPE ON her laptop while eating her dinner. The sun outside sinks towards the horizon, casting the most delicious amber glow on her skin. She is breathtakingly beautiful; even the lines around her eyes are gorgeous. I can tell she's lived a life full of smiles and laughter, and I want to learn the story behind every single one. I want to memorize the freckles that dust her skin and run my fingertips over every curve of her face and neck. I lean my head back and take deep breaths, trying to control the storm raging inside me. I watch her fingers fly over her keyboard and am captivated by her eyes when she glances out the window, the sunlight making them seem like an endless ocean of blue hues. I'm done for. Sunk.

While she cleans up dinner and completes her nightly routine upstairs, I give into my curiosity and slide in front of her open laptop. I picked up that she's a writer, but I want to see what she writes. I loved reading and would usually spend my evenings behind the pages of a book out on the back deck rather than on the couch in front of the TV. I wish I could have read one of her books. My eyes dart across the screen, bulging at the scene she's typed out before me. Holy shit, she's *this* kind of author. A sex scene so detailed plays out on the monitor—I can't believe she wrote this with a straight face. She goes into such great detail about the size and length of the male character that I'm suddenly jealous and impressed at the same time. Her steps make their way back down the stairs and I slide my aroused self back to my spot around the table.

I have to force myself to take deep breaths as I watch her go back and forth from the kitchen to the living room. She popped popcorn and filled a giant tumbler with ice, multiple cans of Dr. Pepper, and added in a grotesque amount of cream. It's movie night and I am so game. I ease myself around the table and make my way to the couch. I'll give it to her—her taste in furniture is just what I pictured for this house when I first had it remodeled. After Peter's horrific redecorating, I'm happy to see this house look as it should. In place of the uninviting nightmare of a couch Peter awkwardly placed in this room, is an off white, deep seat sectional, sitting on a colorful rug that covers part of the hard-wood. In the space behind the couch against the wall she installed bookshelves that are filled with not only her favorite authors, but books about a wide range of topics. To my delight, she's included every title she's published. I pictured so many layouts in this space, but she's the one who has brought it to life.

I lean back on the couch and almost fall off the side when she settles in and stretches her feet out, just about touching me. After about ten minutes of watching her scroll past countless movies, I have to hold myself back from snatching the remote out of her hand. Before I can reach out and grab her, she sits up and heads into the kitchen, no doubt searching for another snack. While she is gone, I take the remote she's laid next to me and take control of the evening. I've watched her scroll mindlessly past too many great movies to waste any more time. When she comes back in and pulls the blanket around her, she hesitates for only a moment, no doubt confused as to why *10 Things I Hate About You* is ready to play. It's a timeless film and one of my favorites. To my delight she shrugs, clicks start, and settles in. I wait a few minutes before scooting a few inches towards her, then a few more until I close the small space between us completely. I'm right next to her. I can feel her relax as she absentmindedly leans towards me. I'm in heaven. I just wish it were *real*.

We're about half way through the movie and she's dozing off. I watch her a few more minutes before I decide it's time to get her to bed. I slide one arm under her knees and another behind her lower back, scooping her up into my arms and heading up the stairs. When I turn the lamp off, the room is washed in pale light filtering in from the moon behind the blinds. As I'm about to walk away and take up my usual spot in the chair across the room, she opens her eyes and stares straight into mine.

*"Stay."* That one word will be my undoing. Without even thinking, I round the bed and slip under the covers, staying a good foot away, watching her nestle into the sheets and pillows. Slowly, I move towards her and wrap an arm around her waist, sliding her carefully towards me. She doesn't wake and her breathing stays even, so I rest my head next to hers and breathe her in. Rose and gardenia wash over me and I allow myself to drift off in a dreamless sleep, holding her in my arms.

Ella shifts in her sleep, waking me from mine. "More, baby, I need more." It takes me a moment to remember where I am. I'm not sure I heard her right and I'm worried she's having another nightmare, so I tighten my grip across her body and hold her back tight against my chest. *Fuck. Me.* She moans and her body grinds back against me. I should leave, but I can't control myself around this woman. I let her move her ass back and forth against me, closing my eyes and biting my lip with so much force between my teeth that I taste blood. She moves over me again, sending waves of pleasure through me. I tease the hem of her shirt, wanting nothing more than to slip my hands underneath it. She does it for me when she moves again, shifting her body just enough that my hand is now on bare skin. I suck in a breath and do my best to control myself, but my fingertips glide across her smooth skin while every naughty thing I want to do to her flashes through my mind.

Her breathing grows heavy and frantic, like she's chasing her high and can't quite reach it. Fuck it. What kind of man would I be to deny her some pleasure? I slide my hand down between her legs, under her cotton shorts. She's bare and so fucking wet that I can't stop, my fingers slipping through her arousal. My body reacts to her unlike anyone else I've been with as a feral groan rips through me. Loosening the grip of my other arm, she rolls onto her back, her chest heaving with need and back arching slightly off the bed. I ease my fingers lower and rub my fingers against her. I can't control myself as I slowly sink one finger in her, my eyes rolling back and my heart beating wildly. She lifts her hips and pushes onto me, taking that as my cue for more. I pull my finger out and suck it into my mouth, groaning loudly as her taste slides over my tongue.

She whimpers with the loss of my touch and I smile, pulling my fingers from my mouth with a wet pop. I slide my fingers from my mouth and trail them down her body. The mixture of us on both of my fingers creates a trail of moisture across her skin. Goosebumps raise as the gentle breeze from the fan touches her skin. I'm paralyzed with lust, soaking in the sight beneath me. She shifts her hips back and forth, bringing me back to the task at hand. I continue my path down further, pushing two fingers in when I reach the spot between her legs. She cries out at the pressure, picking up her pace while rocking back and forth with total abandon. Her eyes close while her mouth opens as her climax gets closer. I move my fingers back and forth, running my other fingertips over her body. Shivers chase my touch and she pulls her bottom lip between her teeth. I know she's close so I lean in and whisper near her ear, "Come for me, Ella."

She arches her back and the sexiest moan I've ever had the pleasure of hearing escapes her lips. She rolls once, twice more before I pull my fingers out and readjust her sleep shorts. As I bring my hand to my mouth to lick her off my fingers, a deviant thought crosses my mind. I take my slick coated fingers and gently rub them across her lips. Instinctively, she sticks out her tongue and I'll be damned, *moans* at the taste. I suck my fingers clean, lay back against the pillows, and watch as she rolls over and drifts off into a deep sleep.

# FIFTEEN
## TASTE YOURSELF

ELLA

My phone alarm buzzes on the nightstand next to me and I roll over to turn it off. The half open blinds let the morning sun pour through, casting golden streaks around the room. I spread my arms out to my sides, stretching as my body slowly wakes. When my palm lands on the other side of the bed, I pause and turn to the unoccupied side. It's *warm*. I pull my arm back and then slowly reach over again and feel the empty space. Definitely warm, like someone slept there. I lay back into my pillows and cover my face with my hands, contemplating my sanity. Doing a mental check on my body, I realize I didn't wake up once last night, didn't have any flashbacks, and didn't end up on the bathroom floor retching into the toilet. If anything, I feel relaxed and even a little…sore. I rack my brain and try to remember what I dreamt about. It's not uncommon for me to dream about James and I having sex. When that happens I wake up panting, needing hands on my body, and pissed that my dream ended just before I've reached my climax. I'm trying to figure out if I fingered myself or if I stayed in that dream long enough to imagine James taking care of me, finally getting the release I've been chasing. I stick my tongue out to wet my chapped lips. *Shit.* I lick them again. I must be dreaming, but I know it's real. It's a distinct, heady taste on my lips.

What. The. Fuck.

I roll out of bed, walk to my closet, and stare blankly into it. I'm not sure what to make of my dream or the taste on my lips. Knowing Madi will drop Rone off in a couple hours, I plan to get my workout in early today. I hit play on my playlist and *Snap* by Rosa Linn plays over the speaker as I let my mind wander to last night. I close my eyes and try to remember each detail; I remember watching Heath Ledger and Julia Stiles battle it out on the TV, a warm feeling pulling me close, drifting off to sleep…on the couch. I stumble to the bed to sit down and take slow controlled breaths as I try to ease the panic rising to the surface. I close my eyes and it's as if I can feel the arms gently carrying me up the stairs and putting me under the covers.

*Stay.*

My eyes snap open, and as clear as day, I remember looking up into a pair of familiar, forest green eyes. I jump up from my bed, grabbing the door frame to swing myself into the hallway. I stumble down the steps, tripping on the last one and about land on my face in the foyer. I fly into my office, shaking the mouse to wake up the screen. I pull up my search history and click on the name Cillian Rose. Sinking into the chair, I stare into moss green eyes. His perfectly white teeth smile at me with black hair falling into his eyes calling to me, begging me to reach out and run my fingers through it.

"Cillian," I whisper his name, almost reverently. As if he's been waiting, I feel him—a soothing, warm feeling melts down my back before it wraps around me. I can almost visualize strong arms circling me in and caging me against my desk.

"Ella, sweetheart." I shiver at the soft touch grazing my neck. My hair is piled into a bun on the top of my head and I gasp at the feeling of lips dragging against the exposed skin on my neck.

I lean into the sensation and tilt my head to reveal more skin for my shadow to tease.

"You're not real," I mutter more to myself, trying to pull myself back to reality.

"So you keep saying." His words float over my skin and I can't breathe. "But last night felt real to me." I wasn't delirious this morning. The warm bed, the sweet sore ache between my legs was *real*.

"What is happening?" My voice comes out so soft that I can feel him lean in to hear me. "I can feel you around me, feel your hands on my face, your arms around my waist, and I saw..." I trail off because I know how ridiculous I sound.

"Saw...?" He's so close the heat radiates off him. I want to reach out and grab him, but I'm terrified at what I'd find.

I gesture to the screen with his face smiling back at us. "I saw your eyes!" My voice comes out higher and I sound hysterical. The gentle touch of fingertips brush across my cheek and I lean into the touch, confused and comforted. His voice is just as I remember, deep and calm. I squeeze my legs together, trying to force my mind to stop replaying last night. I should feel violated, now that I know it wasn't my fingers that brought me so much pleasure, but I can't stop the rush of desire that settles into my core.

His voice washes over me. "I wish I could explain it, but I'm as shocked as you are, sweetheart. I've never been able to touch or be heard before." I want him to keep talking, so I keep asking the questions that have been swirling in my mind since our first encounter in the garden.

"Why me?"

After a brief pause, his voice ghosts over my skin. "I don't have the answer to that, other than since the moment you stepped out of your car, I can't stay away. I've been stuck in this space between life and death for ten years, yet I've never had such a physical reaction to anyone before. Even before I died, I've never been so..." There is a long silence, when he responds it's almost a whisper. "...drawn to someone." It's the most conversation I've been able to pull from him and I have to dig my nails into my palms to make sure I'm not imagining it.

"What about the other voices? I haven't heard them since that night in my bedroom." I had almost forgotten about the cold whispers of the other spirits that I met in the garden and the night he built my nightstand. I try to shake myself out of the haze I'm in, realizing now that the feeling I got from them was so much more menacing than the feeling he brings me. He could be playing me, drawing me in just so they can hurt me and Rone. As if he can sense my inner struggle, the warmth settles closer to my body. Featherlight fingers resume their trail across my exposed neck and shoulders.

"I'm sorry they scared you. After I died, I woke up in this house. I couldn't understand what was happening to me, so I ran out to the woods. And they were just there. I had never seen them before. They were the ones who helped me understand that I was in fact dead. Well, not really dead, but not really alive." I rub my face, trying to absorb what he is saying. "We're all just kind of *stuck*. They know what happened to me, but I don't know anything about their story."

He takes a deep breath and when he lets it out, I can't help but breathe him in. "It was comforting in a way to have someone else here with me. We made a promise to help each other find a way to move on." The sudden thought of him moving on to whatever is next has my stomach turning over with dread. It hasn't been long since I first felt his presence and I don't want it to end. Not yet.

"And did you...find a way to move on?" A soft chuckle ruffles my hair and he leans in to whisper in my ear.

"Careful, Ella, sweetheart. It's starting to sound like you'd miss me?" He nips at the other side of my neck and I yelp at the sharp sting on my ear.

"Did you just...bite me?" I reach my hand up and rub the soft spot of my ear.

"I want to do so much more than bite you. Feeling you rub your perfect ass on me last night and your pussy clenching around my fingers before you came all over my hand? God, Ella," he groans into my neck, his heavy breaths sending my loose strands of hair flying in front of my face. "Did you taste yourself this morning on your lips? It was fucking heaven." I gasp and my hand flies to my mouth, running my fingers over my lips. I'm so turned on, almost positive I've left a wet mark on my office chair. As I'm trying to figure out my next move, my chair is spun around so the back is now facing the monitor.

"Do you want a repeat of last night?" I can feel him lean into my front, and for the first time, I notice the most intoxicating smell overwhelm me. I close my eyes and let out a moan at how sexy it is. It's been a long time since I've been so close to a man that I can smell him around me. I'm instantly horny, damn near begging him to touch me again. He smells like tea tree and mint, like he's just walked out of the shower. I close my eyes and breathe him in. I feel the chair slowly turn back around, the heavy feeling of hands and fingers sliding over my shoulders, between my breasts, and down to the band of my workout shorts.

"Open your eyes." His demand scrapes deliciously over my nerves. When he speaks near my ear, I don't hesitate to follow his command. In front of me is his picture. My eyelids flutter and my breathing picks up. The feeling of his hands slide into my shorts and work their way between my legs. I'm damn near panting, eyes locked on the man on the screen. Green eyes pulling me under. If I'm the ocean, he's the moon. Shining through the darkest parts of my life, gravity pulling me to him. And I'll let him.

A car horn sounds outside and I jump up from my chair. I look out the window and see Madi waving from the driver side as she pulls her car up to the front of the house. I run my hands over my arms, the loss of his body around me leaving me feeling cold and empty. I settle my hands on my chest and try to center myself, questions still running through my mind. I *did not* almost get off with ghost hands in my pants. I shiver at the creepy but delicious thought and head to the door to open it, just as Rone hops out of the car. He runs up to me, gives me a quick hug, and dashes up the steps to his room. Madi walks up the front steps and then comes to stop staring at me.

I bounce from foot to foot, uncomfortably as her eyes take in my face and move to my shorts. I look down and frantically turn my back to her, noticing that my shorts are pulled down in the front and one side almost exposes my thong.

"Shit, I'm so sorry. I was in the bathroom and heard you pull up. Clearly, I didn't put myself back together before coming out," I lie around a laugh, feeling my cheeks flame in embarrassment. Shifting the waistband back into place, I turn back around. She gives me a lopsided smile, no doubt reading my lie. *Great, she totally thinks I was getting myself off with my vibrator. Good one, Ella.*

### SIXTEEN
# TREEHOUSE

CILLIAN

FUUUCK ME, THAT WAS THE HOTTEST THING OF MY ENTIRE LIFE, living or deceased. If I thought last night was my undoing, this morning in her office was a new level. She called my name and like a moth to a flame, I was there. I didn't know what to expect, but that was most definitely not it. I watched her from the foyer as she opened the door and greeted Rone and Madi. When the car had pulled up and she leapt from her chair, I noticed a split second too late that her shorts were pulled down and damn me her ass was almost hanging out. I loved the show, but I didn't want anyone else to see her like that.

She moves effortlessly around the kitchen, getting lunch ready for Rone while he once again chats her up about the sleep-over at Ty's house. Watching Madi drive away brought up feelings I have tried so hard to keep locked away. A piece of me that is missing lives on around me and it's agonizing to watch. I miss Madi and Mike. They were my best friends all through childhood, but it makes my heart burst knowing that they befriended Ella. I'm zoning out when I hear Rone.

"Mom, I want a treehouse. Not like a baby tree house, but a real wooden one, in a tree!" He's bouncing around excitedly and Ella's eyes go big.

"We'll see, honey, but I'm not sure if I can do that on my own." My heart cracks wide open. Split down the middle with blood pooling in my chest.

"Daddy would have built the biggest, most awesomest tree house in the whole wide world." His comment makes Ella's face fall and she ducks into the fridge before Rone can notice the tears filling her eyes. When she closes the door, she turns to face Rone and puts her forehead on his.

"You know it! Your daddy was the most awesomest guy in the whole world." My heart bleeds at her words. They stay like that for a moment longer before she pulls away and goes back to making lunch.

Her disposition has shifted and I can sense the mood in the room fading and slipping into old memories, such a dark contrast from the happy buzz it was a few minutes ago. I want to reach my hand out and ruffle Rone's hair as I walk by, but I hold my arms against my body as I walk to the door. Ella's phone lays on the counter and catches my eye. I've noticed Ella loves to have music playing in the background, no matter what she's doing. If she's like me, it helps her mind from wandering to sad places. The screen is unlocked and opened to Spotify. She's busy at the island, so I quickly type in the search bar. Within a few seconds, *I'll Be There* by Walk off the Earth begins to play through the speakers.

I watch as the music filters through the room, breaking the tension. I wait until Ella makes her way over to where Rone is sitting and then quickly tucks him into her arms and starts to dance around the kitchen. He giggles as she tickles him and then she tilts her head back, hair flying around her, and lets out the most beautiful laugh I've ever heard. The sound makes me smile and I'm wondering how this woman before me can laugh through the pain of everything she has been through. I lean on the doorframe and watch in awe at the beautiful moment taking place in my kitchen. Vividly I remember sitting at my desk, sketching out a dozen different designs for this space. I must have spent hours at my desk, only stopping when I had finally finished a design so that I could see a moment just like this one. I looked down at that drawing and had dreams of standing in this same spot watching my wife spin our kids around, laughing, living.

Needing to distance myself from the two of them, I turn and head up the stairs. As I reach the middle of the staircase, I stop and look for the first time at the photographs hung on the wall. Love drunk teenagers smile back at me. Leaning over a younger version of Ella with his arms around her shoulders, is a grown up version of Rone. I remember her whispering his name. *James.* I look from one to the next and in most of them, they aren't even looking at the camera, too caught up in each other to care. My heart aches. What I wouldn't give to look at someone like he is looking at her and have someone look back at me like Ella did him. She looked at him with the most genuine love I've ever seen from someone. I take another step up and follow through a lifetime of memories behind the glass panes. College football games, a proposal on a hike overlooking a beautiful lake, wedding pictures, their first house, her holding her first published book, maternity pictures, family photos, they seem endless, but I take them all in. Love oozing from the glass as they smile back at me. Rone's first bath, first steps, first trip to Disneyland, first day of kindergarten. They stop and I'm left staring at the rest of the staircase leading up to the next floor. I let myself sink to the steps, overcome with emotion as I feel for Ella. I let myself mourn with her and Rone. A love like that should never end, it should continue on for eternity.

I make it back to my room and close the door softly behind me. Overwhelmed and sad, I walk over to my window that overlooks the backyard. I let the sun shine in on me and try not to dwell on my own despair. Instead, I look out over the manicured lawn and into the trees beyond. *Trees.* I almost smash my face into the glass as I look out at the large, southern red oak tree that stands just off to the side of the house. My fingers itch and I about knock my desk over as I reach into the drawers to pull out my paper and pen. Sitting at my desk, my pen scratches across the paper. The sun slides lower and lower as the hours pass. My hand begins to cramp, but I push through the pain. The design on the paper comes to life. I don't stop drawing until it's dark outside. Pushing myself back from my desk, I smile at the design before me.

I sneak out of my door and peek in to check on Rone, passed out and snoring softly. I move down the hall, drawn to the next door that is left open. I slip inside and begin to make my way to the chair that I have now made my bed. But as I cross the foot of the bed, I notice the covers on the other side of the bed are thrown back. Instead of facing the wall like she normally does when she sleeps, she's turned facing the empty side. Streaks of moonlight illuminate her sleeping face just enough to make out the soft rise and fall of her breathing. I pause and look between the chair and bed. *Could it be a coincidence?* But like the stalker I am, I've watched her sleep enough to know that this is not the normal routine. With tentative steps, I round the bed and ease myself onto my side, facing her. As if she can sense me, she scoots closer and the softest smile creeps across her face. She tucks her cold feet between my legs and we lay there, tangled in each other. As I'm drifting off to sleep, I swear I hear her whisper:

"Stay."

## SEVENTEEN
# FEELINGS

ELLA

IT'S BEEN A LONG TIME SINCE I'VE SLEPT THROUGH THE NIGHT consecutively. Usually my sleep is restless, interrupted by my nightmares or cries from Rone's room as he calls for his dad. But this is the second night I haven't woken up in terror or wishing I hadn't woken up at all. I grab a pillow and hug it to my chest, looking out the window on the other side of the room. Letting the sound of birds and the soft warmth of the sun wake me further. I take a deep breath and can't help the smile that lights my face. Tea tree and mint. *It was him.* I had left the covers thrown back, searching for another physical sign that I wasn't making all this up. The steaming cup of tea, the nightstand, the note, my bed. Reaching out I rest my hand on the other side of the bed, wondering why he could touch me. I could feel him when he touched me, but I couldn't touch him. Even when I *knew* he was next to me I still couldn't touch him back, but his touch felt real, *was* real.

I get out of bed and head down the hall to check on Rone. It's still early for him and he's nestled down in his covers sleeping soundly. Totally oblivious to the fact that his mom is having conversations and, *shit*, feelings for a ghost. *Feelings.* That thought stops me dead in my tracks. I'm in love with James. I will always be in love with James. There is no room in my life, in my heart, for a love like what I had with James.

*Safe.*

*Live.*

The soft voice whispers from the deep part of my mind. My heart stutters at the idea that I could find safety, could live a new life with someone who makes me *feel* again.

I shake the thoughts away and walk back to my room to change into my work out clothes, thinking the whole time about what is happening to me. Do I really have feelings? Do I even remember what *feelings* beyond a platonic relationship feel like? I met James when I was seventeen and never needed anything more from anyone else.

As I tie my hair up, I settle with the fact that I'm just finding comfort in whatever Cillian has to offer. Nothing more, as I have nothing more to give. But I allow myself to applaud my progress to even consider the idea of giving even a small piece of myself to someone else. I stare at my reflection in the mirror. My eyes have lost a bit of their shine. My skin doesn't glow like it used to. My heart has nothing else to give. I can't risk giving it to someone just to have it broken all over again. I wouldn't survive it. My hand reaches out and slides across the mirror where the message from Cillian was written in the steam, *I like what I see.* As much as it hurts to come to the realization, I know that I need to help him move on. I can't get twisted up in some ghost bride horror story.

———

"Shit! I think I'm dying!" I collapse back on to the mat after my workout, throwing my hands over my face and breathing heavily. I stripped out of my warmup cover about thirty mins ago and lay on the ground in my leggings and sports bra, unable to move as I try to catch my breath.

"Tough workout, sweetheart?" I sit up, my hands smacking the mat as Cillian's voice rolls across the gym.

"Cillian…" I close my eyes and try to ignore the butterflies that have taken flight in my stomach. I need to stay strong, help him move on, heal my heart, and move on myself. *I am not afraid* my mantra repeats over and over in my mind. Although, I'm not sure if I'm trying to convince myself that I'm not afraid of him or if I'm afraid of living without him. That thought scares the shit out of me. I feel him settle next to me, not touching me, but close enough that I can feel his warmth seep into my skin.

"I don't know what this is. I can't explain what is happening. But I can't give anything to you," I say the words that have been bouncing around in my brain since my pep talk in the mirror this morning.

There is a hint of sadness in his voice when he whispers, "I don't want anything from you." I swallow my emotion, willing myself to follow through with what I've decided is best, for us both.

"I have nothing to give, Cillian. I'm broken and lost. I'm hanging on by a thread, just trying to survive every day for Rone." My heart beats wildly in my ears and I have to take a deep breath before I ask. "Can I be totally honest with you?"

"To give me anything less would be a disservice to us both." I let his calming tone wash over me, taking even breaths before I go on.

"If I had my way, I would have died in that crash with them." I wipe the tears threatening to spill from my eyes. "It breaks my fucking heart to admit it because then I would have left Rone behind. But I don't know how to live this life without James by my side." I'm rambling, but I let the words go. I've learned the best way through this tragedy is to just walk through it. So I'm walking. "I should be living my life watching Paige grow up, watching Rone make memories with his sister and dad. But I'm here, me!" I slam a palm against my chest. "My heart is either broken in a million pieces and blowing away in the wind or it's locked up so tight I can't allow it to feel anything. I'm numb, I'm hurting, I will never be whole again. And to top it all off, I'm sitting on the floor talking to nothing. It just doesn't make sense!" Now the tears flow freely with my words and I'm shaking my head, feeling completely ridiculous. I can feel him, hear him, see the physical things he moves around, but it cannot be real.

A soft touch wipes the tears from my cheeks and then moves to my shoulders, grounding me as I try and calm my breathing. "Ella, breathe for me. Just take a second and breathe." I pull my knees to my chest and force air into my lungs, sucking big breaths between hiccups. "I wish I could explain what is happening, I really do. I'm not asking for your heart, Ella. If you want me to stay away I will, as much as it may hurt. I'll leave you alone and try to figure out how to move on." His words shouldn't make my heart ache, but they do. The tears turn into full on sobs.

"I should want that. But I won't deny that you bring me a sense of comfort and peace that I so desperately have been miss-ing." I wipe at my face, his touch still gently holding my shoulders.

"Then let me be that for you. No strings attached, no expecta-tions, just let me be what you need." His voice is soft and low, making its way past my defenses and gently picking the bleeding bits of my heart off the ground and holding them together.

I sit there for a few minutes before I feel like I can speak again. "I can't lose again, I can't open my heart if there is any chance of it being torn apart again. And you're, I mean, what even are you!" I sigh in defeat and lay back on the floor.

I feel his movement as he lays down next to me. The hairs on my arm raise and I know he's right there. His response is quiet. Short, but quiet. Like he almost doesn't want me to hear it.

"Yours."

"I thought you said no strings attached?" I sound more sarcastic than I intend to.

I can feel the smile in his words when he says, "Like I said, just let me be what you need me to be."

"What happens when you finally, you know." I wave my hand in the air. "Move on." There is a long stretch of silence, and if it wasn't for my body's reaction to him, I would have thought he'd left me laying there alone.

"You'll be ok." He doesn't hide the sadness in his voice.

I flip my hand over so my palm is facing the ceiling. "So friends, then?"

"If that's what you want from me." Fingers slide between mine and squeeze gently.

"Can I do anything to help you find closure? A seance or whatever it is." As much as I admit that I'd hate not having his company, I know the right thing to do is get him to move on. Neither one of us can continue in this weird back and forth, occupying different dimensions.

"I'm not sure what needs to be done. If I think of anything, I'll let you know." He gives my hand another squeeze and then it's gone.

I sit back up and rest my hands on my crossed legs. I can still feel him so I call out, "Cillian?"

His response is immediate, like he was waiting for me to reach back out.

"Yes, sweetheart?" *Sweetheart* doesn't quite fall in the category of nicknames you'd use for a friend. I let it slide, just this once, I tell myself.

"Thank you for being here for me. I don't know what this is or why we are drawn together, but, just thank you. I'll do anything I can to help you find the peace you've given to me." If I have the chance to help him find it, I'll happily give it.

"You promise?" That response he has so often given me still

makes me pause. Like he knows what it means to me. Instead of questioning it, my eyes are pulled to a spot by the door and I keep them fixed there when I say,

"I promise."

# EIGHTEEN
# LOOPHOLES

## CILLIAN

DOES SHE KNOW THE PEACE THAT I NEED, THAT I'VE BEEN CHASING down for ten years, is her? Lying next to her last night, I tried to walk through every scenario about what was happening between us. I've never been able to speak to anyone, let alone feel them. Even though I could annoy the shit out of Peter when he lived here, I'd never been able to physically touch him. And here I was, slowly stroking Ella's hair while she slept. I drifted off while exhausting my brain, trying to solve this problem we were stuck in.

After our conversation in the gym, I came back up to my room to get away from the pull she has on me. Even though she'd plainly put me in the friend zone, I hadn't been completely shut out. She'd given me some loopholes that I fully intend to slip through. But I kept pausing on her comment about not wanting to be broken again. I'd never hurt her, I'm connected to her in a way I can't fathom. But what kind of life, what kind of love, can I offer her when I'm not alive but not quite dead, either? I want to be there for her, in any way she needs me, but at the same time, I can't answer any of her questions. And if I end up slipping away one day, I'll never forgive myself for leaving her feeling alone again.

Over the years, I've tried everything I know of to get to whatever is on the other side. Everything. I've tried stepping in front of cars, hoping that maybe I just needed a repeat to finish the job. They just kept plowing straight through me like I wasn't even there. Because I'm not there, not really. I've tried reliving every moment in my memory from my mortal life; maybe I missed a sign or made a mistake I needed to right in order for my sins to be erased and the gates to open before me. Each time I kept waking up right back where I started, like a horrible replay of *Groundhog Day*, over and over for ten years. I have lamented in this cycle—until a few months ago when I saw her. The world paused, my urgency to move on faded away, and I couldn't wait until the next day to see what she would do. What would make her smile, make her laugh. I longed to be the reason for all of those things.

I slipped out the back door while Ella and Rone were getting ready to head to the park and made my way to the tree line at the back of the property. Before I see them, I can feel the breeze slow and steady moving across the ground, blowing the fallen leaves on the ground around me. Standing before me are the twins holding hands, pale skin and sad eyes staring back at me. They freak me the fuck out. Have they always been this creepy or is it something I'm just now noticing?

"We need to figure this out, it's been too long. We must be missing something." I look at them and give them what I hope is a comforting smile. To my surprise, they aren't angry, but it doesn't ease the restlessness I feel radiating from the pair.

"We have done everything. It's her and that boy." The one sister spits at me. "They need to leave."

"Leave the boy out of this." I bite back. They aren't alarmed in the slightest at my outburst and continue on.

"It has to be them. This is our home, we need to be in it to move on."

"How do you know that? It's my home, too, and I've lived there since I woke up after my death." I throw an arm out in the direction of the house. "There has to be something we haven't tried." I kneel down before them so we are eye to eye and plead with them as gently as I can. "Can you please tell me what happened to you?" I have to remind myself that they are just kids. They never knew a full life, never had to grow up, never had the unfortunate chance to understand death. And if myself at thirty-seven-years-old can't figure this shit out, I can't expect them to. One of the sisters opens her mouth, but before she can get the words out, the other slaps a hand over her mouth and glares at her. Slowly turning her attention back to me she says,

"We've already told you all we know. Forcing us to relive our death will only cause us more pain." She wraps her arm around her sister and turns them to leave. I'm left kneeling on the ground, even more confused than I was when I came out here.

Watching them walk off into the trees, I can't help the odd feeling that they know more than they are telling me. And that makes the rage inside build up to a point of explosion. I'm so angry, deprived of any happiness or hope. I've done a damn good job of just walking through every day, hoping that one day it will come to an end. Like maybe I'm just waiting my turn and one morning I'll wake up, sun shining on my face and look around to see that I've finally moved on. But each day I wake up and it's the same room, same feeling of spinning my wheels, same useless attempt to understand what's going on. And I'm tired, so fucking tired. I smash my fists into the ground, sending dirt flying around me. I let it all out, pain, confusion, anger, despair, everything that I've tried to bottle up for ten years. I've always had a calm disposition; nothing really riled me up. But since Ella walked into my space, I've been wrapped so tight it's only been a matter of time before I snapped.

My moment in the woods wiped me out and put me in a mood. I retreated to my room and have been here for most of the day. The sun has started slipping towards the horizon and not long ago, the doorbell rang constantly as Rone's friends were dropped off for the sleepover they are hosting tonight. I'm lying here, listening to little feet run rampant through the house. I smile to myself because damn, it makes me happy to feel this house full of so much love and laughter. The pain and exhaustion I felt earlier melts away as little voices filter through the halls. Before too long, the voices move out to the backyard and I stand to watch from my window. Down below are probably eight six-year-old boys running wild in the yard. I laugh as Ella chases them around in circles and collapses in a heap as they pile on top of her. Her laughter floats up to me and I allow myself a few more minutes to watch from my window. The house is quiet except for a few shouts and giggles making their way through the house from the back.

Taking advantage of the empty house, I make my way to the office and sit in the desk chair as the computer comes to life. My mind flashes back to the moment I shared with Ella in here the other day. I have to rub my eyes and take deep breaths to stop my body's reaction to the thought of her sitting where I am now, panting and needing my touch. Stomping feet and rowdy voices rush in from the back door and I stand quickly to slide the barn doors to the office closed. I make my way back to the desk, reminding myself I can't be seen and shouldn't be worrying about having doors open or closed. But I need this time. Closing the doors makes me feel closed off, alone. I need that reminder, this is how it has to be, how I'll go on existing. Closed off. Alone.

Sitting back at the computer, I pull up the web browser and type in *Death of twins in Spring Hill, TN*. I'm not surprised that the search results load hundreds of links. I rack my brain, remembering any detail that the twins have given me over the years and try to pull together the pieces to their story.

# NINETEEN
# EPIC FORTS AND EPIC BRUISES

ELLA

I HAVEN'T HEARD OR FELT CILLIAN SINCE OUR MOMENT IN THE GYM this morning and my heart hurts a little. I try to tuck that feeling away and refocus on what we talked about: we're friends and I'm helping him find closure. Thankfully, the house is full of wild boys getting ready to devour the pizza that was delivered as they yell over each other, deciding what movie to watch. They have somewhat successfully built the largest fort I've ever seen in the living room. Although with their limited height capability, it's falling apart for the fifth time and they are getting frustrated.

"Pizza is ready, come and get it!" A stampede of feet coming from all directions answers my call and I slip out of the way into the living room. I watch one of the blankets slip from under the pillow weight and fall to the floor. Dropping my head back, I let out a defeated sigh. I move around the massive pile of blankets and pillows in the middle of the floor, grabbing the corner of the blanket to pull back into place. After multiple failed attempts, I'm ready to give in until I feel him. A hand wraps around my waist and tugs me close. A shiver runs up my spine when I lean into him. I missed the tenderness that I feel when he's near. His sense of calm washes over me and makes all the stress and sadness drift away.

"This is a mess now isn't it, sweetheart?" I can feel his smile close to my ear and his hand holds me a bit tighter like he's afraid to let go. "Would you like some help?"

I roll my eyes and playfully shrug. "I think I can manage."

I swear I feel his eyes roll back at me and he spins me around, arms snaking their way around my back.

"I've been watching you *manage* for a while now and I can't take it anymore." I wish I could see his face. Bask in his green eyes and feel them pull me under. Reach out and brush his black hair off his face. Without another word, he moves away and then I see the corner of the blanket on the other side of the couch lift. He gives it a shake, a silent command to grab my corner, and together we move around the living room, lifting and tucking blankets under couch cushions and heavy books, securing it all in place. We work in comfortable silence. I follow his instructions and blush each time his hands brush against my body when he moves around me. Slowly, the fort takes shape and I'm in awe. I never knew a fort of this magnitude could be made. Suddenly I'm jealous of all the lackluster forts I made as a child. I'm standing back with my mouth open when I finally feel him sneak up beside me.

"How did you do this?" I ask in amazement, gesturing to what we just created.

"I built forts in this very room when I was Rone's age. I guess it's where my love for designing and building first started." I had forgotten that Madi and Mike mentioned he was an architect. Scrapping stools sound from the kitchen and little voices grow louder. I feel Cillian's warmth move closer to the door. I glance towards the doorway, hoping and praying one day I'll be able to see him and not just feel him. The herd of boys run into the living room, now finished with their pizza and ready to pass out in front of the TV. All their feet come to a stop and their eyes bug out of their small, adorable heads.

"Holy cow, Ms. Carter, how did you build this?" The boys all look at me like I have some kind of fort building superpower. In a way, I guess I sort of do.

I smile back at them and give them a little shrug. "I have my ways." That seems to do the trick and they all rush under, getting settled in the pillows and blankets.

I keep busy cleaning up the kitchen, leaving a few water bottles and snacks on the counter in case anyone gets hungry before they fall asleep. After locking up and checking on the boys, I head into the office to get a few chapters done to send in to Mabel. When I sit down, I notice the notepad beside the keyboard. The handwriting is very clearly not mine. Where my handwriting is rushed because I can't keep up with the thoughts racing through my brain, this is neat, like the person writing it had all the time in the world. Images of his fingers gliding over the paper infiltrate my mind. I imagine his fingers long and slender, years of drawing, stretching each one. Those fingers moving down my neck, across my throat, squeezing lightly before they drift down, stopping at my breasts to hold them before continuing on lower, teasing their way under my clothes. I shake my head and readjust in the seat. *Dammit.* He is taking over every innocent thought. I turn my attention back to the notepad before me and look at the notes scribbled all over the page.

- ~~*Drunk driver kills twin high school students, stuns small town Tennessee 1960*~~
- ~~*Mom and twin boys during birth 1966*~~
- *Twins die in house fire Spring Hill Highlights-1967*
- *Burglary gone wrong, results in death of teenage twin girls-1970*
- ~~*Second set of twins born in Spring Hill in the past decade-1974*~~
- **Identical twins go missing from home near Rose Manor-1976**

.  .  .

There must be at least twenty more articles listed after, but this one in particular is bolded. Like he wrote each letter multiple times, tracing and retracing them over and over. I pull up my web browser typing in *Rose Manor 1976*, tapping my pen anxiously as I wait. When the page loads, I scroll through the different articles and find the one about the missing sisters from the area around Rose Manor.

### *Spring Hill Tribune-June 25<sup>th</sup>, 1976*

*The twin girls of Rosemary and Peter Connely have been missing for three days. Reports came in early on Tuesday, June 22nd from their parents that the girls had not been seen since earlier the night before. Their mother states that she sent them off to play with friends after dinner. The girls came home later that evening to tell her they would be spending the night at their friends house on the next street over. The sisters, Jane and Emma, have not been heard from or seen since. Their parents are asking for any information about the whereabouts of their eleven-year-old girls.*

I feel like the wind has been kicked from me. Sitting back in my chair, I cover my mouth with my hands, reading the article over and over again. I grab the pen and write notes underneath Cillian's neat handwriting. This is where he must have been for most of the day—researching what happened to the two sisters who have kept him company over the past decade. The two who do not feel welcoming or happy in the slightest that we're here. I save the article and go back to search for the name of the twins, hoping it narrows down the results. I don't know if this is them, but it's worth a shot. I feel awful that they have withheld their story from Cillian for so long and I'm committed to helping them all move on.

．　．　．

### *Spring Hill Tribune-June 29<sup>th</sup>, 1976*

*Bodies of Connely twins have been recovered. Jane and Emma went missing on the evening of June 21st when they told their mother, Rosemary, they would be spending the night at a friend's house. The next day, their parents reported them missing after discovering that they never made it to the house they said they would be sleeping at. After days of searching the woods surrounding their home, the bodies of the two young girls were found not far from each other. Police have interviewed neighbors in the area, however no reports of suspicious activity were noted. There is an advisory for this area to keep a close eye on your children and make sure all doors and windows are locked while the investigation continues.*

I can't read anymore. The contents of my dinner are threatening to come back up. I dash through the house, being as careful as I can not to wake the boys, and shove my way out the back door into the cool summer night. I fall to my knees in the damp grass and will myself to take slow, calming breaths, gulping down as much air as I can. Being a mother has brought a whole new set of worries into my life. I'm always thinking ten steps ahead, never wanting to do anything to risk something unthinkable happening to Rone. But the fact that terrible things happen every day, even when you try your best to protect your kids, is awful and an unfair part of life. I'm sick for those girls, I'm sick for their mother. That is a pain no parent should ever have to live with. No child should ever experience that kind of terror.

My arms erupt in goosebumps and the feeling that I am being watched is overwhelming. I break out in a cold sweat, looking up into the tree line. Squinting into the darkness, I can't shake the feeling that something is out there, watching me. The trees are so dark and everything is suddenly deafeningly quiet.

Before moving here, I was so worried that it wouldn't feel

like home, nervous that I'd be a wreck and jump at every new sound. But from the moment I looked at the listing online, something felt right about this place. It *felt* like home. But, until this night, I've never felt as uneasy as I do right now. Spring Hill has a low crime rate, our neighborhood is quiet, and the people are kind. But regardless of all the positives to this place, the article I just read wiggles its way back to the front of my mind. I'm instantly so terrified I can't move. Like when you see a spider or snake and you want to run away, but your body freezes. I'm an easy target; it's late at night and I'm alone, except for the group of young boys sleeping peacefully inside. I'm all too aware of how vulnerable and responsible I am.

Standing on shaky legs, I force myself to move toward the safety of my house. Ice cold fingers wrap around my ankles, holding me in place. A heavy weight is shoved against my back, causing me to fall over roughly as my legs are ripped out from under me. I slam into the ground so hard the air is knocked from me. My knees ache from the landing and I can feel the cold ground soak through my pants. A chill breaks out over my skin. Stars dance in my eyes and I gulp for air, struggling to fill my lungs. I'm gasping for breath as I turn onto my stomach, coughing and trying to push myself back up to my feet. Lifting my head, my eyes land on my bleeding palms, scratched from catching some of my weight in the fall. I try to look around at who has gotten to me so quickly, but all I see is darkness from the tree line inching its way closer to me. To say I am petrified is a huge understatement. I've never felt this kind of terror before and I lost my fucking husband and unborn daughter.

The darkness creeps closer and I scramble on hands and bruised knees. I don't make it far before I feel thin, cold fingers thread their way through my hair. They pull so hard that I'm lifted onto my knees. I let out a scream at the pain and rip at the hands holding my hair, trying to find something to grab, but my fingers slip through the cool air. My scalp burns and I feel strands of my hair, one by one, being plucked from the skin. I try to scream for help, but when I open my mouth, all that comes out is a mangled whimper. Another set of hands grabs my arms in a bruising grip and pulls my arms forward with so much force that my hand snaps back. Just as the hold on my hair lets go, my body flies forward. Landing hard, my face ricochets forward and bounces violently off the ground. Cartilage crunches and a sharp pain slices across my cheek. My body sags to the ground, coughing and choking. I try to comprehend what is happening.

The harrowing feeling that had surrounded me melts away, back into the trees. I hear the sound of crickets slowly grow louder until the sounds of the night once again fill the air. Rolling to my side the best I can, I try to assess the state of my body: warm liquid runs down from my nose, the top of my head is on fire, and my arms sting. My vision blurs around the edges. I'm so tired. If I could just rest here for a few minutes, I'll be ok. The last thing I remember is the slam of the backdoor, just as everything fades to black.

## TWENTY
# LOOSE ENDS

### CILLIAN

I KNEW DEATH WOULD BE PEACEFUL, BUT I DIDN'T THINK I'D actually be aware of it. I thought I'd be, well, dead. I'm lying in my room, smiling to myself and feeling completely content. If this is death, then I might be ok with it. There is something about the feeling in this house with Ella and Rone that makes it feel like home. Helping her build the fort for the gang of boys sleeping over has been the highlight of my immortal life so far. The look on their faces when they came running into the room gave me a sense of pride I haven't felt in a long time. Not pride in myself for what I had contributed, but a sense of pride in the woman before me. I didn't mind one bit that she took ownership of what we had built together. I'd happily let her shine while I stood in the corner. After my conversation with the twins in the woods and then my unsuccessful research in the office earlier that day, I needed something to bring a smile to my face. I had looked through countless articles, jotting down which ones may have potential and crossing out any that clearly didn't fit the little information I knew about the sisters. There was one in particular I needed to look into more when I had the chance.

I had given up once I peeked through the office doors and saw Ella, clearly out of her depth, rebuilding the fort. It felt so easy and natural to work alongside her. Even without any words, we just flowed. When I had relationships before, I always felt the overwhelming need to fill any empty space. Silence felt uncomfortable, stifling. It felt like failure. But with Ella, silence feels whole. There is no need to fill gaps with awkward conversation or lame jokes. With her, it's like all my loose ends are tied up neatly in a bow.

The house had been quiet for a while now, so I decided to get on with my nightly routine of making sure the house was locked up and Ella and Rone were in bed. I made my way out of my room and noticed the lights were still on in Ella's room. Taking a quick look inside, I noticed she wasn't there. Quietly, I shuffled down the steps and into the living room, ducking under the top blanket to check on the boys. They were all strewn across the floor in different positions that would make any adult need an appointment with a chiropractor if they spent the night like that. After double checking the front door was locked and switching on the porch light, I stepped into the office to turn the lamp off. On the desk was my notepad that I had forgotten to tuck away. But I noticed on the bottom were notes in Ella's handwriting. I sat down and read through the articles she had pulled up on the screen and the notes on the paper.

A feeling of dread washed over me and I couldn't fight the feeling of loss that snuck in. I should be happy that she was following through on her promise to help me, but I also couldn't help that I felt upset that she wanted me to move on. As I sat here wrestling with these emotions, a sound from the back yard had me snapping my head up. I strained to listen for anything else. After a few moments, I stood and made my way to the kitchen to check that the back door had been locked up for the night. It was then that I heard a muffled scream and my blood ran cold.

Moving through the hallway to the kitchen, I scanned the backyard as I passed the wall of windows overlooking the back of the property. It was *so* dark outside, dark and quiet. That was enough to make me pick up my pace, something pulling me out of the house. I slammed through the door, darting across the small deck and down the steps to the grass. Looking to the side I saw her, laid out on the grass, not moving. I scanned the trees for any sign that danger was still present and dropped to my knees beside her.

"Ella! Ella!" I screamed for her, but she didn't move. Gently turning her over, I fought the animalistic growl that threatened to break free. Her face was battered, bruises starting to turn her skin an ugly purple. Her hair was tangled and her nose was bleeding, running down the side of her face and dripping into the grass. Deep red stained her lips and cheek as blood made a gory trail down her tan skin. I laid her head in my lap and shook her shoulders, firmly calling her name. *Please, please, please.* Panic wrapped its claws around my heart and I had to swallow my own sobs that worked their way up my throat. She gasped for air and reached her hands up to grab her face. I wrapped my fingers around her wrist and she flinched, struggling to pull away from me.

"No! No, get off me!" She thrashed back and forth, screaming at me.

"Ella, sweetheart it's me. It's me, baby, I'm here." I tried not to let panic lace my words as I gently brushed her matted hair from her face. I carefully tucked her into my arms and made my way back up the steps and across the deck into the open door, stopping only to close and lock it behind me.

"Baby, do I need to call the police?" I wasn't sure how to pull that off. All I knew is I would do whatever I needed to do to take care of her.

Her response was a painful whisper that I had to lean close to hear. "I couldn't see them." I held her closer as my rage tried to break free again. I knew exactly who was responsible for this. Even though I hoped more than anything that I was wrong, I knew I wasn't.

As we passed the living room, I quickly made sure none of

the boys had been woken up by the noise. Even though I didn't see the twins outside, I wasn't sure if there was still a threat. The possibility of anyone hurting my girl or these boys had my blood pressure building. Ella rested her head against my chest as I climbed the steps two at a time and turned into her room. I took her straight into the bathroom and sat her on the counter, settling myself between her thighs. She was shaking and wouldn't lift her head from my chest. My arms wrapped around her and I stroked her hair, whispering soft words of comfort over and over until her breathing evened out and she lifted her head. My fists clenched and I had to do my best to hide my anger before I accidentally pulled her hair that was still intertwined in my fingers.

Softly tipping her chin so I could look at her better, I brushed my hand across her cheek. "I'm going to run you a bath, can you sit here for a minute?" She nodded and I moved from between her legs to start the water in the tub. When I was sure the temperature was perfect, I crossed the floor back to her.

"Can you get undressed or would you like some help?" She didn't respond, but simply lifted her arms above her head, wincing in pain. It was then that I noticed the long, slender bruises already marking her beautiful skin. I reached out and grabbed the hem of her shirt and slowly lifted it over her head, careful not to bump her nose in the process. Next, I knelt down and removed her socks, rubbing her feet, cold and wet from the grass, between my hands. Helping her stand, she leaned towards me and I reached behind her to unclasp her bra. She pushed off me slightly just enough to let it slide down her arms and land with a wet smack on the floor between us. I reached down and pushed the waistband of her sweats and underwear down her legs. Turning her around, I keep one hand holding her waist steady and the other helping lift her feet free. I walked her to the bathtub and held her gently as she stepped into the water and settled beneath the surface. She took a long, shaky breath before staring up at the ceiling.

I carefully wiped her face, cleaning off the blood from her

nose along with the remaining dirt and grass before moving behind her to clean her dirty hair. I gently poured water over her head, careful not to dump it over her face. She leaned into my touch as I washed her hair, avoiding the red spots on the crown of her head where hair had been ripped out. When the water began to turn cold, I reached into the tub to let the water drain, helped her stand, and wrapped her in the towel from the hook.

"What do you want to wear, sweetheart? Tell me what to get you and I'll get it." Ella sat on the chair by the window and pointed to her closet at a pile of clothes on the floor. She wasn't shaking anymore, but I could still see the fear in her eyes and the way her arms hugged her body. I grabbed some sleep shorts and her oversized Dolly shirt that she loved so much. She gave a little laugh as I walked closer to her and I smiled at the sound, immediately feeling lighter.

Tilting my head to the side I ask, "What's so funny?" She rested her head back against the oversized chair and nodded towards the clothes in my hand.

"All I can see are floating clothes." I hadn't stopped to think how strange it must look from her perspective, but now that I have the image in my mind, I laugh at the thought. We laugh together as I slowly help her get dressed, paying close attention not to touch her too intimately. I've wanted to see her naked again for so long, but at this moment, all I can think about is keeping her safe. I get her settled under the covers and go to move to the chair to keep my nightly watch, but she rolls to face the open side of the bed and whispers,

"Cillian, please stay by me." I sink into the mattress and shift over so we're almost nose to nose. I look into her ocean eyes and she stares back. We stay like that for a long time until her eyelids drop closed. She turns on to her other side with her back facing me, and without hesitating, I reach under her and slide her back against my chest. Breathing in tandem, I drift off with her in my arms.

# TWENTY-ONE
## SOAKED, NOT IN A GOOD WAY

ELLA

Cold fingers slide over my skin, gripping my wrists so tightly they leave bruises in their path. Hands slide up my arms, over my shoulders, and wrap around my neck. My face turns horrific shades of red, morphing into a disgusting purple as the air leaves my body. My eyes ache from the pressure and I'm sure my head is about to explode. For a moment, my vision becomes clear and I can see him perfectly, sitting before me. *Rone.* He smiles at me and for the briefest moment, I smile back. Then his eyes turn from their perfect shade of chocolate brown, darker, darker, until they are completely black. His smile morphs into a sickly, demonic sneer. Black dots dance in front of my eyes and slowly turn into a wave of darkness that washes over my existence. I'm dying, finally, drifting closer to the end.

"Sweetheart, I'm right here. Breathe for me, you're alright. It was a nightmare."

In a panic I sit up, instantly dizzy and gasping for air. I'm drenched in sweat, my clothes plastered to my body like I've just climbed out of a pool. Grabbing my neck and face I wince in pain, my fingers unknowingly jabbing at my sore nose and dry eyes. Then the warmth I've become so accustomed to floats around me. I can feel his body move behind and around me, pulling me back to reality in a wave of calm. I shiver from the instant change in temperature and lean back into my shadow of comfort. It's as if he's really there, legs draped around my waist, his arms pulling me back against his chest. I close my eyes and envision what it would look like if he was actually here.

"Tell me what you're thinking." His voice is so real. It tickles my ear when his face nuzzles into my neck. I want to turn into him and pull him against me, but I don't want to disrupt the comfortable hold he has on me.

"I'm thinking about what you look like," I admit. His hold tugs me a little closer, so I continue. "I know what you look like, at least from the neck up. I envision your black hair, unkempt and disheveled from sleep, falling down just over your green eyes. Maybe a little hint of a beard coming in." I can almost feel it against my skin. "Your lips are obnoxiously full, I'm wondering if you pay for fillers or if they are natural." I shift a little bit, trying to get as close to him as possible. Then because I'm feeling bold, or maybe delirious, I go on. "Maybe you can fill me in on what the rest looks like?"

"Mmmm…" I swear I can feel his nose run up my neck and the slight touch of his lips when he speaks against my skin.

"You covered most of the important features." His breath tickles my ear and I have to fight back the tremor that tries to roll through me. "I like to keep my hair a little longer. I have a nervous tick of running my hands through it when I'm drafting designs, so I never bother to do it." He continues his path over my skin and the shiver I've been pushing back finally breaks free. The pain and fear long gone.

"You can thank my mother for the lips and my dad for the perfectly straight nose. I did break it once in a fight in college, but didn't get the signature bad boy bump I hoped for." I try to pull away and scoff in mock disbelief that life was so unfair to his perfect nose. His low laugh has heat pooling between my legs as he pulls me back against his chest.

"I like this, keep going. It's unfair you know what I look like and I don't know anything about how you look."

His fingers dig into my hips when he playfully says, "Don't forget, sweetheart. I know what all of you looks like." I laugh and struggle playfully in his hold.

Shuffling back into position, I wave my hand for him to continue. His lips smile against my neck and he goes on.

"I like to work out, but I'm not a calorie counter. My favorite thing to eat is brownies. I probably ate a whole tray once a week, I can't help myself. But I'm blessed with good metabolism and it shows." As if he can feel my eye roll, he nips at my shoulder. I shiver, the dampness of my clothes now seeping into my bones. He pulls back and before I know it, I'm lifted in the air.

"What are you doing?"

"Sweetheart, you're shivering. And you're soaked—not in a good way, either." God, is this man dirty without even trying? "What would you prefer, shower or bath?" He gently sets me down in the bathroom, but his hands never leave my body. He holds me, one hand on my waist with the other on my arm, gently rubbing over the angry, purple bruises.

"That sounds great. Shower, please." There is no use arguing with him. Hilariously, the glass door opens on its own and suddenly the water turns on, steam slowly filling the room. I turn and tug the clothes free from my body. Not the least bit self-conscious, I turn and enter the shower. The door closes behind me and I expect to feel alone while I warm under the water. I almost scream in surprise when I feel him push me up to the wall. The cold tile on my back and hot water pouring over me are at war with each other against my skin.

"Do you want me to tell you what I'd make you feel like right now?" His once soft and deep voice has turned dark and thick. Even under the hot spray of the water, I shiver.

"No…" He stills and I feel him pull away, but I smile and finish the sentence.

"I want you to show me." There is a brief pause before I feel his hands grip my face and he turns my head away from the shower spray. Teeth graze my neck. He stops at my collarbone and pulls my skin between his lips, sucking and leaving marks in his wake. His broad hands drop to my waist and he pushes me harder against the wall. Goosebumps pop up along my skin as his mouth works its way from my shoulder, down to my chest, and between my breasts. A hot, soft, wet motion works between my heaving chest and over the top of my right nipple. Without any warning, it's sucked roughly into his mouth, pinching and rolling it between his teeth and lips. I let out a low moan and arch my back, pushing myself further into him. He lets out a growl of approval and moves to the other side. I'm melting and the hot water suddenly doesn't compete with the heat of my skin. I'm on fire, burning for this man. A man I cannot see but can feel all around me. *Inside me*, I beg.

"Cillian.." I whisper his name. He mumbles something against my skin that I can't hear over the sound of the water. His hands continue their path down my hips, over my thighs, massaging and soothing their way to my ankles. My mind has barely caught up to his movement before my legs are lifted into the air. If I didn't feel them thrown over what I'm assuming are his shoulders, I'd be terrified I'd fall to the floor. The sight must be baffling, like I'm hovering in an invisible chair, legs spread wide.

His hot mouth leaves my skin and I want to cry in protest. He plants a soft kiss on my stomach before pleading, "I'm holding on by a thread here, baby. Tell me you want this." I reach my hands down and almost jump in surprise when my hands vividly feel the texture of wet hair. Up until this moment, I've only ever felt him when he's near me or when he touches *me*. I've never been able to reach out and touch *him*. His mouth between my legs distracts me from trying to reason it all out in my mind, but a brief thought crosses my mind that the closer we get to one another, the thinner the veil between life and death becomes.

I don't risk opening my eyes, happy to live in this dream. Even if it's just that, a dream. I pull tightly and push my back harder against the wall, which in turn pushes me up more against his body. His hot breath drifts over my aching skin. I'm unsure if I'm more wet from the shower or from this man kneeling before me. His big hands and long fingers grip my ass and he pulls me away from the wall. In any other situation I'd be anticipating the fall, but something about the way my body instinctively trusts him has me begging for more.

He dives between my thighs, a slight scruff scratches delightfully against the sensitive skin of my inner thighs and I sigh at the sensation. My clit is sucked in the most eye rolling, orgasmic pull I've ever felt in my life. *Holy shit, holy shit, holy shit.* I'm not thinking clearly, but I don't give a fuck. I haven't felt on fire like this in the longest time. The sensible part of my brain is telling me to wake up from this impossible dream while the other is begging me to cave. And like the slut I am, I jump in, head first. I rock back and forth against his mouth, pulling his hair harder every time he moans in approval. His tongue flicking and sucking my clit as his hands massage my ass. I'm writhing and wiggling in his grasp and then, I'm detonated. One hand moves to the center of my back, holding me firmly in place, while the other moves to my clit, pressing and rubbing in the perfect motion. His tongue takes the place of his fingers on my clit and in one swift motion, he plunges two fingers inside me. The scream I let loose can only be described as other worldly, the sound of a woman coming undone and coming together at the same time. In tandem, he works his fingers and tongue until I'm pulsing around him, sobbing with pleasure as my hands and thighs hold him tightly against me. If he wasn't already dead, I'd be worried I'd suffocate him. His hold on my back loosens, his fingers slide out of me, and they move to my back. As I come down from the most delicious high, he slowly rubs up and down my spine, dropping my legs back to the floor and pushing his chest up against me. I lose track of how long we stand there, his forehead resting on mine.

"Fuck, Ella, that was incredible."

Words evade me and all I can do is nod my head against his. He turns me to the water and holds my back to his chest, his arms encircling my waist. When I've come down, I turn in his arms, sensing his gaze on my face.

"How can I return the favor?" Apparently, I'm still feeling bold, desperate to feel him again. His hands slide up to my shoulders and he grips them gently, slowly and carefully walking me backward to the bench at the back of the shower.

"Show me what I designed this shower for." The back of my knees hit the edge of the stone bench and I sit down. The seat is warmed from the hot water that has drenched it, doing nothing to calm my body that is now shaking with anticipation. The glass of the shower is fogged over with steam and as I feel his body move to the other side of the shower, handprints drag across the glass causing the water to collect together and drip down the glass. It's like a scene from a movie. I'm so turned on by the idea of his eyes on me.

"Tell me what you had in mind and I'll do it." I'm shocked by how forward I've become but I lean into it, ready to play my part.

"Lean back." His voice is husky and without seeing him, I am spurred on by the hunger in his voice. I tilt my head back against the glass wall and stare towards the sound of his voice.

"Do you like it when I talk dirty to you, sweetheart?" I nod my head, slowly running my hands up and down my breasts.

"You're so sexy, baby. Breathtaking, earth shattering, gorgeous." His words encourage me and I tease my nipples with my fingers, rolling and pinching them, hissing at the pleasure that snaps through me.

"That's it, touch yourself. Show me how you make yourself feel good." When was the last time I touched myself like this? It's had to be since before James passed. The thought of him should make me feel guilty. I should be ashamed, but something in my heart tells me that he would be proud of me for feeling sexy again, proud of me for finding something or someone to help hold the shattered pieces of my heart together again. I shake the image of James from my mind and let my hands wander. I can hear Cillian panting from the other side of the shower. The hot water raining on the ground and our heavy breathing are the only sounds filling the hot and humid room. I put both of my palms on the ends of my knees and slowly turn them inwards, pushing my legs apart as far as they'll go, raising up on my toes.

My smooth hands drift up my inner thighs and I whisper to him, "Like what you see, sweetheart?" Repeating the words he wrote on the sticky note not that long ago.

"God, yes. I worship you, Ella." If I wasn't so turned on I'd stop and marinate in those words, but I want nothing more than to bring him to the edge with me, so I keep my hands moving. When I reach the soft spot between my legs I almost climax from my first touch, but I focus on the spot in the corner where if I look hard enough, I can almost see hooded, green eyes feasting on me. I circle my index finger over my clit, smiling to myself as I hear him curse from across the shower. The idea of him getting off simply because of how I look and touch myself makes me feel powerful. I circle faster, my breath matching the pace of my finger.

"More, baby, I need more." The words from my dream float through me.

"Tell me what you want, guide me." I'm in control here, but I want to hear his voice, already missing the feel of him around me.

"Fuck me, Ella. You're everything. Finger yourself, make yourself come on your hand. Show me how many fingers you can fit in your tight pussy." The filth flowing from his mouth easily does me in. I circle faster, pushing a finger from my other hand into me slowly, curling as it slides it. Pumping and circling until I'm lost in a daze.

"Another one!" His commanding tone is so unlike the gentleness I've heard from him before. Nearing my climax, I remove my one finger and fold my three middle fingers together so they wrap around each other, pushing them into me. I groan as I stretch myself around them.

"Holy hell that is so hot. I'm about to come, baby."

"Cillian…" Tears run from my eyes, buzzing fills my ears. My body coils tighter and tighter with each pass and stroke of my fingers. "I'm so close."

His voice is instantly in my ear, his arms braced on either side of my body. Lips work their way over my shoulders and up my neck. Nipping and leaving open mouthed, wet kisses on their way up my body.

"Come for me." Like I've grabbed an electric fence, my body shakes and trembles. My orgasm rips through my body. I feel him smile against my skin as I float in a blissful haze.

# TWENTY-TWO
# PANCAKE GOD

### CILLIAN

THE SOFT GLOW OF THE RISING SUN SEEPS THROUGH THE BLINDS AND I stare at the gorgeous woman sleeping next to me. Her face is still a little swollen from the beating last night, but her cheeks have some color back to them. I hate to leave her, but I want to make sure the boys haven't woken and raided the pantry. I silently slip from the covers and head to the bathroom to get some Tylenol and a glass of water for her to wake up to. When I enter the bathroom, I'm assaulted by the memory of our time in the shower. I have to grip the counter to keep from doubling over in pain as my dick starts to relive each glorious moan and whimper.

Ella is beautiful every moment of every day, but Ella with her legs spread and head tipped back in pleasure is something I'll never have words for. When she was too sated to move, body limp from her orgasms, I gently lifted her from the shower bench and wrapped her in a towel. Once she was dry, I tucked her under the covers and slipped in beside her. My own orgasm from watching her finger herself was so divine that I almost passed out when I came. I barely had enough energy to take care of her and get us both in bed. I almost laugh out loud when the memory of her sleepily whispering comes back to mind. I was just about asleep when she mumbled, "I wish I could feel you."

I don't know in what context she meant that, but I am assuming it was in a sexual way based solely off of the filthy way we got off last night. My eyes wander around the bathroom, letting my mind replay the way she tasted on my tongue. How I licked her off my fingers when I set her back on the floor. My eyes land on a can of shaving gel. That's about the right size, I think to myself. I reach in the shower, grab the can, and set it by the sink. I pull open the drawers of the vanity until I find a tube of red lipstick. I don't have a stack of sticky notes, so I uncap the tube and write directly on the countertop,

*Now you know what to expect.*

Proud of my frat boy behavior, I fill a glass with water and shake out a couple Tylenol. Returning to the bed, I give her a soft kiss on her head and set down the pills and water on the nightstand.

Making my way downstairs, it's quiet. I take that as a good sign that the boys are still asleep. I peek under the fort and the boys are snoring gently, miraculously in the same positions as last night. I head into the kitchen and come to a dead stop. Sitting at the island, swinging his legs back and forth with his chin in his hand, gazing hungrily into the pantry, is Rone. His little head swivels to look in my direction and I have never been happier to be invisible than I am right now. I blush as thoughts of the things I did to his mom last night creep back into my mind.

"Who are you?" he asks. I step sideways and look behind me, expecting to see one of his friends who has woken up and made their way into the kitchen. When I don't see anyone and turn my attention back to him, I freeze. His Hershey brown eyes look at me intently, waiting for a response. Knowing that he can't see me, I quietly step towards the door, but his gaze tracks my every move.

What. The. Fuck.

"Can you see me?" I whisper. There is no way, absolutely no way this is happening.

"Of course, silly." Then looking down at himself, he looks and back up again says, "Can you see me?"

"Umm, yes I can see you. But how can *you* see *me*?" His mouth raises in a lopsided grin and he gestures to his face.

"With these, duh!" He puts his thumb and index fingers over both eyes and lifts them open as wide as he can. I'm not sure how to respond. I can't leave and run out the back door, I can't tell him who I am or that I live here. I'm in shock, on shaking legs I move over to the microwave and look at my reflection in the door. Nothing. Just like always, I never see myself staring back.

"What are you doing? Are you mommy's friend?" His voice startles me back to the reality that this boy can see me. I turn around and brace my hands on the other side of the island facing him.

Do friends have absolutely filthy shower sex? I'm unsure how to answer him, but he doesn't look away from me. His head tilts to the side, waiting for my answer. "I am your mommy's friend. I used to live around here." I've never been more nervous than I am right now. I haven't been around many kids in my lifetime and I'm suddenly very aware that his answer has a lot of weight to it. "Is it ok that I'm here?"

His answer does little to ease my hysteria. "That depends…"

"On?"

"Do you know how to make pancakes?" I let out the breath I didn't realize I was holding in and gave him a big smile.

"The most awesomest." Rone and I get started on making pancakes together and he chats my ear off like we've been friends forever. It feels unbelievable to be seen, feelings of belonging and acceptance wash over me despite my best efforts to push them aside. I'm finishing cleaning up the kitchen when noises start coming from the living room as the other boys start to wake up. Not wanting to risk any of the others seeing me, I start to slip out the door to the backyard, but Rone's sweet voice stops me.

"You never told me what your name is, I'm Rone!"

I grin back at him. "Hey, buddy, I'm Cillian." His mouth opens and closes. I can almost see the wheels in his head turning as he tries his best to say my name. I walk closer to him and pull his head under my arm, ruffling his hair. "You can call me Ian, buddy."

"Ahh good, your name is hard to say. I like Ian better." He shakes his head out from under my arm, his little hands flattening his messed up hair. "Thanks for making us breakfast."

"Anytime." I release my hold on him and start to walk away when he asks.

"Promise?" My heart stutters and I can't help the emotion misting over my eyes.

"Anything you need, I'm here. I promise." And with that I finally make it through the door, closing it behind me.

# TWENTY-THREE
## DON'T LET YOUR LIGHT FADE

ELLA

My whole body hurts, I feel like I've been run over by a truck. I peel my eyes open and turn my stiff body in bed. There is a glass of water and Tylenol on my nightstand. Leaning over to grab them, I sit myself up in bed and instantly feel the pressure of a massive headache building behind my eyes. I feel like shit, but I slept like heaven. I tip my head back, swallowing the pills as last night's horror and pleasure runs back through my mind. The news article about the twins tragic death, the attack outside, strong arms carrying me, bathing me, taking care of me. And everything that happened after I woke from my nightmare. His voice, his laugh, his fingers. God, I'm a mess. Everything about what we did in my shower is a scene from one of the books I write. And it's at this moment I realize that I can't deny the way we are pulled together. I keep comparing him to the moon. I'm the ocean. We move together, we belong together. One cannot exist without the other. He's the gravitational pull to the chaos of my waves. Pulling me to him and pushing me to heal.

I lean my head back on the pillow and allow myself a few moments to collect my thoughts before I force my sore body from bed. I wish I had time to shower, but I know the boys will be awake soon and their parents will be arriving to take them home. When my eyes meet my reflection in the mirror, I let out a small cry. My eyes are red and swollen, like I spent the whole night crying. My arms have bruises that are undeniably from fingers that held me so punishingly the night before. My nose is puffy from the beating it took when my face became so well acquainted to the ground. My hair is surprisingly the only thing that looks like it has survived, although I can feel the sore spots on my scalp where there is no doubt a few bald patches from the hair that was pulled out. I wince and do my best to wash my face, grabbing a long sleeve sweater off the back of the door to cover my bruised arms.

Reaching for my toothbrush, I knock a can of shaving gel off the counter. Confused, I kneel down to pick it up. Rolling the cold metal in my hand, I reach up and hold it to my head, sighing as the cold eases the pain throbbing against my skull. When I turn to lean against the counter, my other hand slips against something slick on the surface. Red coats my fingertips and for a split second I almost mistake it for blood, but the sticky waxy feel reminds me of lip gloss. I look down to where I had just touched and the can falls from my hand, landing with a loud clang on the tile floor. *That bastard.* I'm equal parts disgusted at his crudeness, impressed with his opinion of himself, and curious to know if it's even remotely close to accurate. I grab the can from the floor and take a closer look at how it looks in my small hand. My fingers barely reach around and the length has got to be close to eight inches from top to bottom. I've read and written my fair share of smut to know how much we exaggerate this part of a man. So without too much hesitation, I grab the tube of lip gloss from my drawer and write him back.

*Prove. It.*

I throw on some sweats and tenderly pull my hair up into a bun. I can't do much about the bruising on my face and even my most expensive eye cream couldn't solve my puffy eyes. About half way down the stairs, I'm met with the delicious smell of pancakes and the sound of happy voices makes me feel warmer. The chill from everything that happened last night fades with the sun that now shines through the windows, sending the dust particles floating through the air into a golden dance. I step into the kitchen to find the entire island and kitchen nook table covered in sticky syrupy plates and chocolate milk cartons drained dry.

"Rone?" I call out for him, trying to keep my surprise hidden. After a few calls, he finally drags himself into the kitchen with peanut butter smeared across his adorable face. "Baby, I'm so proud of you for taking care of yourself and your friends, but we've talked about cooking without mommy." Wetting a paper towel, I bend down to wipe his face.

"Ian helped me, I didn't do it on my own. And I didn't even get burned, he did all the cooking. I just helped mix the batter." The look on his face is pure satisfaction and I'm so happy to see how proud he is of himself. But as I run through the names of his friends, I pause.

"Who is Ian? I don't think any of your friends' names are Ian."

"Not my friend, Mom, your friend. He was here before you woke up." He gives me a quick hug and bounds back into the living room to join his friends, leaving me kneeling on the floor blinking in confusion.

*Who the fuck is Ian?*

It takes me a solid hour to clean up the mess the boys left behind and I'm still mulling around the different scenarios from my conversation with Rone.

1. He is making it up, which is very likely. But the mess would definitely be a hundred times worse if he did this himself.

2. I don't remember all the boys names and there really is
   an Ian in the group.
3. There is another spirit in the house, a pancake God
   named Ian.

I'm still debating my options when the doorbell rings and I make my way to answer. Madi is standing on my porch with a to-go cup of coffee. Her smile quickly fades when she takes in my face. "Oh my gosh, Ella!!" She moves past me and sets her bag and cup on the entryway table. Her perfectly manicured fingers gently tug me in to her and she hugs me tightly. "What happened, are you ok?"

"I am so embarrassed, Madi. I slipped going down the stairs and my face caught me before my hands could. Does it look that bad?" The lie slips easily from me and I watch her, waiting to see if she buys it.

"You should have called me, I would have come and helped with the boys. Do you need me to take you to the clinic?" Her cool fingers gently cup my face, turning it side to side. "Is your nose broken?"

I run my index finger and thumb softly across the bone of my nose. The pain is already less than it was when I woke up. "I don't think it's broken, just my pride. I hope I didn't scare the boys. They seem to think it's pretty cool." Rone hadn't noticed my face this morning when I asked him about the pancakes, but when I went in to get the boys ready for pickup, a few of them looked at me like they couldn't quite understand if I've always looked like I am part of a fight club or if it was just my normal face.

"You know kids, they will say whatever is on their mind. They would have said something earlier if they wanted to. Are you sure you're ok? Do you want me to take Rone for a while so you can rest?" I feel guilty pawning him off, but a nap sounds divine.

"If you're sure it's not too much trouble. He'd be bored here, anyway."

"We love having him. He keeps Ty busy so I can get stuff done, so it works out. Do you need anything before we go?"

"Actually, yeah. Do you know if any of the boys have a dad named Ian?" She taps her chin with the magenta nail of her index finger.

"I don't think so, why?" I wish I could sit her down and tell her all the bizarre things that are going on around here, but I know how crazy it all sounds and I don't want her more concerned than she already is.

"Rone made breakfast this morning before I got up and said that Ian helped him. When I asked if it was one of his friends, he told me it was one of *my* friends. I'm not sure what to make of it."

Her hazel eyes crinkle at the edges when she lets out a soft laugh. "Kids are hilarious. If I think of any Ian I'll let you know." When she turns to the living room she stops short, gives a little shake of her head, but reaches out to grab her things. I reach out and tug her back.

"Madi, what is it?"

"Oh, it's nothing. I was just thinking about that name. It's what we used to call Cillian. Ian was so much easier to pronounce when we were kids and it kinda stuck as we got older. But only me and Michael called him that. To everyone else, he was Cillian."

I can feel the blood drain from my face and Madi must take it as a sign of fear, not recognition that my son somehow met the spirit of a man I have fallen for. Shit, *fallen for*? Not sure how to process this, I forgot to reply to her.

"Ella, I didn't mean to scare you. This house is perfectly safe, no ghosts." She laughs a little to lighten the mood and I give her a tight smile. "I was more thinking how adorable Cillian would look cooking breakfast with Rone and that thought made me smile. He would be drawn to you, Ella. You radiate with light." I shift uncomfortably under the weight of her compliment. She tilts her head and gives me a knowing smile. "Which I know you don't believe because of what you're going through. But I see it, I'm drawn to you. Don't let your light fade, even if your reason for it is gone." She pulls me into her and I allow myself to sag into her familiarity. She gives me one more squeeze before heading into the living room, clapping her hands and herding the boys out the front door. Once they are piled in her car, she gives me a bright smile before taking off down the driveway to drop each boy off on her way home. Girl is a fucking saint. I can't help but laugh at the memory of her compliment, *you radiate light*. I'm a disaster, a tornado, a cluster fuck of confusion and questions. One day I'll figure it all out. Not today, though. Today, I'll rest.

# TWENTY-FOUR
## FUCKING FEELINGS

CILLIAN

I HEAR TIRES CRUNCHING OVER THE GRAVEL DRIVEWAY AS I MAKE MY way back, the house is quiet when I let myself in the backdoor. The kitchen is spotless as always and I breathe in the clean smell that has replaced the sweet, sticky aroma of pancakes. I couldn't stop grinning, even when I walked into the trees to try and find the twins. My conversation with Rone this morning reminded me how cute kids can be and I hoped that I could remember that when I spoke to the girls. Images of Ella laying on the grass, breath shallow and face broken, threatens to bubble over any sense of calm I'm trying to keep on the surface. When normally I can feel their presence and hear them giggling off in the trees, today is quiet. Peaceful, in a way. I waited and waited, but nothing. No footsteps, no giggles, no eerie draft of cool breeze when they make their way to me. I stayed out there for a while before giving in and turning back, walking the pathway up to the house.

I make my way into the living room, blankets and pillows strewn across the floor with the TV still playing some obnoxious kid's show. Looking around the corner to the office I expect to see Ella, sitting in her chair working on her draft. But no smiling face or sea blue eyes look back at me. My heart sinks a little bit.

Every time I see her my heart swells, so I'm not surprised at the sadness that she isn't there. I'm slowly beginning to cave into the idea that even if I can't have her in a living sense, I'll take any stolen moment I can get with her. No matter what stage of life or death I'm in. I take my time folding each blanket and tucking it away in the basket it was pulled from, neatly placing the pillows back on the couch.

Once the living room is put back into order, I softly walk up the steps, smiling at each picture as I pass. Her door is left open and I lean against the doorframe and take in the woman laying before me. She didn't change out of her sweats or sweater and her hair is still in its messy bun piled on her head. I stand here for a while just watching her, looking around the room that never felt more like mine than it does right now. Not wanting to disturb the sleep she so desperately needs, I take my seat in the chair across the room. For a while I just sit here, listening to the gentle whirl of the fan mingling with soft snores from the bed. As much as I want to pull her to me and hold her while she sleeps, I feel restless. Standing from the chair, I head to the bathroom to clean it up, hoping that any small chore I do will help her feel less stressed or overwhelmed when she wakes.

I move around the bathroom, picking her clothes and towels off the ground and tossing them in the hamper. The bloody washcloth hangs over the edge of the tub, now dry and crusted over. Not wanting any memories of the night before, I chuck it in the trash, more aggressively than I intend to. I turn my attention to the counter to straighten up her face creams and oils. It's then that I remember the note I left her this morning and I cringe at how childish I was. I shouldn't have added to the morning and just left our night alone. It was magic, but would most likely never happen again. I grab the can and before I can set it back in the shower, I notice a new message written on the counter. My fingers grip the container so tightly I'm surprised it hasn't crushed under the pressure. Every time I feel like I need to back off, like I'm making something out of nothing, she does this. She reaches out and yanks me back. There is no place I'd rather be than in her grasp, no place I wouldn't walk as long as she was pulling me along with her.

I slide down the vanity and sit on the floor, resting my head back against the drawers. Something warm and wet slides down my face as little droplets of tears roll off my cheeks and splash to the floor. I try to recall the last time I cried, *actually really cried*. I've been angry since my death, but never sad. I did my best to cram that emotion in a little box, close the lid, and put it in a corner to deal with another time. I've never been sorry for myself. My parents passed away before I did so I didn't have to watch others mourn my loss. I never cried for the life that I left behind. I channeled all of that into a funnel of anger and denial. But for the first time in ten years, I let that box open, just a crack, and some of that sadness spills out.

Tears trek down my cheeks and before long, I'm sobbing. Fat, ugly sobs accompanied by the occasional hiccup. I let myself *feel*. And not just anger at the driver who killed me, not anger for the life I left behind, not anger for the life I'll never have, but sadness. Sadness for the driver who has to live with the guilt of taking someone's life. Sadness that I never got to experience just one more day. Sadness that I'll never have blue eyes, deep like the ocean and soft like the sky, staring into mine with so much love and tenderness. For a while, I'll let myself feel.

Just for today.

# TWENTY-FIVE

# FIND YOU ALONG THE WAY
## ELLA

"Never leave me."

"Do you think I have any chance at surviving without you?"

"You'd be alright."

"Don't say that!"

"I don't foresee there being a day that we aren't together, but you'd find a way to survive if we weren't. That's just who you are. You're strong and capable. More than you give yourself credit for."

"I don't want to be any of those things if I don't have you."

"You won't have to be as long as I'm with you. I'll let you lean on me, even though I know you can stand on your own two feet."

The sun cast crescent shaped shadows around us, dancing through the leaves of the tree above us. The park is busy this time of year, but we found our own hideout in the shade, laying on a large blanket with our lunch spread out around us. James leans over and rests his head on my stomach.

"Ouch! Every time you do that he kicks you." I rub a hand over the tender spot. "Either that's his way of telling you he loves you or that you need to give his mama some space." I laugh when James tickles my ribs. "Stop, you'll make me pee!"

"I think he's telling me that you are no longer mine. He's taken you *from me." Those brown eyes that I have fallen for over and over again since we met stare into mine.*

*"No one could ever take me from you. I'm yours."*

*"And I'm yours, sweet girl." He gives my pregnant belly one more quick kiss then lays down beside me. Hand in hand, we look up at the clouds drifting carelessly across the sky. I blame it on the pregnancy hormones, but my eyes begin to fill with tears and I let them overflow and run down my cheeks. Some moments are so beautiful that you can't believe you're living them in real life. I run my thumb over the back of his hand and let myself sit in this moment, praying that we'll have a lifetime of these little moments together, forever.*

———

Sniffing and the sounds of crying, which I've become so accustomed to, wake me from my dream. It takes me a couple minutes to realize that for once, it's not me. I look around the room, trying to find where the sound is coming from. My heart is racing from my dream, like it always does when I live out little moments I had with James. I get out of bed and quietly make my way to the bathroom door, the crying growing louder the closer I get. Now my heart breaks for an entirely different reason than when I woke, expecting to find James lying next to me and the bed is actually empty. These sobs sound familiar—heartbroken and lost. Feelings I know all too well. Another jab lands squarely to my already tender soul. I stand there for a moment listening, not wanting to disrupt the moment happening just around the corner. I know what it's like to work through your emotions. Sometimes the best remedy is to let it out. So I wait, silently sending all my energy through the open door, hoping that it reaches out and wraps around the man that I know is sitting inside.

A couple big sighs give me the sign that he is starting to calm down. I slip through the doorway and walk across the floor. Even without seeing where he is, the moment I sit down I know

I've landed right next to him. A heavy weight lands on my shoulder. I can be this for him. I can be the shoulder that someone needs when their life is falling apart.

"Talk to me," I say softly.

He takes a shaky breath. "I'm so fucking lost Ella." I lean my head back against the wood doors of the vanity and close my eyes. What kind of advice can I offer him, when I'm still wading through my own trauma?

I want to know him, every detail about his life, his story, every piece that made him the person he once was, and I guess, still is. "Start from the beginning, maybe we can find you along the way." A gentle kiss is placed on my shoulder before he begins.

"Once upon a time…" I jerk my shoulder, tossing his head. A soft laugh glides across my skin and I feel his lips lift in a smile. A small victory. "What do you want to know?"

"Everything." I sigh and rest my head against his. "What was your childhood like, did you play sports, your favorite color, first crush, what makes you laugh?" I close my eyes and breathe him in. "Anything, just tell me about yourself."

He shifts next to me before tugging me to my feet. I feel his hands wind around my waist and he pulls me into him. I close my eyes to picture the man before me, holding me, comforting each other while we walk aimlessly along this path that never seems to lead us where we want to be. Together. Whole.

"Can we go sit on the bed? I'm too old to sit on the floor any longer." It didn't even occur to me to think about his age. I just assumed since he grew up with Madi and Michael that he would be my age. Suddenly, I'm wondering if I'd still be ok with this situation if he was some fifty-year-old with a young, single mom fetish. As if he can sense the irrational thoughts racing around in my mind his fingers dig in a little deeper, pulling me back to him. "Don't worry, sweetheart. I'm only twenty-seven." I freeze. Twenty-seven? An old man is one thing I could maybe jump on board with, but a child? I was twenty-seven when I had Rone.

Cillian is practically a baby. I instantly feel creepy and try to back away, but his hold stays firm. "When I died…I was twenty-seven when I was killed." There is a hint of amusement to his voice and I lean back into his touch. "So technically, I'd be thirty-seven." My breath leaves my body in one big whoosh. His forehead leans down to rest on mine and he laughs. His tea tree and mint smell wrapping me up in the comfort I've slowly become addicted to.

"Geez, you gave me a heart attack. I didn't know what was worse: an old man or a teenager with wandering hands."

"You love these hands." He walks me to the bed and we settle in next to each other.

"What else?" The pillows rustle next to me and he lays beside me, our arms brushing against each other.

"I was born and raised here in Spring Hill. My dad grew up in this house, so did his dad before him. This house has, well was, been in our family since around the Civil War. I loved my childhood; my parents let me run wild in the woods and get dirty. They were hard on me and my wild ways when it came to being kind and respectful. It was always *yes, ma'am* in this house. Which as an adult, I respect. They raised me to be kind and accepting, but also to be sure of the person I was. I went to Spring Hill High School, GO RAIDERS." I can feel the air move around him like he's fist pumping the air and I giggle at the image.

"Go raiders!" I echo and he nudges my arm playfully.

"I played football like any good ol' southern boy. Wasn't very good, but it gave me and my dad something to talk about, so I was happy with it. I've always loved drawing and when I was in high school I took some art classes."

"You draw? Like more than houses and shit." I slap a hand over my mouth. "I'm so sorry, sometimes the sailor in me comes out."

My sweater has slipped down my arm and I feel his mouth brush over the exposed skin. "Now you in a sailor's outfit is something *I need to see.*" I roll my eyes, but he keeps talking so I let him. "I can draw, but I'm better at designing houses *and shit.*"

I smile. Not even trying to hide how much I love being in his company. "Wow, that is so cool. I wish I was artistic."

"I've read your smut scenes. And trust me, baby, that is its own form of art."

The thought of Cillian reading my books has my face burning. "When did you read my books?"

"You left your laptop open before movie night and I read some of what you'd written." His lips drop to my shoulder again and I close my eyes at the feeling washing over me, heat building between my legs. But the moment disappears when he keeps telling his story, a smile coating his words like he knows what I was imaging. "Anyway." He drags out the last syllable and I huff in response. "When I was a senior, my parents took me to Alabama to look at college options. We took a tour of Frank Lloyd Wright's famous Rosenbaum House. I remember that exact moment—it all clicked together. I knew I wanted to be an architect. The idea of making someone's forever home was a feeling I needed to chase. So, I was accepted into the program at Cornell. I did my time, loved being there, but couldn't wait to come home. The city life wasn't for me. I missed the quiet, missed the stars, missed being home."

Here in this moment, I feel peace. My heart isn't bleeding from the loss that I've experienced or the pain that I've gone through in the past year. I feel like for the first time in so long, it's resting. It's not trying to outrun the past or sprint to the finish line. I'm just existing and happy. He goes on for what feels like hours, but I live for each minute. Every memory that he relives and retells shapes the outline of the man I so desperately want to see.

# TWENTY-SIX
## BUSTED

CILLIAN

Reliving my past used to make me feel empty, like I have become a shell of the person I was. But something about the safe space that Ella created for me made it feel liberating. Like I was taking a deep breath after resurfacing from cold water on a summer day. Gasping for oxygen through the adrenaline after jumping off a cliff into a lake. Usually, I feel like I need to sleep for a few days after crying that hard, but when she sat next to me, I felt calm. We laid next to each other for the better part of the afternoon. I did most of the talking, but I watched her as she listened, noted every smile, every eye roll at my lame jokes. I told her about my childhood, about my passion for architecture, she laughed when I told her about my first kiss and cringed when I went into detail about my mom walking in on me and my first girlfriend getting caught making out on the living room couch. Everything about our time together is healing. My frayed edges slowly pulled together again.

Rone was dropped off not long ago and I'm sitting around the corner stealing glances at them in the garden together. Knowing Rone can see me has left me feeling unsettled and I'm not sure how Ella would feel if I came around the two of them together. She points out all the different vegetables and herbs she's planted and picks a purple lavender stem, rolling the small flowers between her fingers so he can lean in and smell the soothing scent that I've come to love so much. It brings back memories of my mom doing the same exact thing when I was a kid. Lavender was her favorite, hence why there are multiple bushes planted around the house and garden. He laughs at something she says and takes off through the gate and into the house. I lean back on my hands and watch her work her away around the garden, watering the planter beds and leaning in to smell the roses that have bloomed around the fence line. Her face is that of total serenity and it makes me smile. I can almost see her shattered pieces snapping back together.

"Mom!" Rone comes bounding down the steps waving a paper in his hand. Ella looks up at him, a hint of panic in her eyes.

"What's wrong?" She drops to her knees in front of him, the watering can falling to the ground beside her. She grabs his shoulders and inspects him from head to toe.

"You're building me a treehouse?" She blinks in surprise and shakes her head in confusion.

"Rone, what are you talking about?" He waves the paper that he's holding in his hand, eyes big and round like he's just found the secret stash of hidden Christmas presents. I'm smiling at the mischief behind his eyes until I take a closer look at the paper that he is shoving in Ella's face. I sit up and my jaw drops. *He found my treehouse design.*

"This!!" The edges of my design brush against her face as he waves it at her. "It's perfect, Mom, thank you, thank you!"

She takes the paper from him and stands up, looking over the paper with disbelief. I want to walk over and explain myself, but I don't know how to work around Rone now that I know he can see me.

Ella rests a hand on his shoulder, holding his bouncing body down. "Where did you find this?"

"In the guest room, I went inside to go to the bathroom and

the door was open, so I went inside." He gives a little shrug and keeps going. "It has everything I want, Mom, see." He takes the paper from her and walks to the bench, spreading it out on his lap as he points at my design. Of course it has everything he wants. For thirty minutes I listened intently while he told his mom about every detail. And then I put them all down on paper. She sits beside him and nods along while he animatedly jabs his chubby finger at the paper. Before long, he jumps up and starts running around the house, carefully inspecting each tree that has any sense of potential. I walk over to her when he rounds the corner and slowly approach the bench. She lifts her head when she feels me cross the pebble walkway.

In a hushed voice she asks, "Cillian, did you do this?" She lifts the paper, my design waving in the gentle breeze.

"I didn't think he'd find it," I admit, tugging on the back of my neck, a bit embarrassed. "I didn't even think anything would come of it. I heard how excited he was and I haven't been inspired like that in so long. I sat down and before I knew what I was doing it was done." She doesn't answer, just stares at the paper in her lap. "Shit, are you mad?" I sit down beside her and run my hands through my hair like I always do when I'm nervous or anxious. I know she can't build this on her own, but I'll do anything to make sure it happens, if that's what she wants. All she has to do is say the word and I'd gladly walk to the edge of the Earth for her.

"How can I be mad? This is…incredible."

"Really?"

"Of course it is, I mean, I have no idea how to make this happen, but wow! You are so talented." I watch her delicate fingers trace over the lines of the treehouse. My chest puffs with pride and I want to spin her around in my arms. I take a minute to settle my racing heart.

"Mike can help you. He's in construction and we used to build treehouses all the time when we were kids. Not as big as this one, but I'm sure he'd love the excuse to make our childhood dream come to life."

"I haven't seen Rone this excited since before." Her voice trails off, shoulders sagging. Before she can fall into whatever memory is threatening to come up, I grab her hand in mine, intertwining our fingers and tugging her to her feet.

"Come with me, I found the perfect tree."

# TWENTY-SEVEN
# HANG ON BABY

ELLA

TUGGING THE BLANKET AROUND ME, I LOOK DOWN AT RONE WHO IS snoring quietly on my lap. He passed out about thirty minutes into our movie night. I tuck his blonde hair behind his ear and smile at the memory of him spending close to an hour running from tree to tree, trying to pick the perfect one for his new tree house. Cillian guided me around the house while Rone was busy with his tree inspection. I can still feel his breath on my neck and the heat from his chest pressed against my back as he leaned around me to show me which oak he had in mind.

"It's tall and wide, but the branches are low enough to the ground that it won't be too high." Without even knowing that was one of my fears, he addressed it like it was one of his own. He pointed out which branches would need to be cut back to make room for the base and even showed me a wide, thick branch that could support a swing. His vision slowly came to life before me and it was magic. When Rone's voice grew closer, he gave my waist a gentle squeeze and kissed the place where my neck met my shoulder before I felt him move away.

I look back down at Rone, smoothing down his wild hair, lost in thought.

"What are you thinking about, sweetheart?" His soft, deep

voice doesn't send me jumping in surprise like it used to. It's like my soul is waiting for him when he's not around. When he does speak to me, it finally releases the breath it's been holding.

He chuckles softly when I reply with a simple, "You." The couch dips on the other side of Rone, his little body curled up between us. "I invited Mike and Madi over for dinner later this week. I plan to ask him if he can help with the treehouse. Which is incredible, by the way. I'm jealous I don't get to have a treehouse of my own."

The other end of the blanket shifts like he's moving some of it over his legs. I so badly want to see the person on the other side. I want to talk face to face, feel his body—not just his presence, or the brush of his fingers across my cheek, or the squeeze of his arms around my waist. I'm reminded that there is no ending where I wake up and he is real. Those pieces of my heart that have slowly come back together quake at the thought, threatening to break apart all over again. I swallow the emotion that is quickly building behind my eyes and settle my head back against the cushions.

"This may sound strange, but hear me out." I give a soft smile and nod my head. "When I designed this house, I was finally ready to settle down. In the few years after my parents passed, I lived a pretty wild life in college. I was young, single, and had a bit of money to throw around." I feel his arm reach across the back of the couch as a hand threads through my hair, twisting a lock of it around his finger.

"One day I woke up to the house a mess with friends were passed out in the living room and guest room. Usually I'd shower, wake everyone up, hit the gym, then head back into Nashville for another night out. But one morning in particular, I woke up feeling empty." He pauses and I want so badly to reach out and nuzzle into him, to smell him, feel his heartbeat against my cheek. I never knew what being lonely felt like. James and I were inseparable, there was no space to feel alone. The thought of Cillian feeling like that makes me want to wrap him in a big hug and promise to never let him feel like that again.

"So you thought that you needed a remodel and your life would feel whole?"

He tugs my hair playfully before he goes on. "No. I woke everyone up, we hit the gym, and then we went out on Broadway and got totally drunk."

I sit forward and look towards him as he drops my hair and his throaty laugh settles between my legs, making me readjust in my seat. "Ok, then what?"

"The next morning I woke up with a blonde I didn't recognize on one side of me and a redhead on the other." I want to punch him, but I roll my eyes and cover my face with my hands instead. "That's when it clicked that my life had so little meaning. I needed to make some changes. I ordered the girls an Uber, politely kicked them out, and made my friends go back to their apartments." I hear him take a deep inhale. "Then I spent three straight days drawing up the design for this new house. I pictured everything that I wanted in my new future. The big master bedroom with enough room for a huge bed for my wife and I to sleep in and one day cuddle our kids in. Big, cozy chairs to curl up in and read under the windows. The bathroom had to have all the features that would make it a sanctuary after a long day. A kitchen to cook and to fill with friends and family."

I can't help but interrupt him, "I love this house." I look at the living room around me and the soft light that spills in through the kitchen doorway. It's breathtaking, every inch painstakingly stressed over until it was just right. "Everything about this house is perfect, it's a dream. If I could have designed it, I would have done everything just how you made it." His hand comes back to my hair, but instead of twisting it around his fingers, he cups the back of my head.

"Ella, in some weird way, I think I designed this house for you." I let my head drop back fully into his embrace and his fingers hold my head softly.

"It's beautiful." My voice comes out as a whisper, I'm almost not sure if I spoke it aloud or thought it to myself.

"Yes, you are." That emotion I've worked so hard to keep tucked beneath the surface begins to trickle over the top. Before the waves can pull me under, I change the subject. Sitting forward I wring my hands in my lap, suddenly nervous to ask the question that has been on the tip of my tongue all day.

"Cillian, this morning…" The energy in the room shifts.

"I'm sorry I broke down like that, I didn't mean to wake you or to be a burden on you when you were already feeling so many emotions. Forgive me?" I drop my hands and tip my head to the side. I can't help the laugh that escapes me and I have to cover my mouth so I don't wake Rone.

"You think I'm upset about you crying?"

His voice is unsure when he responds. "Aren't you? I should have been taking care of you, not the other way around."

"Never apologize for feeling how you do, it's healthy. I can't imagine how stuck and confused you feel." I run my hands down my face, surprised that he thinks I would be upset at him for showing emotion or letting me comfort him when he needed it. "You've been there for me in the worst moments over the past few months, why can't I be there for you?"

"I'm confused," he trails off. "If I didn't scare you off with my snotty sobs, what did I do?"

"First of all, I can't even see your face, so…" My shoulder gets pushed and I fall against the armrest of the couch. "I'm talking about the mysterious pancake breakfast that happened to appear while I was asleep."

"Oh, that." His voice is thoughtful when he goes on. "I swear I just went down to check on the boys. I didn't notice that Rone wasn't in the fort. When I walked into the kitchen he was sitting at the island, so I tried to move out the door." He's talking so fast he has to stop and take a second before he goes on. "But shit, Ella, he…"

"Language!" I whisper-shout, motioning to the snoring body between us.

"Right." I can sense the smile in his voice. "Ella, he looked right at me and it scared the shit out of me." I roll my eyes and drop my head back with a sigh. This man.

I cup my chin in my hands. "How can he see you?" Dropping my head back against the couch I let out a groan of frustration. "I mean, he told me he saw you, talked to you, cooked with you! How is that possible when I can only feel you when you touch me, but *I* can't feel you? I can't even see you!"

The unanswered lingers between us. "I have no idea, but I have heard that because kids are still so innocent in life, they can see things that we as adults can't. I haven't been around many kids before, but he wasn't scared. He just wanted pancakes." A soft laugh escapes him like he can't believe it, either. "He's a good kid, Ella. You've done such a great job raising him." The emotion that I had managed to trap back in its little box bangs on the walls inside me. I can't help the tear that slips down my cheek. A soft finger trails up my cheek, catching the drop before it can fall.

"I'm so scared I'll mess this up." Admitting that out loud doesn't feel as terrible as I had expected. It feels like I'm popping a hole in a balloon, letting out a small bit of pressure that has built up inside me since James passed.

"You love him. You give him reasons to laugh and smile. I have no doubt he misses James and his sister, but I promise you, Ella, he will be alright. He loves you." It's in that moment that I lose it; the box melts away and all my emotions break free. This time, it's my turn to sob. The couch dips and a breeze moves my hair softly as he circles the back of the couch. I feel him move to my side before strong arms wrap around me and pull me against his firm but soft body. His warmth and smell ease their way into the place of my emotions, pushing my fear and sadness back. I want to wrap my arms around him, cling to him, but I can't. And that makes me cry harder. "I've got you sweetheart, let it out." I fall, stumble, crash, submit. All the feelings I've held inside are at war with each other to get out first, fighting to find release while they can.

I'm not sure how long I sat there, butt on the edge of the couch and leaning into my shadow. Letting him hold me, soothe me, comfort me, fix me, heal me. He didn't need to say anything. Our souls are intertwined, one clutching to the other. Little splinters of my heart lifting once again.

---

Quiet voices wake me from my sleep and it takes me a minute to realize I'm in my bed. The house is quiet, lights off and closed up for the night. I smile at the thought of Cillian tucking me and Rone in our beds, moving around the house to shut off the lights, close the blinds, and lock the doors. It feels nice to have someone to do that for us again. More soft murmurs make their way through the open door and I tip toe out into the hallway. It's been a little while since Rone has woken from a nightmare and I'm mentally kicking myself that I didn't wake when he called out for me. I move closer to his door and the whispers come into focus.

"It's ok to be sad, buddy. Don't be embarrassed to cry or be sad, it's normal."

"But I don't want to be a baby, Ian." Rone's sweet voice floats out the door and I slide down the wall to sit outside his room. "You wouldn't cry, you're big."

"I cry all the time." Cillian's voice is soft, but reassuring. There isn't a hint of judgment or shame.

Rone sounds surprised when he asks. "Really?"

"Oh yeah, just this morning I cried really hard. I was sad and mad, but after I cried I felt a lot better. I cry when I'm sad, I cry when I'm happy, or if I laugh too hard." I hear Rone giggle and wish I could be part of this moment. I should feel guilty I'm not the one comforting my son, but I'm relieved that Cillian can be there for him. Especially after what he went through this morning to finally sit in his feelings and work through them.

"Maybe one day I can make you laugh so hard you cry, that would be funny!" Rone lights up.

"It would be, huh? Ok, buddy. Get some rest so you can look up some good jokes tomorrow after camp, ok?"

"Hey, Ian?"

"Yeah, bud?"

"Will you stay with me until I go back to sleep?"

There is the quickest beat of silence like, Cillian was caught off guard by the question. "You bet, I'll stay right here." The sheets rustle and I can picture Rone snuggling down in his bed, peeking over at Cillian to make sure he didn't sneak out. The tears running from my eyes don't stop the smile that breaks out across my face.

*Hang on baby, you're going to be ok. I promise!* James' voice encourages as I close my eyes. For the first time, I feel peace wrap around my heart. Not the pain or regret, or consuming emptiness that used to tangle around it like barbed wire.

# TWENTY-EIGHT

# ROSE COLORED BUTTERFLY

## CILLIAN

I HAD JUST LAID ELLA IN HER BED, COVERED HER UP IN THE SOFT covers and turned out the light, when I heard Rone calling for her. I watched her for a few seconds to see if she'd wake, but she didn't move, exhausted from the day. When he called out again, I didn't think twice before I was moving down the hallway and into his room. He was sitting up in bed holding the covers to his chest, big fat tears rolling down his chubby cheeks. I knelt beside him and gently reached out to hold his hands in mine. He didn't jump away or ask why I was there, instead he took all the air out of my lungs when he leaned over and threw his arms around me.

"It's ok, buddy. I've got you." After years of being alone, it felt nice to be there for someone and give the comfort that I had ached for so long. He sat there for a while, taking deep breaths between wet hiccups. I think back to earlier in the evening when I held Ella while she broke down. It felt like a flash flood had run through her, all these emotions that she had been trying to shove deep down for so long finally spilling over the surface. Her whole body shook, tears rained down where our hands twisted together. All I could do was hold her and whisper over and over again, *I've got you, sweetheart. Let it out.* The best way through something was to just walk through it. I was proud of her for leaning into the fear, the sadness, the pain. My only hope is she keeps walking until she makes it out on the other side. I'm praying that I can walk through it with her, for as long as she needs me. Rone's quiet whisper broke through my thoughts.

"Sometimes I have scary dreams." My heart broke in half.

"Everyone has scary dreams, do you want to tell me about yours?" His little head shook back and forth so fast that I thought it was going to fall off his body. I reached my hand out to hold it steady. But before I could tell him that it was alright not to share, he opened up and told me everything in one breath.

"In my dream I'm walking, walking, walking, forever on this sidewalk that just keeps going. I'm tired but I can't sit down, so I just keep walking. Then I hear someone behind me but I can't look back, but I know I need to run. They get closer and closer to me, but I still can't see who it is. Then all of a sudden, I'm running so fast my legs are on fire and I can't breathe. And then the sidewalk ends and I'm falling. Then I woke up!"

I stifle a laugh at the way his chest heaves when he finally stops talking. "Man, that is scary. What do you think you're running from?" He picks his head up off my shoulder and looks me in the eyes. It still shocks me that he can see me, but I find solace in his little, brown eyes. Like he's grounding me, holding me in place so I don't drift off. I wish Ella could see me like Rone does. I understand that kids are more prone to seeing ghosts and spirits, but my heart aches with the possibility that one day maybe Ella could look back at me. Then he lays back in bed throwing his arms behind his head. I can see the gears turning so I push a little more. "Maybe you're running from a dragon and if you looked back, his teeth would be snapping trying to eat you up!" I make a chomping motion with my hand and tickle his stomach. He giggles and tries to squirm away.

"Maybe it's a giant spider trying to trap me in a web! OH! Maybe it's a river of slime and if it catches me I'll turn into goo!"

I smile at him and rub his head. "You're very creative! Do you feel better now?"

"Yeah, sorry I cried." His mom's words from earlier come back to me.

"It's ok to be sad, buddy. Don't be embarrassed to cry or be sad, it's normal."

"But I don't want to be a baby, Ian. You wouldn't cry, you're big." Oh if he only knew.

"I cry all the time." My admission must shock him because he rolls over, mouth hanging open.

"Really?"

"Oh yeah." I lean back against his nightstand, pushing a truck out from behind my back. "Just this morning I cried, really hard. I was sad and mad, but after I cried I felt a lot better. I cry when I'm sad, I cry when I'm happy, or if I laugh too hard." He giggles again and damn what I wouldn't do to hear that sound every day for the rest of my life.

"Maybe one day I can make you laugh so hard you cry, that would be funny!"

"It would be." I lean over and pull the covers up to his chin. "Get some rest so you can look up some good jokes tomorrow after camp, ok?"

"Ok." He pulls his stuffed animal into his arms. "Hey, Ian?"

"Yeah, bud?"

"Will you stay with me until I go back to sleep?" I was planning on staying here for a while anyway just to make sure he was ok, but I will definitely be staying here all night now. How could I deny him that comfort?

"You bet, I'll stay right here." And so I did, dozing off as I leaned against his little nightstand. The nightlight made shadows dance on the ceiling and I have never felt more at peace in my entire life.

———

Car doors slamming and tires rolling down the drive wake me from my place on the floor. Checking the clock in Rone's bedroom, I knew Ella was taking Rone to camp. I find myself wandering through the house, looking at all the details Ella had added to it. It was perfectly put together. Perfect in a sense that the house looked clean, but lived in. Shoes neatly placed by the front door. Her sneakers and flip flops on either side of Rone's adorable, little shoes. I lay down on the couch in the living room, the sun filtering in through the big windows, and just listened. Birds chirping and singing outside, wind chimes ringing softly in the breeze, the whirling of the dishwasher, all the sounds mixed together made me overwhelmed with a feeling I haven't felt in a long time. *I was home.* I hadn't thought about moving on in what felt like ages and now the idea of even entertaining the thought made me sick to my stomach, so I pushed it away. Happy for the moment to just exist.

I hear Ella come in and take her shoes off by the front door. She drops her keys in the dish on the entryway table and makes her way into the office. I don't want to interrupt her, so I lay my head back on the couch and listen as she clicks the computer to life and joins a virtual meeting. She talks with her agent about the progress of her book and how the characters and storyline are developing. They go back and forth, tossing ideas around, and I marvel at how well she handles herself. She is accepting of new ideas, but quick to stand up for herself and defend pieces of the book that she feels need to remain untouched. When her call ends, she stays in her office and I let the quick clacking of her fingers against the keyboard lull me back to sleep.

A muffled moan wakes me from my place on the couch. Rubbing my eyes and running a hand down my face, I lift my head and look up towards the office, but Ella isn't in her chair. Standing up and stretching, I walk into the entryway, trying to figure out where the sound is coming from. Upstairs, I hear it again and my curiosity gets the best of me. I quietly walk up the stairs, listening as the rustle of sheets and moans grow louder. It can't possibly be what I think it is, but I peek through the open doorway anyway. I swear my jaw hits the floor. My sleepy self is fully awake now and I can't help but stare. Ella is laying in the middle of the bed, naked, legs spread wide. An obscene amount of sex toys lay on the covers around her with her auburn hair strewn around her head looking like a goddamn halo. My fingers itch at the thought of wrapping my fingers in it and tugging her head back so I can lick my way up her throat. Her jagged breathing pulls me back to the scene in front of me and I lean against the door frame palming my growing erection as I watch the show before me. I've always been a participant, but at this moment, I'm content to be the voyeur.

Arching her back against the bed and pushing her ankles into the sheets, she rubs one of the small, pink vibrators against herself, moaning and shaking. She's close. Then she lets out a frustrated sigh, blowing the hair out of her face with the angry puff of air, and tosses the vibrator to the side. Her breasts bounce as she tries to slow her shaky breaths. I'm taken back to that night in the shower where I held them in my hands, just big enough to fill my palms. Her nipples were soft and sharp in my mouth.

"Not you, not you, not you." I look up just in time to see Ella throwing toy after toy to the other side of the bed like they have personally offended her. She eyes a rose colored toy that looks like a butterfly with a giant dick. I tilt my head, eyeing the pink silicone toy, trying to figure out how the hell that thing works and where it is supposed to go. She pops the top on a bottle of lube, pours a small amount in her palm, and rubs it on the end. I drop my head back and fight back the groan that is slowly making its way up my throat. Then she leans back into the pillows and spreads her legs open again. Laid out before me, glistening, I'm gone. She moans loudly as she slowly slides the long end of the butterfly into her. It's torture, one I'll happily suffer through over and over again. I notice a small remote on her nightstand and look back at her while she continues the slow push inside.

I carefully move to the nightstand and grab the remote, then walk over to my chair under the window. The sun streams in through the blinds that are half open, gold lines are cast across the floor and up over the curves of her body as she settles the butterfly against her clit. Her hand reaches out to her nightstand and she blindly slaps around, looking for the exact thing I'm holding in my hand.

*Fuck. Me.* This will be fun.

# TWENTY-NINE
# RESEARCH
## ELLA

Whenever I write a sex scene in my book, I like to do a little *research*. I hate reading books where they *switch positions in one movement*. Not possible, believe me I've tried. I want my readers to feel like they can recreate what I write without feeling inadequate. Sometimes the scene just flows and I can write it in one sitting, blushing and giggling the whole time. When I would get stuck I'd walk up to James, grab his hand, and pull him down the hall to our room, rolling my hips against him and kissing his neck. He always laughed when he'd read what I wrote, but never complained about the part he played. I needed him then and I need him today. It's awkward now; weird and uncomfortable. I try to picture him, trying to imagine his hands running up my legs, rubbing against me, pushing the toy deeper. Blonde hair and dark brown eyes stare back at me from behind my eyelids. I can almost feel his rough hands softly sliding over my skin, his calloused fingertips scratching my skin in the most delicious way. It's never good enough, it's never close enough to the real thing.

After multiple attempts, I swear his mouth gives me a little smirk and his eyes morph into a deep green, hair changing from his bright blonde shaggy locks to perfectly straight, inky strands.

It catches me off guard, my hand stills on the vibrator still wedged between my legs. I brace for the impact of shame that usually slams into me. I wait and wait, but those feelings don't come. I almost feel turned on. So I settle back into the pillows and clench around the butterfly vibrator, pushing it the rest of the way inside. I let my mind reminisce about soft hands gripping my ass, fingers pushing into me, filling me. Just picturing him has my orgasm building, spine tingling and toes curling. I blindly reach to the nightstand to grab the remote, knocking my lotion and ChapStick off in the process. Before I can open my eyes and roll over to find the fucking thing, I'm thrown onto my back as the vibrator comes to life.

My eyes fly open and I battle through the vibration that is quickly pulling me under. I glance at my nightstand, but the remote isn't there. I try to roll myself over to look at the floor by my side of the bed, but the vibration changes from the steady pressure to an agonizingly slow pulse. My legs shake and I reach between my legs to hit the button on the side that will turn it off.

"Don't you fucking dare." The vibrator cuts off and the loss of sensation makes me want to scream. His voice sends chills over my whole being. I feel them erupt on my soul, flow through my blood, and push their way to the surface. I shiver and try to pull the covers over myself, suddenly very aware of how naked and open I am. As quickly as it shuts off, the butterfly flutters back to life, massaging against me in the most delectable way. I moan and grip the sheets tighter in my fingers as my body begins to race towards my climax. Just as I start to lose myself in the feeling, it turns off again and this time, I don't hold back my grunt of frustration. His dark chuckle bounces around the room, assaulting me with another wave of goosebumps. "Drop those sheets, sweetheart. I don't want to miss a thing." It takes me a few seconds longer to overcome my embarrassment. Then I give into the tension in the room and give a wicked smile in the direction of his voice, letting the sheets slip from my grip and pool around my waist. The buzzing begins again, a soft pulse. "Good girl." His praise is almost as good as the feeling of the butterfly pulsing inside me and the dainty butterfly wings fluttering against my clit.

"You're torturing me," I pant out. The image of him sitting back watching me again has me shifting my hips to chase my climax. The pulsing speeds up and I hold back a laugh when I realize that he knows exactly what he's doing.

"Consider it payback for torturing me every day since you arrived here." The vibration intensifies and I lift my back, attempting to push my body further into the feeling. "What are you doing, playing by yourself, when you have a willing party waiting for an invite?" His voice is deep and breathy, like he's trying to hold himself together. I can't give him a reply, I'm too busy drifting away into oblivion. Stars start to crowd my vision, my lungs burn from holding my breath. I'm there, so close, and then.

Nothing.

"Cillian!! You asshole!" I wipe the damp strands of my hair from my forehead and sit up. I go to reach for my covers—his teasing has officially pissed me off. The bed dips under his weight before I am shoved back into the bed. My pillows have been thrown around and the covers are bunched at the foot of the bed. My hair falls over my face with my wrists trapped firmly in one of his large, warm hands. His other reaches up to brush the hair out of my face. His touch burns against my skin and I'm fully willing to accept the idea that my flesh will melt away in his presence. He pushes my legs apart, his weight settling between them, lifting my still trapped wrists above my head and caging me in with the other arm against my head.

"You don't get to walk away," he whispers against my neck. "Not until we've finished what you started." I fight the shiver that threatens to roll through me. His voice is low and sounds like he's speaking around a mouth full of broken glass. It's raw, grating, and so damn sexy.

"Watch me!" I try to wiggle free, but he chuckles when I

barely move an inch. He leans his full weight into me, his heat is stifling. Tea tree and mint washes over me and I can't help the whimper that slips out when I breathe him in. I want to wrap my legs around him and pull him into me. I want to hold him, run my fingers through his hair and tug it. I want to hear him groan against me. His tongue works its way up and down the slopes of my neck and the hollows of my collarbone. I can feel his smile on my skin when he says,

"I told you to use me. If you need a release, all you have to do is ask."

"I got stuck writing a scene in my book and needed to work out some kinks."

He bites down hard on the flesh just above my left breast. "I'll be your kink, baby." I scream out in pain, but just as quickly as the pain came, he licks it away. I'm an inferno. Sweat clings to my skin, pent up tension rolls through me, and I can't help but lift my hips and try to move the toy still inside me, hoping some kind of friction will give me my release. He lifts off me the slightest bit as if he's looking down to where I'm trying to work myself around the butterfly shaft. I feel him move by my head and with a soft click, the vibrator comes back to life. I moan at the instant pleasure that courses through my body. He releases my hands and the blood rushes back into them, making me groan at the tingle in my fingertips. His hands wander down my body, stopping to weigh each breast while rolling the nipples at the same time. The heat from his body drifts away, if it wasn't for the feel of his hand still massaging a breast I'd have thought he left. His weight shifts back slightly and then there is a sharp sting as his other hand slaps my breast, *hard*. Goosebumps pebble my skin and a bright pink handprint stains my creamy skin. Both hands are back on me, rubbing at the print, massaging the pain away. I love a good spank, something I had to convince James wouldn't hurt me. But a smack to my tits, holy shit, *again* please.

# THIRTY
## SHATTERED

CILLIAN

I WASN'T SURE HOW SHE WOULD REACT, BUT IT HONESTLY HAPPENED before I could stop myself. The way her tits bounce has me gritting my teeth. I'm glad she can't see my face as I eye her, waiting for her to yell at me and cuss me out. My dick pushes painfully against my pants. Her eyelids flutter and her cheeks flush, she liked it. I can feel my body buzz with lust and I hold her in my hand, rubbing soft circles over the mark. I lift my hand and land a firm smack to the other one. The vibrator hums sweetly from its nook between her legs and if I lean into her just a bit more, I can feel it vibrate against me as well. My eyes roll back in my head as I massage her breasts, alleviating some of the pain and giving her nipples one last roll between my fingertips. I trail my hands down her stomach, noticing for the first time a small scar just above her perfectly trimmed core. I gently brush my fingers over the scar, leaning down to give it a kiss. She lets out a small exhale, eyes falling closed and head tilted back, with the most adorable blush on her cheeks that shine with a light layer of sweat. I've edged her enough.

I place one hand on her hip bone and dig my fingers in, not hard enough to bruise, but enough to hold her in place. I reach down to the silicone butterfly laying flush against her and give it a gentle tug back and forth. Her back arches, causing her to push up against me. I groan out loud and push her back into the bed. We repeat this motion a few times before I roughly push her legs apart and grab the butterfly, rotating it 180 degrees. Her eyes fly open at the sharp turn, making her gasp in shock. The shaft inside her is now rotated at an angle that stretches and rubs her in a different way with the butterfly wings now resting between her ass. The feeling causes her to shift on the bed and change her breathing as the new sensation works its way through her body.

"Tell me what you want, sweetheart. I'll give you anything." She rolls back and forth, slowly picking up speed before she responds.

Her lips part and I have to lean down to hear her. "Touch me." Smiling, I release her hip from my grip, little red dots marking where my fingers held her. I move to her center, looking down at the rose colored shaft moving inside her. I rub slow circles over her clit, alternating the pressure. My other hand works its way slowly up over her hips, again giving that scar a gentle caress as I pass over it. I slide between her breasts, but don't touch them. She moans in protest and my hand encircles her neck. Her breath catches, but she doesn't open her eyes. To my surprise and satisfaction, she grabs my hand with both of hers and pushes down to apply more pressure. I give her a squeeze, not hard enough to cut off her air supply, but enough to let her know I'm in charge. She's close as I work my fingers, rubbing and pushing until she is panting, chasing her climax. This time, I let her catch it.

She falls apart under me in a wave of tremors and curses. Her body slick with sweat, little droplets colliding and cascading down the crease between her breasts. I release her neck and watch as my handprint fades away. A little disappointing, but I make a mental note to do it again. I turn off the vibrator and reach down, slowly pulling it from her and tossing it on the other side of the bed. I cage her in again, arms resting on either side of her, hoping to keep her warm as her high fades.

A soft smile breaks out on her face. "That will definitely make it in the book." I roll her so we're laying with her back pulled tightly against my chest. I stroke her hair and kiss her neck softly, perfectly content to lay here for the rest of my days. Holding this woman feels like home. I can't escape her and I don't think I ever want to.

"You felt my hands." It's a statement, not a question. She grabbed my hands, pushed them into her. There is no logical answer for what is happening between us, I've spent countless hours trying to make it all make sense. She trails her fingers down the forearm I have wrapped around her.

"I did." She smiles against my skin and I want to drink her in, live in this moment for however long I can. "I didn't think about it, I just reached out." There is a stretch of silence where we both sit in our thoughts. If being intimate with her brings us closer to being together in a more real sense, then I'll happily oblige.

After a few minutes, she pulls the covers up around her shoulders and slowly slips under them, her hands wandering down my thick thighs. "Sweetheart," I caution, but make no move to pull her back. "What are you doing?" The smile dies on my lips when I feel her hands stroke me over my pants before her fingers start to undo the button at my waist. She pulls my zipper down so slowly I'm about to reach down and pull myself out if she doesn't hurry up. As if she senses my frustration at her slow pace, she runs her hands up the front of my legs and digs her fingers into my waist. I pull away sharply as she begins to tickle me, but before I can get too far, she pulls me back to her. One arm wraps around me to run her nails up and down my lower back while the other pushes my pants and briefs out of the way. I feel my cock spring free from my pants and before my brain has time to catch up, her wet, hot mouth is sliding over me.

*"Holy. Shit,"* I pant out. I can't form complete sentences, not when her lips move over me in leisurely passes. Her tongue plays with the vein on the bottom of my shaft. Her fingers slide over my balls, massaging them before she drags a nail achingly slowly along the seam between my balls and ass. "You're punishing me, aren't you?" Her hum is the only reply I get as she works her way up and down me while getting dangerously close to my backside. I clench out of response and I feel her laugh against me, the vibration moving against my sensitive skin. Her mouth picks up pace and she tugs against my back, pulling me into her. I'm always pulled to her, and this is no different. I slide my hands under the covers, fingers twisting in her hair and palms holding the back of her head. She nods in a silent confirmation and we move in tandem. Her hand carefully rolls my balls in her palm, fingers dig in my back, tongue licking, lips sucking. I move her up and down, pushing her as deep as she'll let me. My eyes roll when I feel myself nudge the back of her throat.

"Fuck, baby. You're so good at this." She doesn't respond but gives me more, teeth grazing slightly as she pulls back, almost releasing me before she plunges back down. I'm gone. I don't remember much other than holding her perfect head in my hands, pulling and pushing her back and forth over me, pulling strands of hair softly in my fingers. Her moans of pleasure mix with mine and I'm tripping and falling, careening off the cliff as my orgasm washes over me. She takes all of me, licking me clean before kissing her way up my body.

Rolling to her side again she snuggles her back up against me. "I've gone mad." Letting go of my arms, she runs a hand through her tangled hair. "How are we doing this?" We hold each other for a long time, neither one of us able to explain the intimacy we've just shared. Our bodies stay wrapped around each other, hearts beating together, souls mingling and fusing together. I don't feel so lost when I'm with her. I feel seen, I feel *alive.*

————

Glass shattering jolts me awake at the same time as Ella. She jumps from the bed, grabbing for her clothes on the floor, jumping wildly as she sticks one leg through her pants before the other. I beat her to the doorway right as she's pulling her sweat-shirt over her head.

My hands land on her hips, stopping her in place. "Ella, wait. Let me take a look, please stay here." She has a look of determination on her face, but I don't miss the way her hands tremble when she pushes her hair out of her eyes.

"What do you think it is?" I listen for any sound of movement downstairs, but I don't hear anything. "Something probably fell over, it's nothing. But let me check just to be sure." She gives two sharp nods and takes a step back into the room. I release her hips and press a soft kiss to her cheek before stepping out into the hallway. The pictures that used to line the staircase are scattered all across the steps, glass shards glinting off each stair. I peek over the railing just in time to see two blonde heads disappear below me, their quiet, shrill giggles make their way through the kitchen and out the back door.

"What the fuck was that?" I whip around and find Ella peeking out from around the doorway. Her face that not long ago was bound and determined to take care of whatever had happened is now drained of all color.

"Ella I'm so sorry..." I trail off as she walks further into the hallway and takes in the damage on the stairs. All her memories, happy smiles, and milestones lay strewn across the floor. Her beautiful eyes well with tears and one by one they slip down her cheeks. I move to her but as she feels me push into her space, she puts her hands out and I almost trip over myself with how quickly I come to a stop.

"I can't do this, Cillian. If Rone was here, what if something happened to him? It's one thing what they did to me outside, but this?" She waves her hand over the mess, tremors working their way over her hands and through her body.

"It won't!" I grit the words out and flinch even thinking about the possibility of him getting hurt.

"You don't know that!" She raises her voice in finality as she wipes her hands down her face, clearing away the trails of tears left behind. In all honesty, I don't know that they won't hurt her or Rone. I didn't think they had it in them to be malicious. But then they attacked her and now they've come into the house and caused this destruction.

"Ella, I will never allow anything to happen to you." My voice shakes. I give myself a second, swallowing the lump in my throat. "You or Rone." I want to hold her, to comfort her and promise that this was a mistake. But I can't lie to her. She moves forward, her bare toes stopping just in front of mine. We stand like that for a moment, basking in each other's comfort. Her phone chimes from the bedroom and she lets out a tired sigh.

"I need to get this cleaned up and get Rone from camp."

"Go, I'll take care of this. I'll talk to the twins, get this figured out."

"Are you sure?" Her voice isn't angry anymore, but worry etches every word. I reach out and run my hand over her face. She leans into it and I want to hold her like that forever.

"Yes, go." She slowly makes her way down the steps, carefully avoiding the pieces of broken glass. When she makes it to the bottom she turns back towards me, finally looking in my direction. She gives a sad smile, then walks out the door.

A chill I hadn't noticed before soaks through me and I wish I could rewind to thirty minutes ago and hit pause. Both of us finding release in each other, whispering the other's name. Instead, I pick my way through the damage, collecting photos as I go. After the glass is swept up and I'm sure nothing is left behind, I take a seat on the bottom step. Flipping through the photos in my hand, I take in the faces smiling back at me. One photo in particular makes me pause. Ella looks up at James as he leans over her, wrapping her up in his arms. Her painted nails grip on his forearms, holding him to her. But his gaze looks directly at me. I feel sweat slick my palms as if he's standing right in front of me. I brush his face softly with my thumb and make a silent promise that I'll never let anything, or anyone, hurt Ella or his little boy. With that I stand up, place the photos neatly on her desk, and walk out the back door.

# THIRTY-ONE
# SHIRTLESS AND SEXY

## ELLA

"THIS IS GOING TO BE AWESOME!" RONE AND TY RUN IN CIRCLES while Madi and I sit on a blanket in the backyard. A charcuterie board full of meats, cheese, and fruit sits between us. Our glasses full of wine, heads buzzing, and smiles wide as we watch the boys help Michael plan out the first steps for the treehouse.

"Tell me again where Rone found this?" Micheal looks up at me from his place on the blanket. When I first laid the design out in front of him, I couldn't look away from the gleam of childhood excitement that took over his expression. I almost expected him to start running around with the boys. He can't wait to build it, just like Cillian said.

"He was playing in the guest room one day and found this design on the table in there. He was so excited to show me. I don't remember seeing it in there, so it must have been in one of the drawers." I do my best to bend the story a little bit and hide the fact that Cillian overheard Rone telling me about his dream treehouse, then went upstairs and drew it out. Every little detail.

"No, it was right on top, Mom!" I wince a little as Rone jumps in to correct me.

"Either way, this thing is epic. Ian must have drawn this up before his accident. I can't believe he didn't show it to me." He runs his hands for the hundredth time along the sketches. "Man, I would have loved to build this with him." Michaels words fade out as he looks toward the big tree across the yard. I look over to where Rone is munching on some grapes, juice running down his chin. He didn't catch Micheal calling Cillian *Ian*, thankfully.

"Thank you again for helping with it, I know you're busy. So please don't work on it unless you feel up to it." I stand and walk with Michael who is still eying the tree in question.

"Are you kidding me? I'll stay up all night to work on this thing. We used to build treehouses when we were kids. Nothing amazing or even sturdy, though." He laughs and I see a whole lifetime of memories flash behind his eyes. "Ian fell out of so many trees when we were younger, I'm surprised he didn't kill himself. He couldn't contain his excitement sometimes and he paid for his clumsiness." The image of a younger, lanky Cillian falling out of trees makes me laugh.

I gently place my hand on his arm. "I wish I could have seen that." He shakes his head as if he can clear out all the memories of the past. Then he gives my hand a squeeze and makes his way back to the blanket. Flopping down next to Madi, he steals the bite out of her hand and tosses it in his mouth. She laughs and smacks his arm playfully. I smile and turn my attention back to the tree, closing my eyes and soaking in the moment around me. Spring has turned to summer. The air is not quite as heavy with humidity this evening, but warm enough that the cold grass feels heavenly under my feet. I sigh and sink my feet deeper into the blades, letting them tickle my ankles.

It's been a week since the twins walked into my house and shattered all my photos on the stairs. After I got home from picking up Rone from camp, the glass was cleaned up like it never happened and the pictures were stacked neatly on the corner of my desk. On top was one of my favorite pictures of James. I remember the exact day and time we took that picture. We'd been dating for a couple months and it was the last football game of his senior year. We went and watched together as some of his best friends played on the team. Even though they lost, James took it upon himself to lighten the mood, cracking jokes so his friends would smile. By the end of the night, he'd successfully gotten them all to forget the sting of losing. All of us were hanging out in some parking lot, music blaring from one of the parked cars. I was talking to one of the other girlfriends and James came up from behind me, grabbing me and pulling me into him. *"Say losers!"* he yelled over my shoulder. Even that got a laugh from his friends and I couldn't help but fall in love with him all over again. Just as I looked up at him, wrapping my hand around the arms holding me to him, I can still feel the ache in my cheeks from smiling so big at him. A flash went off somewhere in front of us, but I didn't look away. The slight stubble on his face accented by the streetlights, his blonde hair blowing lightly in the breeze, his chocolate brown eyes turning almost honey colored in the flash. A face frozen in time, in that photo and in my mind. Gosh, he was beautiful. I love that picture because I can remember looking at him. And when I look at his face, I feel as if he's looking at me.

When I look down at my feet wiggling in the grass, the green reminds me of another set of eyes and I'm taken back to that afternoon in my room. I still feel the stifling heat of him around me, his smell overwhelming, his hands seeking refuge on my skin. When he caged me in and my eyes rolled back in my head I swear I saw him, licking and kissing his way over my body. He went in and out of focus, but if I let my mind fill in the gaps, I can picture him clear as day. Black hair spilling over his face and tickling my skin as he moved over me. Shirtless and effortlessly sexy as I fell into his gravity yet again. When he bent down to catch my nipple in his mouth, his smooth skin stretched over his broad shoulders, freckles dotted his toned muscles and tumbled down over his chest. I remember eyeing the hollow line of his spine, wanting nothing more than to climb over him and run my tongue down it. White briefs poked out from his jeans. I clench my hands into fists, digging my nails into my palm at the memory of slipping under the covers and feeling his thick thighs under my fingertips with another thick thing in my mouth.

That moment is shadowed by the sound of breaking glass, a sound that already holds too many painful memories. I wanted so badly to fold into him, to have him tell me it was a silly prank and nothing else would come from it. But even I know that he wouldn't lie to me. The attack in this backyard and the shattered pictures was a clear message that I am not welcome here. And they didn't stop there; I feel like they are slowly making their way to me again. Closer to Rone. I can't bear the thought of anything happening to him. We've lost so much, but if it comes down to losing each other or losing this new life we've built here, I won't hesitate to choose him.

"What are you thinking about over here?" Madi's sweet voice startles me and I push a hand to my heart to slow it.

"Geez, Madi. Give a girl a warning before you scare the shit outta me." I laugh and give her a shove with my shoulder. She leans into me, then wraps her arm around my waist, pulling me into her.

"Talk to me, Ella. You don't have to go through this alone, I'm here for you."

"Ah, I'm just thinking about how happy we are here. Our whole lives, our futures, were changed in an instant. But I'm happy, I feel light, like maybe I'll actually be ok."

Her soft gaze moves past me and she looks up at the clouds that are painted pink and purple from the setting sun. "I can't imagine what you've gone through. But I know you'll be ok. I just have a feeling." And with those parting words, she gives me a hug and turns back to the blanket.

After I say our goodbyes, I get Rone and myself ready for bed. I lay under the covers and turn out the light. Like every day this week, Cillian hasn't been around. But every night as I'm just about asleep, I feel the bed sink under his weight and a soft, warm hand reaches out and holds mine. When I wake he's gone, but my bed smells like tea tree and mint. All of a sudden, I'm angry. I don't know what game he's playing at, giving me space during the day but curling up next to me each night. What we had that afternoon went beyond sex, then he just disappeared when what I needed was protection. I know I told him I needed space, but I hoped he'd still let me know that he was close by. An irrational rage builds inside me. So I lay there, pretending to be asleep, taking even breaths despite the anger that builds just under the surface. And I wait.

# THIRTY-TWO
## DOG MAN
### CILLIAN

A week. I've been trying to fix this for seven days. I've spent every waking minute researching more about what happened to the twins, trying to track them down to get to the bottom of this. Their temper tantrum is pushing me into uncharted territory when it comes to my anger and I don't like feeling out of control. I keep a close eye on Rone when he plays outside, never letting him see me, but never letting him out of my sight, either. I told Ella I'd keep him safe and I'm determined to do just that. Even at night I can't rest. I check and recheck all the doors making sure they are locked, that the blinds are lowered and curtains are drawn. Then I sit by Rone for hours until I'm sure he's asleep and the nightmares don't creep into his dreams. It's only when I feel like my body is shutting down that I make my way into Ella's room and crawl under the covers next to her. I get drunk off of the gardenia and rose smell that wraps around me as I doze off to sleep, reaching out and holding her hand in mine.

Tonight is no different. After Madi and Micheal left, I sat outside and looked at the tree before me, tall and strong. I want nothing more than to climb it and watch the sun sink lower and lower, so I do. I rise to my feet and pad my way across the grass, dew already collecting and making my bare feet slick. I grab the lowest branch with one hand and pull myself up. Memories of me and Michael climbing this same tree plow into me. My tears mix with the stupid smile I can't wipe off my face. Once I'm dangerously high, I look out over the rolling hills and take in the clouds that are now fading into a deep purple and blue as the sun drops lower in the sky. I sit there for hours, thinking about absolutely nothing. Breathing, just existing.

By the time I decide to head inside, it's dark enough that I can't see the branches below me. I laugh at myself when I realize that I'm a little bit scared that I'll slip and fall, but I'm dead. What's the worst that can happen? I jump what I hope is the last foot or two to the ground and land awkwardly, rolling onto my back and staring up at the night sky. Twigs crunching at the tree line draws my attention, my whole body on edge. Where I used to feel a sense of protection over the girls, now I only feel anger and disappointment. I sit up and listen as leaves rustling and hushed voices grow louder, the hot summer air turning chilly the closer they get to me.

"Where have you two been?" I stand and stalk towards them, feeling like a father scolding his children.

"Who do you think you are? You're the one playing house when we are trying to move on." The bolder sister's face is so pale. She looks like she's aged since I first met them, not at all like the face a sweet, innocent eleven-year-old should have.

"Have you forgotten about us?" The other sister, who usually stays quiet, peeks up at me from under her icy blonde bangs. Her eyes look so sad and a wave of compassion washes over me. I kneel before them and reach for their small hands, but the angry one pulls hers back. I let her and slowly reach for the quiet one's hands. She hesitates for a moment before reaching for me. Her hands are so cold, like she soaked them in ice water. I subconsciously rub them in mine to warm them and her eyes fill with tears. "We trusted him, too, and look what he did to us." Her admission catches me off guard and her sister snags her hands out of mine, pulling her away from me and into herself.

I tilt my head, dropping my hands into my lap. "Who? Who did you trust?" I feel closer to answers than I ever have and my voice comes out more demanding than I intend it to.

The shy one peeks out from under her sister's arms and whispers, "The dog man." Chills break out across my skin and I can feel sweat pooling under my arms. They turn sharply and walk towards the tree line, the shy sister getting a quiet reprimand from the other. But I follow. I can't let this moment to find answers slip away. When I get close enough, I reach out and grab the shy one by the shoulders, turning her away from her over protective sister and crouch down in front of her.

"Tell me, *please*. I can help you!" I'm pleading with her, holding her frail shoulders in mine. My thumbs rub in slow circles, trying to help her see that I do care about them, that I would never hurt them. She looks at her sister who is glaring at the side of my face. "Please."

She rolls her lips between her teeth, fingers wrapping into mine.

"I don't want to say his name. His little dog would follow us down the street. Dolly was her name. She was so cute. All the kids on the block loved to play with her and he would sit on his porch and watch us." Her eyes flick to her sister before going on. "One day all the other kids ran off to play, but Dolly was still outside so I walked her home. He wasn't on the porch, so I knocked on the door." She trails off and tries to pull her hands from mine. I gently hold them tighter.

"Did he hurt you?" I whisper quietly, hoping she'll continue. This is the most information I've gotten from them in a decade and I'm itching for more.

Her eyes well up with tears and before her sister can pull her away, she whispers, "Not that time." Then with what I can only guess is a sneer from the other twin, they walk off into the dark. I sit in silence, knees soaked from the damp grass, my mind reeling for what feels like eternity. I try to piece together this new information. I need to find out who the hell *dog man* is. I wipe the grass from my pants and take long strides across the lawn to the backdoor. When it clicks open, I groan quietly and make a mental note to lay into Ella about locking up more carefully. That is, when I build up the courage to approach her.

I make sure the front door is locked before pulling up behind the desk. I grab the notepad that I've been keeping my notes on from the drawer off to the side and begin a deeper dive into the new information I was given. I stare at the screen until my eyes burn with exhaustion, then I trudge up the steps, turning into the master bedroom without thinking. The moon casts lines across Ella's sleeping body and I take a moment to let her peaceful face calm my racing heart. Then I slide into my spot and reach out for her hand. Like every other night, she gently wraps her fingers around mine, but after a split moment her grip becomes painful. I look up to her face, expecting to see her eyes scrunched and body shaking from a nightmare. Only this time I'm met with wild, blue eyes, shooting daggers straight through me.

I try to tug my hand away. "Ella, what are you doing? Are you alright?" Her grip stays firm. "Shit, babe, you're strong." I try to lighten the mood and laugh a little, but it dies quickly when she grasps my palm even tighter. I'm a big guy, but she holds onto my hand like it's nothing but putty ready to be smashed in her grip. I don't think she's blinked. Her eyes are wide and full of fire. I have no prior reason to be terrified of the woman in front of me, but I am. Totally, irrationally, terrified.

Anger bleeds into every word she speaks. "Where have you been? You come into my bed, touch me, hold me, tell me you'll take care of me, and then leave?" Her voice rises as she finishes her sentence, not once loosening her hold on me. Before I can respond, she throws the covers back and rolls on top of me, her thighs holding my sides tightly. Her hair falls around her. When I reach up to push it back, she grabs that hand and slams it down into the bed, like she saw my hand before it touched her. I could easily push her off of me, pin her down and make her listen to me, but I can't deny the fact that her on top of me is the only place I'll ever want her to be.

"Ella, sweetheart."

"Don't *sweetheart* me." She bares her teeth a bit and I can't help but choke back a laugh. She may think she looks threatening, but I think she looks down right gorgeous. If she keeps looking at me like this, I'll happily give her a fight anytime she'd like.

"*Sweetheart...*" I don't miss the way her eyes narrow as she stares down at me. Her blue eyes are almost iridescent in the moonlight. For a moment, I wonder if she can really see me. If she can see the effect she has on me, over me. "Let me explain." She finally releases my wrists and I move my hands to grip her hips, keeping her in place. She blinks at me a few times before rolling her eyes and sitting back, crossing her arms over her chest.

It takes a great deal of effort to pull my focus from the feeling of her pressed over the length of me. My eyes start to go dry with the effort I'm putting into not looking at her breasts pushed up between her folded arms. Nothing but a thin, oversized shirt covering her from me.

I take a deep inhale then dive in, telling her about how horrible I felt the afternoon with the twins. How I left the house planning to come back with answers. Leaving out the part where I sat on the bottom step making a silent promise to James to take care of her and Rone. I don't skip over any other details about my research into the twins' death or the odd conversation I had a few moments ago outside. The more I tell her, the more she relaxes, nodding along as I go on. When I finish, there is a long pause, both of us looking at each other. I'm unsure where to go from here. I open and close my mouth a few times. It's on the tip of my tongue to ask her why she wants me here. Or why she even took notice that I wasn't around as much. But I don't want to push her away, I don't want to lose the heat that radiates between us. I don't want to lose *her*.

# THIRTY-THREE
# SWEETHEART

## ELLA

My resolve has melted away. From the second he first laid next to me, I had a plan. I was angry, ready to lay into him and push him away. I was tired of waiting on him, tired of feeling like he was using me and leaving me behind. Afraid of feeling empty and alone again. But when the bed sunk down and he held my hand, everything faded away. He was here, he's always been here. Even if it isn't the way I want, he came back. I knew I'd feel him, but I didn't expect to open my eyes and see him so clearly. Even through the fading light of my room with little moonlight shining in, casting shadows over my bed, I had to blink a few times to make sure I was actually seeing who was next to me. I felt his fingers wrapped around mine, but more than just feeling him, I can *see* the muscled forearms stretched between us, the veins that wrap tightly around them. I let my eyes wander over the black ink I could just make out on his wrist. His green eyes seemed to shine in the dim light, black hair falling over his forehead. *Holy. Shit.* He's here, not just a presence or a feeling. *Real.* The picture of his smiling face I've looked at so often on my computer doesn't do him justice. He is breathtaking. I'm not sure why tonight I can see him like he's a living person and not just the ghost living in my house. My breath gets stuck in my throat at the realization that he is here before me.

His eyes twinkled in amusement when I grabbed hold of his hand as tightly as I could. When I rolled on top of him without thinking about it, I could feel him grow underneath me. His strong stomach flexed under me as I held him down. The simple, white shirt he wore stretched over his broad chest. He's devastatingly handsome, with a strong nose and straight, white teeth that peek through full lips as he tries not to smile up at me. It takes everything in me not to reach out and thread my fingers through his hair again. It's messed up from running his hands through it and I want to rough it up more. Dark, full eyebrows frame those deep, green eyes and his eyelashes brush his cheeks when he blinks. His skin is smooth and I can just make out the small lines that crinkle around his eyes when he smiles at me. I try not to shift on his lap despite how much I want to. *I cannot give in,* I repeat over and over, even though I'm pulled into his orbit. Tea tree and mint floating around me as I stare down at him.

"Sweetheart..." I narrow my eyes at him and I squeeze his wrists tighter. He bites down on his bottom lip and I feel a tug in my stomach. "Let me explain." I let his wrists go and shift back onto my legs, which is a big mistake, I didn't think it through before I straddled him. Now that I've pushed my weight back onto his lap, I am painfully aware of how my attempt to scare him was received in an entirely different way. He rubs his wrists, smiling at me playfully like I actually hurt him. Then his hands land on my waist , not missing the subtle way he moves me back and forth over him a few times before he holds me still.

I try to move off of him after he tells me about his week of waiting and researching. "I don't know what to say." The conversation he had with the girls gives me second hand horror and I rub my arms to chase off the chill that washes over me. "That's horrifying. And she didn't give you any other information about who this *dog man* is?" He moves his hands up and down my thighs, mirroring my movements on my arms. His touch is comforting and I want to lean into him, lay down and have him wrap his body around me.

"Her sister took her away pretty quickly. It was clear that she didn't want her to give me any more details. I tried to look up any articles on who this guy could be, but I didn't find anything. It happened back in the 70's, so news isn't as accessible as I'd like it to be." He sighs and puts his hands behind his head, staring at the ceiling. I can't pull my eyes away from the way his muscles bunch in his arms as he lays there. How is it fair that he looks like he does? My eyes wander over his arms, down to his body beneath me. When I look back at his face, he raises an eyebrow at me. He totally caught me, but I can't find it in me to even be embarrassed. He's beautiful and I can't believe I can see him.

*Holy shit, I can see him!* Again, I'm shocked that this isn't something I've imagined. That he is here, under me, *real*. My eyes widen and I open my mouth to say something. Just before I can get the words out, there is a blood chilling scream from Rone's room. I move to get off Cillian, but he has already pushed me to the side and is racing out of the room. Before I make it to my doorway, Cillian is rushing past me back into my room with a sobbing Rone in his arms. As I turn to follow them, an icy chill drifts past me in the hallway. Turning to look in that direction, I feel a hand run down one of my arms. My skin breaks out in goosebumps and a cold sweat beads along my spine. *Them.*

I dart back into my room, closing the door behind me. When I make it to the bathroom, Cillian has gently sat Rone on the counter, bent over so he's nose to nose with him. I can't hear what he's whispering to him as I rush towards them. Cillian moves to the side ever so slightly, like he's afraid to be too far away, giving me space to hold my boy.

"Rone, what's wrong?" His face is covered in streaks of tears and snot runs from his nose. I reach for him and wrap him in my arms, holding him tight to my chest and running my hands over his hair. Cillian eyes us for a minute before he takes off out of the bathroom. I hear his footsteps on the steps and the backdoor slamming. A few minutes later, I hear him come back up the stairway, his footsteps disappearing into Rone's room before he comes back to us. He stands in the doorway for a moment, running his hands through his hair. He shakes his head before walking over to us, his hand sliding over my waist as he goes back to his spot on the other side of Rone.

"Hey, buddy, I just turned on the nightlight in your room. I'm sorry I didn't notice it was off when you went to bed." I look over at him with wide eyes. *How does he know that Rone can't sleep without his nightlight on?* Looking at me, he gives me a small smile, a hint of pink tints his cheeks like he's embarrassed that he let the detail slip out so casually. My heart hums at the thought of him checking on Rone and I after we've gone to sleep. I look back at Rone, my eyes snag on the reflection of his back in the mirror. All the blood drains from my face and I feel faint. It's happened, they've reached him.

"Baby, what happened to your back?" His pj top is stretched out like someone grabbed it and pulled. Lifting the material up, I let out a sharp gasp before dropping his shirt back down to cover my mouth with my hands. There are long scratches all down his back, not deep enough to draw blood, but angry, red, puffy lines mark his smooth soft skin. My eyes fill with tears and I turn my head into Cillian's shoulder while I hug Rone to my chest. When I look up to him, his eyes are full of apology, begging for forgiveness. Despite the emotion in his eyes, his body vibrates with anger. He bends down to wipe Rone's face, not caring about the snot and tears.

"Tell me what happened while we get you cleaned up and tucked in with Mom for the night, ok?" *Mom. He called me Mom.* Not your mom, but *Mom*, like the title was something he gave me. Before this moment, hearing any man say that would have made me angry. I should feel awkward, but all I feel is peace, like I'm not alone in this. I give him a small smile and begin to take Rone's top off while Cillian digs through the drawers for some ointment to put on the scratches.

"My night light was on." His small voice makes us pause. "It was on when I went to sleep. Then I had a scary dream."

"Keep going." Cillian's voice is calm and reassuring. I watch as Rone turns his little eyes up to Cillian and nods his head.

"I was outside playing in my new treehouse, the one that you drew for me." Cillian smiles and nods his head, encouraging Rone to continue. "These girls came out of the trees to play with me, so we ran around and climbed into the tree house. They were nice for a while and then..." His eyes fill with tears again and I hold onto him, kissing the top of his head. "Then, they pushed me. The tree branches scratched my back when I fell, I landed so hard that I couldn't breathe. Then I woke up." Biting back tears, I look over at Cillian—his face is cold and void of emotion.

As I stare, I have to blink a few times to get him into focus. Only an hour ago, he was so real. I could see every detail, every freckle on his nose, every indent of the muscles in his arms. But now, he's fading around the edges like he's slipping away again. I wish I could reach out and hold him in this moment, keep him here with us. By the time he tucks an exhausted Rone into the bed beside me, he is nothing more than the warm presence I felt that first afternoon. I can still feel his body move behind me in the bed, smell his familiar odor, but gone are his verdant eyes, the feel of his smooth, black hair against my skin. I can't bring myself to have the conversation I was so close to having before we heard Rone's scream. I can't find it in me to admit to him that I could see him perfectly only an hour ago.

Thankfully, the light clicks off before my tears hit the pillow. Tears that I finally had him here in reality and not just a shadow only to slip away again, tears that my boy has now been the victim in another attempt to get us to leave, tears because this might be the thing that breaks me, tears that I let myself believe that I could ever be truly happy again.

# THIRTY-FOUR
# BOB MARLEY

## CILLIAN

I HELD ELLA WHILE SHE CRIED. EVEN AFTER SHE FELL ASLEEP, I couldn't find it in myself to leave them. I watched them sleep for hours, memorizing every detail. Rone's long eyelashes and his little hands holding onto Ella's. The freckles that scatter across her nose and cheeks. I don't think she wanted me to know she was crying, so I did the only thing I could and held her to me, trying to give her comfort in the only way I knew how. I fought back tears of my own; tonight feels different. It started playful, the two of us clinging to each other and lost in one another. It felt real. At one moment, I swear she could see all of me with the way it felt like her eyes roamed over my body. I'll keep that soft expression on her face and the fire that burned in her eyes in my memory for the rest of my life. In a split second, it all changed. After what happened with Rone and the way she quietly cried in my arms, it felt like a goodbye. I bury my nose in her hair and hold her tighter, allowing myself to picture a life where this is my reality. Happier, of course. Getting to hold my family at night, watching them laugh, smile, watching them *live*. It only makes my heart break more, so I give in and let my body drift off.

Ella's phone buzzes on the nightstand at the same time

knocking comes from the front door. She shifts in bed and rubs her eyes.

Voice thick from sleep, I mumble into her hair, "Morning, sweetheart." I pull her into me for a quick moment, then let go to move off the bed.

"Hi." Her voice is soft and she looks over at Rone who has starfished in the middle of the bed. "Will you stay with him while I answer the door? Mike is here to start on the treehouse," she says as she looks down at her phone, texting a reply.

"Of course I will. He's safe with me, sweetheart." She looks down at her hands, twisting them in her lap before letting out a soft sigh.

"I hope so, Cillian. I trust you with him, I really do. I just..." She trails off and it feels like a punch to the chest. I know she's upset. I am, too, but last night felt different, like she was slipping away. But to hear it from her has my bile rising in my throat. I swallow it down and bend down in front of her, reaching out to stop her fingers from fidgeting more.

"I promise I'll figure this out. I want you here. I don't know what I would do without you. Without both of you." The thought of them leaving is almost too much to bear. I brush her hair out of her face before pressing my lips to her forehead.

"Don't promise things you have no control over." She pushes past me and walks out the door. I settle back on the bed beside Rone and listen to the voices below move outside. I stare at the fan spinning lazily above me.

"Ian?" I didn't even notice Rone had woken up and is now laying on his side facing me. His deep, brown eyes bounce across my face. I roll on my side and prop my head up on a pillow.

"Hey, buddy, how are you feeling today?"

"Good, no more nightmares." He looks me dead in the eyes when he says, "You look sad." *Fucking kids.* I give him a small smile and let out a deep breath.

"I guess I am kind of sad. I don't like seeing you get hurt."

"I'm ok now." He reaches out and wraps his little hand

around mine. I stare at the place where our hands intertwine and can't stop the tears that start to run down my cheeks. "It's ok to be sad, Ian. Remember?"

"I know, buddy. I just really like being around you and your mom. I don't want you to get hurt because of me." His little hand squeezes mine and my heart fractures all over again.

"My daddy was in my dream last night." My whole body freezes and I look over at his little face. His eyes look up at the ceiling now, like he's replaying his dream. "It was after I fell asleep next to you and Mommy."

I'm caught off guard. Clearing my throat roughly, I ask, "Oh yeah? What did he say?"

"He was holding this baby, I think it was my baby sister. They died together and it made me happy that he was holding her so she wasn't scared." His eyelashes graze his sun kissed cheeks. "He was singing some song I've never heard before. Then he looked at me and winked. He always winked at me, it made me laugh because he'd always close both eyes." His own eyes twinkle with laughter and he lets out a small giggle, which in turn makes me smile through my tears.

"Do you remember what song he was singing to your sister?" I can see his little mind thinking, nose scrunching before he starts singing the chorus to *Three Little Birds* by Bob Marley and the Wailers.

I'm still sitting there in shock when Rone finally lets my hand go, gives a big stretch, and rolls out of bed like he's ready to take on the day. After a few minutes, I cross the hall into my room and lean against the window frame, watching Mike get to work below. I rub the hurt in my chest as I watch him. All the memories that we no longer get to make together constricts my heart in a painful grasp.

"Cillian?" Ella's soft voice from the hallway instantly has me moving to her. She's looking around and I start to rethink her expression from last night. Laying in her bed with her on top of me, she looked at me as if she really saw me. I could feel the path of heat as her eyes took in every inch of my face and body. I don't let myself believe that I imagined it. I know she felt my hands. Felt it in my blood when she looked into my eyes that she could see me, see past whatever barrier there is between us and looked into my broken heart. I walk into her space and pull her into a hug, her surprised gasp gives me the answer I needed. She can't see me now. Now that things are falling apart between us, I've gone back to the other side of the divide.

"Hi." I'm not sure what else to say.

"I don't want to leave..." My heart skips a few beats with excitement and I let out a sigh of relief. "But..." *Shit.* I shouldn't have gotten my hopes up. It feels like that moment before you get broken up with. You know it's coming, but deep down you try to reason it away. Before she can break my heart, I cut her off.

"I know. I'll try again, I'll find them and figure this out. Please don't leave. Please let me try to help them."

"Help them!" She moves away from me, pointing a finger towards Rone's room. "Did you not see what they did to Rone?" Her voice rises and she pinches her nose with her fingers. "Cillian, I can't be here if that's what they will do to him every time I turn my back. I can't put him in this position to get hurt again." Her eyes fill with tears and she angrily wipes them away before they can spill over.

"That's not what I meant. Of course I don't want anything to happen to him, or you..."

"But it did!!" She's yelling at me now and I'm grasping at anything to help get through to her.

"Ella, please."

"No. Cillian, stop. I need time to process whatever all this is." She waves her hand around in front of her. "I don't know what is going on, but you can't be here anymore. I'm sick over what happened last night."

"You think I'm not?" I take a breath and try to calm down the rampage of emotions building within me.

"He's not your son, there is a difference!" I stagger back like she physically slapped me. Of course I knew that, but it still stings. I care about the two of them. If I'm being honest, I probably care more than I thought was possible. She covers her face with her hands and her shoulders slump forward. "I won't leave. But I won't stay if this happens again. And I do need you to leave us alone for a while."

*Leave them alone?* I'm shattered all over again. Nodding my head as if she can see me, I whisper, "I'll leave, but only to figure this shit out and then I'm coming back to you." Her shoulders shake now as new tears slide down her freckled face.

"Why, Cillian?"

"You're my ocean, Ella." I move to her and carefully wrap my arms around her. She doesn't pull away so I tug her into me. "I'm drawn to you. No matter how much distance I give you, you will always pull me back to you. Please let me fix this."

"I'll try to give you time, but I need it, too."

"I'll try, too. Trust me." She nods against my chest, tears soaking through to my skin. "Can I ask you something?" She sniffs before nodding her head again. "How does Rone know who Bob Marley is?" Her whole body goes still and she looks up toward me with a confused look.

"What do you mean?" I tell her about the dream that Rone told me about this morning and her face pales before a fresh wave of tears pours down her beautiful face. Between sobs she says,

"That was the song playing in the car when we crashed."

## THIRTY-FIVE
# NEVER LET GO

### ELLA

Summer has reached peak heat and humidity, but I can't shake the chill that clings to me. I told Cillian to give me space. I know it's what I need, but I'm stuck trying to convince my mind and body of the fact. My mind is consumed by him. Thoughts of feeling him against me plague my waking moments. My stomach flips in anticipation for the moment I'll feel him. I can't convince that part of me that misses him, his smell on my pillows and his heavy arm wrapped around me every night, to let him go.

The days stretch longer. The smell of freshly cut grass and blooming flowers ambushes me every morning when I step outside. It's so peaceful it makes me sick. I want to scream at the world to stop being so fucking beautiful when everything around me is so ugly. I wake up earlier these days to avoid the heat. I get my workout in and water the garden, making it inside just as the sun peaks over the trees that shade the house. Rone has been sleeping in my bed for the past couple weeks, neither of us risking another incident like the last time he slept in his room. Every morning I wake up and I know that Cillian is in the room with us. He never comes to me, never says anything, but I can feel him. The chair under the window that I used to curl up in and read, now belongs to him. I should be angry he hasn't left, but knowing he sits there every night to watch us and keep us safe brings me the comfort I'm so desperately denying myself. I can't risk the heartbreak that will inevitably come if I allow myself to drift any further in his pull.

I've just stepped back inside the house from dropping Rone off at camp, put my keys on the entryway, and placed my shoes by the door. It's not even mid-morning yet and my shirt is soaked through from the summer heat. My phone pings in my bag and I dig to the bottom, pulling it out to see a text from Mike.

> We'll be back by tonight to work on the treehouse! Madi is wondering if you'd like to picnic in the backyard? I can let the boys help with some things tonight.

Mike and some of the guys from his crew have come by every few nights to work on the treehouse for the boys and it's finally taking shape. I have to remind Rone multiple times a day to leave it alone.

> That sounds perfect, thanks!

I place my phone on the table in the hall and make my way upstairs to change. While I'm changing, *Never Let Go* by Blake Rose starts to play from my phone. My body freezes as a chill washes over me. For a brief second I'm too terrified to move, bracing for the impact of another attack. But after a few moments when nothing happens except for a warm feeling washing over me, it all clicks together. The music in the gym, the song that played in the kitchen when I felt like someone was holding me, the one that turned on when Rone first told me he wished his dad could build him a treehouse. It was always Cillian; listening, being there, trying to talk to me, to be there, any way he could. I sink down into his chair, instantly surrounded by his smell. I close my eyes and relive every little moment we've had together. I can't fight the smile that breaks free and stretches across my face. I *want* him. As ridiculous as it sounds, as impossible as it sounds, I want any piece of him I can have.

Slowly, the happy memories he's brought into my life are overshadowed by the painful reminder that Rone and I are not safe here. Cillian can't be with both of us all the time. That thought alone is enough to shake me from my thoughts. I stand up and slowly walk down the stairway, looking at the photos that I've replaced along the wall. I reach out and run my hand over a picture of James. It's from the day we had Rone. James is standing in the hospital room, head turned down staring at a chunky baby wrapped in a blue blanket. Despite the tears in his eyes, I can see the way he looks at Rone. Like he is the most beautiful thing he's ever seen. His strong arms hold this tiny baby to his chest, one thumb gently stroking a chubby cheek. *God, I miss him.*

Taking a deep breath, I grab my phone just as the song is ending and head into my office. I pull out the notepad that Cillian and I had added notes to about the disappearance and death of the twins. I add the details that he told me about the last time we were together. Tapping the pen on my chin, I stare out the window at the trees around me and shudder at the thought of something so horrific happening just on the other side of the tree line. There has to be someone who remembers what happened. A cat walks across my driveway and lays down in the sun, rolling onto its back and stretching out along the warm gravel. Watching it for a moment, the sun glints off the collar. Cringing at the thought of who it belongs to, I keep an eye on the end of the drive, expecting an angry Ms. Miles to come stomping up my drive, demanding why I stole her cat. After a few minutes, it dawns on me: grouchy Ms. Miles has lived in Spring Hill for a long time. A *long* time. I drop the pen and rush to the front door. It's not until I'm racing down the front steps that I slow down, not wanting to scare the cat away. She's not the least bit bothered, rolling to her stomach and eyeing me as I creep towards her.

"Hi, kitty, I'm going to pick you up and take you home, ok?" She eyes me as I slowly inch closer and scoop her up in my arms. Rubbing her head against my chest, she purrs quietly as I make my way down my long driveway and turn up the road toward Susan Miles' home.

*Here goes nothing.* I hold the orange tabby tighter in my arms like she's my lifeline. Ms. Miles' house is set back a little further than mine and her yard looks like it hasn't been taken care of in years. Dandelions cover her front lawn and chipped paint peels off the front porch. Cats pop out of nowhere and I'm suddenly very aware of the eyes surrounding me as I make my way up the creaky steps. Just as I knock on the door, the cat jumps from my arms and I'm left trying to figure out what to do with myself now that my hands are empty. I hear footsteps slowly making their way to the door and I wring my hands in front of me, so nervous I could puke.

The front door opens a few inches. "What do you want?" Her white hair and pale skin fill the small space between the door and frame. A small, white cat slips past her and darts down the steps. Her eyes narrow on my shirt and I look down, noticing that I am covered in cat hair. "I thought I told you to leave my cats alone." She opens the door a little wider and I'm hit in the face with a hot wave of cat odor. I try to breathe through my mouth, but that only makes it worse. I take a tentative step back to place some distance between me and her open door.

"Oh, you did. I'm sorry, that one," I point to the cat I carried here who has now made her bed on a dilapidated chair, "came over to my house and I just wanted to bring her home safely." I smile, hoping that my lie lands. Her gaze dances over my face and I feel beads of sweat gathering at the base of my spine.

"Ginger knows how to get home." She lets the statement sit

in the air between us. My smile slips a little and I mask my discomfort by looking out over her property. It really is beautiful, if you can look past the weeds and run-down house.

I scramble for something, anything to say to fill the awkward silence. "I feel bad that we got off on the wrong foot. And I really just wanted to come by to check in and see if I could help with anything." The night of Cillian's death comes to me and I remember that he was here, helping her before he was hit on his way home.

"I don't need any help. Never done any good." Taking a step outside, she closes the door behind her and I take a deep inhale of clean air. *I wonder if she's talking about Cillian.*

Before I can think better of it, the words spill out. "Did you know the person who lived in the house before me?"

She huffs and takes a seat in the chair next to Ginger and I have to hold myself back from grabbing on to her when the wood groans under her weight. "That pompous ass should never have been given that house."

*"Cillian?"*

She flinches when I say his name. "No, the other one."

"Oh, you mean Peter, the cousin." I take a seat on the top step and am immediately ambushed by no less than five cats rubbing up on my clothes and fighting for a spot to curl up on my lap. "I heard he was a real piece of work." I mindlessly stroke their ears, letting their soft fur ease the tension between me and the old woman eying me suspiciously from her seat on the porch. She surprises me when she laughs.

"I used to call him Paul whenever I saw him. Drove him mad." My nerves loosen up a bit and I laugh along with her. "Cillian was a good man." She clears her throat before going on. "I've always felt guilty for what happened to him." I look over at her and she stares down the drive absentmindedly, stroking between the ears of a gray cat that has made a home in her lap. "I don't get much company and he was so friendly. I kept him too long that night." Her eyes glaze over and my heart breaks, thinking of the weight and guilt she still carries all these years later.

"It's not your fault that someone was driving reckless. If he didn't want to be here, he wouldn't have been." I reach out and give her knee a gentle squeeze. She looks down the drive a moment longer and then blinks the memories away. Her soft smile is barely noticeable, but I give her one back. "How long have you lived here?" I try to steer the topic away from Cillian and towards the answers I'm so desperately trying to piece together.

"I grew up in this house, it looks a little different now." She waves a hand around the property. "But it was once a very pretty home."

I look into her eyes. "I have no doubt that it was." We both look out over the yard that hugs the house, weeds poking up and grass that has grown knee high.

"My husband passed away before we had any children and I slowly lost any interest in much else."

My heart lurches and I feel tears beginning to form. *I'm so sick of crying.* I close my eyes and pull myself together. "My husband passed away not too long ago. I understand how you feel." I don't add on that I know what it feels like to find a tiny slice of happiness again, to feel cared for. Thoughts of Cillian creep into my mind and my mind drifts to the peace I find between his arms.

"I'm sorry to hear that, dear. I wish I could say it gets easier, but I still miss my Henry every single day."

"I can't imagine a day that I don't think of James, I don't think I ever want to forget him." I smile at the memory of his handsome face. "Susan, can I ask you about something?" She nods her head in response. "It's a bit morbid, but I read an article about something that happened here in Spring Hill back in the 70's and I'm trying to put all the details together."

"Hmmm, I'll try my best to help you."

I think for a moment, kicking myself for not thinking this out before I came over. But to be honest, I didn't expect to end up on her front steps talking like we're old friends. "I was moving out some old boxes from the garage and found a news article about twin girls going missing in the woods around here."

"Horrible," she interrupts me, letting out an angry puff of air and shaking her head. "It wasn't too long after my husband and I found out he was dying of cancer. We were caught up in living out his last few months. I don't remember much other than the search party that went out to look for them and then the police taping off the area when they found the bodies."

"Did you know the girls, did they live at Rose manor?" I remember Cillian mentioning that they said they didn't like Rone and I living here because it was their home.

"No, no. They lived just over there." She points down her drive. Craning my neck in that direction, I can just make out an old yellow home tucked back in the trees across the street. "They were so sweet. They used to sit in my drive and pet the stray cats." I want to ask her about the man with the dog that the kids played with, but try to work out how to word it without letting on that I know more than what was written in articles online.

"It sounds like they loved animals. I'm thinking about getting a dog for Rone. I think he and the other boys on the street would love to play with one."

Her foot stops tapping abruptly, a few moments later she starts up again. I let the silence stretch between us, hoping it'll encourage her to feed me more details.

"Kids do love dogs. You know there is a rumor…neighborhood gossip, I'm sure."

I turn to face her and nod my head. "I do love me some neighborhood gossip."

Turning in her seat, she rolls her lips between her teeth, debating what to tell me. I hold my breath so long that I start to feel lightheaded. Finally, she says, "There was a man, in his thirties or so, who lived alone. Wasn't very social with the adults in the neighborhood, but never missed a chance to talk to the kids. I even noticed him hugging them more often than I liked. He had a dog that would chase the kids up and down the street. Seemed friendly enough and the kids loved to play with her." She pauses for a second and when she speaks next, I feel all the blood drain from my face, chills sweeping over my body. "I remember her name, *Dolly*. Like Dolly Parton."

"Susan, what house is his?" My mind is racing, heart pounding.

"It's not there any longer. Poor guy died in a house fire. It's been rebuilt a few times now. It was three doors down from the Connely's home." My heart sinks, he's dead. Part of me is happy he is no longer around to torment or hurt anyone else, but I wish he had faced justice in this lifetime.

"What was his name?" When I look at her she is gazing off into the trees. Taking a shaky breath, I have to lean in to hear her.

"Arthur Muddle." The name slithers across the space between us and wiggles its way into my mind. *A name.* The horrible, evil man now has a name.

"Why didn't anyone say anything, if they felt like he was odd?"

"Some did, but there was never anything to connect him to it. He was.." she chews her cheek for a moment, *"peculiar,* I guess is a good word. But it didn't make him a murderer." There are too many connections to him and the urge to tell Cillian is over-whelming. I brush my pants off and stand, turning to grab Susan's hand in mine.

"Just like you said, probably some neighborhood gossip," I reassure her. I give her hand a final squeeze between mine. "I'm sorry that I need to run, but could I come back sometime? I enjoyed my time with you today."

Her frail hand holds onto mine, her thumb rubbing over my knuckles. "I'd like that." We say our goodbyes and as I walk away, I look between the shortcut through the trees that leads straight to my backyard and the long drive towards the main road. A shiver runs through me when a breeze causes the trees to bend and sway in such an ominous way that I almost sprint down her drive and back to my place. When I get inside, it's quiet and empty. Usually when I come home, I picture James coming out of the office or kitchen to sweep me into his arms. But today, all I want to see is a freckled face and forest green eyes.

# THIRTY-SIX
# FORGET EVERYTHING

## CILLIAN

SITTING IN THE CHAIR UNDER ELLA'S WINDOWS EACH NIGHT IS A special kind of torture. I get to watch the two of them snuggle together and talk about their day. Rone drifts off and Ella watches him with so much love in her eyes it makes my chest hurt. She gently brushes his hair off his face and kisses his forehead. Then she turns her eyes to the window and looks out at the willow tree that sways in the wind until her eyes drift shut. It's such a special moment that I feel almost unwelcome to witness. But it's a painful reminder that she doesn't want me around. I miss crawling into bed with her, feeling her warmth seep into my cold interior. But I can't stay away no matter how badly she may want me to. So I sit there each night, watching them, listening for any signs of the girls making their way in to cause trouble.

They have avoided me at every turn. I spend most days waiting in the trees for them to come to me, but they never do. When Ella isn't at her computer, I search for any other information about the twins, always coming up empty handed. I was sitting on our bench in the garden when I heard her come running up the driveway, her dirty tennis shoes pounding up the steps and into the house. I wanted to run to her, make sure she was ok. But as I went to stand, I made myself sit back down. *She doesn't want me.* I have to earn her trust, which means staying away and fixing a seemingly impossible mystery.

———

I stare out my bedroom window to the backyard below. Mike and Madi brought Ty over earlier tonight. The boys are helping Mike put the steps on the trunk of the big tree. I laugh when I catch Mike running his hands through his hair, like he's always done when he gets overwhelmed. The boys are narrowly missing their thumbs with each swing of the hammer against the wood. The moment Mike stepped in, the boys gave his hand a nasty smack. I howled with laughter, praying the glass between us muffled my hysteria. Madi and Ella look from the blanket, trying to hide their laughter. My heart aches to be a part of this moment. I rub my hand over my heart to ease the pain that is building inside me. When the boys give up and run away, Mike quickly steps in to finish the project, no doubt wanting to get it done so the boys can't come back over and mess up how he wants it. As the sun dips lower in the sky, the girls clean up the blanket and I watch as Madi rubs her hands up and down Ella's arms. Ella wipes her face and my chest tightens with the realization that she's upset. Mike bends down in front of Rone and asks him something, to which Rone responds by jumping in the air and running to tackle Ty.

A short while later, the back door closes, but I only hear Ella's feet walking up the stairs. Mike and Madi must have taken Rone to their place for a sleepover. I listen as she walks down the hallway and into her room, a few moments later I hear the bath begin to fill. Music plays and I can smell the soothing scent of lavender waft through my open door. Before I can convince myself to stay put, I stand from my bed and move across the hall, through the door, and into her room. The room is almost as humid as it is outside. My skin beads with sweat and I have to resist the urge to pull my shirt over my head to cool down. Peeking into the bathroom, I can't look away from the gorgeous woman, up to her neck in bubbles. Her eyes are closed, but she smiles ever so slightly as the music plays around her.

My mind is at war with itself trying to list out all the reasons not to let her know I'm here. I'm still standing there, debating what I should do when she slips beneath the water, sending a wave of water and bubbles sloshing to the floor. A few moments pass and my heart begins to speed up. A few more and I'm moving to the side of the tub, reaching my arms into the hot water and grabbing her shoulders, pulling her to the surface. She sputters and wipes the suds off her face. "What the hell!"

"What the hell, Ella? What are you doing?" I run my hands over her shoulders. My hand slides against her skin and I'm suddenly very aware of the naked goddess before me.

"Did you think…" She starts to laugh, trailing off. "Did you think I was trying to *drown myself?*"

"You were under water for a really long time!" I can't stop my hands from wandering over her bare skin, my fingertips running up her neck. Smiling, she leans into my touch.

She states matter of fact, "I was on the swim team. Don't worry, I was counting. It was only ten seconds."

It did not feel like ten seconds. A laugh bursts out of me and she rolls her eyes, then tilts her head back and laughs with me.

"You scared the shit out of me, sweetheart."

"You were watching me." It's not a question but a statement. My fingers slide off her and I lean my back against the side of the tub.

"I told you, I can't leave you alone. I tried to give you your space, but when I saw you go under and you didn't come back up, I got really scared."

She lets out a sigh and I hear her sit up in the bath. "I'm sorry I scared you, I just needed to quiet everything for a moment." Her voice is heavy and I turn around. She has her chin resting on her knees above the water, eyes fixed on the bubbles surrounding her. I move behind the tub and wrap my hands around her shoulders, slowly massaging the knots in her muscles. She moans and wiggles back into my grip. The muscles in my stomach flex while my fingers work. I want nothing more than to move them lower below the water.

"Why were you sad, earlier, in the yard with Madi?"

"You're a stalker." I can feel her eyes roll and I give her neck a squeeze.

Leaning in, I whisper against her ear, "You're in my house." Goosebumps pop up along her skin and I lean in, laying a soft kiss where her neck meets her shoulder. "Why are you sad, sweetheart?" She moves her hands to the surface of the water, pushing suds into piles then smoothing them over the surface. "It's our anniversary next month. I'm already starting to forget little things I never thought I'd forget."

I keep my hands moving over her shoulders, neck, and back, trying to ground her in the moment we're in. "Do you want to talk about him?" Normally, hearing a woman I have feelings for talk about another man would have my blood start to boil. But I've already decided I'll do anything for this woman. I'd listen to her talk about him all damn day if it meant I could sit this close to her. She's quiet for so long I peek over her shoulder and steal a glance at her face. Her bottom lip is tucked tightly between her teeth. Finally, she leans back into my hold and lets it all out.

"We met in high school, he was a senior and I was a junior..." She talks for what feels like hours. All the details about their walks home from school, how he made her feel like the only girl in the world. How he proposed at the top of a ten mile hike. That she was sweaty and felt disgusting, but he looked at her like she was the most gorgeous thing on the planet. My heart swells picturing the kind of love they had. I listen to her, smiling to myself at how happy it makes her to relive the memories she made with James. "We were going on a last date before Paige was due. I was so uncomfortable during pregnancy, even sitting through a movie was too much. He was taking me to my favorite restaurant and then...then it all ended. One moment we're laughing, making plans. And the next, he was gone. They both were."

I lean her back against the edge of the bath, releasing her hair from the tie. I massage her scalp, gently tugging her hair. She lets out a ragged breath and I notice tears making their way slowly down her face. Reaching one hand around her, I wipe each tear away. "What can I do for you?"

"Sometimes, I just want to forget it all. It's too painful to sit with all the time and I'm tired."

I don't want to push her feelings away, but I can't ignore the dirty thoughts in my mind, especially the one that whispers, *help her forget*. I brush her hair off her face and lean into her cheek, planting a chaste kiss on her wet skin. "Can I help you forget?" I don't miss the shudder that runs through her and I can't stop the grin that works over my face. "Just for a moment," I say, standing as I walk through her room to her nightstand. It takes a few minutes of digging through her stock pile of toys before I find what I'm looking for. Grabbing a small, thin, bullet vibrator, I don't say anything when I walk back into the bathroom and drop my clothes to the floor. I stand behind her and gently move her forward before climbing into the bath with her. Another wave of water and bubbles overflows, splashing on the floor.

She lets out a startled squeal. "Cillian, what are you doing?" If she asked me to leave I would, but she doesn't so I take that as a green light to press on.

"I told you before to use me, so use me." I hold her neck tightly, pulling her to my mouth. "Let me help you forget, just for a little while." I pull her back to my chest, her ass rubbing between my legs. She lets out a small gasp when she feels how easily I am affected by her, but she doesn't move away. I run my nose along her neck and up behind her ear, licking a path as I go. Her body melts into mine and I fight the urge to lift her up and flip her around on top of me. I dip my hands below the water and grip her hips with my fingers. I press them into her skin until she lets out a moan and subconsciously rocks her body back and forth. I slide the hand with the vibrator over her hips and between her legs. I pat her ass under the water. "Put your legs up, baby." She hesitates for a split second before bringing her legs above the water line and placing them on the sides of the bath. "Good girl." Her eyes close at my praise and I run my fingers through her sex. Clicking the button on the vibrator, a muffled buzz sounds from below the water. I run it softly over her inner thighs and her legs start to slip off the edge. Clicking my tongue in disapproval, I run my other hand down her inner thigh, pushing it back against the side.

The top of her breasts rise out of the water, bubbles and water running down her before they dip below the surface each time she takes a shaky inhale. "That's it, let me make you forget. Forget every painful memory. Forget everything except for how you feel pressed up against me." She nods her head and her lips part. I move the small vibrator over her inner thighs again before sliding it between her swollen lips. She moves forward, trying to push it into her, but I move my other hand to her lower stomach. I hold her against me, warning her to let me take control. Her head falls back against my chest and I kiss any bit of her face and neck that I can reach.

I turn the vibrator up a level and finally press it against her clit. She bucks against me, the sound of water hitting the floor mixing with her moans and my heavy breathing. I hold her firm as her breathing picks up, chest heaving above the water. I reach up and roll one of her nipples between my finger and thumb. "Fucking perfect, Ella." I slip my hand under the soapy water again and press just the pad of my finger into her. I can feel the vibration against her clit inside her and I bite back a groan, dropping my head into her neck, nipping and licking as I work her higher and higher.

# THIRTY-SEVEN
## JUST LET GO

### ELLA

THIS IS NOT HOW I SAW MY EVENING GOING, BUT I CAN'T DENY THAT I wouldn't want it any other way. I'm exhausted from everything going on and the reminder of our anniversary only makes the memory of James and Paige's passing even more painful.

The vibration against my clit and the shallow pressure of his finger has my climax barreling straight towards me. I stop breathing, the spring inside me ready to release. Just as I feel it starting to reach boiling point, my legs shaking, breasts bouncing on top of the water, he curls his finger into me, hitting the spot that sends me flying over the edge. I moan his name as I ride the wave of ecstasy that continues to pull me under. I feel like I haven't even come down from my high before he tosses the vibrator over the side and lifts me above the water, turning me around towards him.

"What are you doing?"

"Stop asking stupid questions and sit on my face." I let out a laugh because I can't even see his face to sit on it, but fuck I want to. As if he can read the confusion on my face, his voice gets softer and he runs his thumbs over the skin on my hips, dripping bubbles into the water below me. "Close your eyes, *feel* me."

I open my mouth to argue, but decide if I'm going to fall, I'll fall headfirst. Closing my eyes, I focus on what I can feel. His hands on my skin. His touch gentle but demanding. Hot breath ghosting over my thighs. A warm, wet sensation working up my calf, over my knee, and up my inner thighs. I reach out and imagine what I would feel if he was really here. My hands sink into strands of silky hair. I follow a lock of his hair that has fallen over his forehead and I let my hands wander over his face. Pulling his head back from between my thighs, I run my fingers over his straight nose and full lips dripping with my arousal. I gather the moisture on my finger and bring it to my mouth.

*"Fuck. Me,"* he breathes. I can feel him watching me pull my finger into my mouth and lick it clean. "Sit. On. Me. Ella." It's not a question, but a demand; each word is said with so much hunger. He pulls me roughly down to him, his tongue instantly diving into me. I grab his hair, my legs going weak. His strong arms hold me up and I run my hands over his forearms, feeling his soft hair and the bumps of his veins. His shoulders are muscular and I dig my fingernails into him when he hits a sensitive spot.

"Yes, don't stop," I pant.

"Never, sweetheart. Just let go." He doesn't stop until I've drenched his face not once, but twice. He eats, and sucks, and nibbles me like he's tasting the most exquisite fruit he's ever had. I'm numb and can't stand when he's through with me. My mind is deliciously blank, my body blissfully exhausted. He lifts me from the bath and wraps me in a towel. When he sits me on the edge of the tub, he pulls the drain and the sound of water swirling down the drain makes my eyes start to fall shut. "I've got you, baby." He wastes no time drying me off before he pulls a shirt over my head and carries me to bed. He turns off the light and tucks me under the blankets. Before I can ask him to stay, I feel him slip in behind me and pull me into him.

———

"No, no, no! Stop, please!" Strong arms wrap around my body, squeezing me, almost painfully. Cillian shakes and twitches behind me. His breath is quick and heavy, moisture builds on my shoulder from where he has buried his head. "I want to stay, please."

"Cillian..." I call his name louder over and over until his body goes still and the arms squeezing the air from my lungs loosen their grip. The silence stretches between us. I give him a few moments before I turn in his arms and stare into his green eyes. They take my breath away and I reach out, tracing the sharp angles of his face with my fingertips. Blinking the nightmare away, his eyes soften as he looks down at me. "Talk to me, love." I'm startled by the affectionate name that slips from between my lips. I look at him, not sure of the reaction I'll see painted on his face, but my heart melts at the softness in his eyes. If he notices, he doesn't give it away. He gives me a weak smile before shifting onto his back. There is an ease between us that comes naturally, like we just fit together. It's in these moments that I'm slowly realizing when I can see him clearly before me. When there is calm and it feels like the way life should feel, he's here. Tangible. And I'm praying that nothing happens again that will pull him back to the other side. I want him here, *I need* him here.

His chest is mesmerizing and I can't help but run my hands over him. The lines of his muscles look like someone sketched his body in a notebook. Soft skin covers hard muscles, dusted with a thin cover of black hair. I lick my lips, wanting to take my time tasting him. He clears his throat and I snap my eyes to his, a smirk telling me that he didn't miss the way I was eye fucking him. Heat floods my cheeks and I rest the side of my face on his chest to avoid looking into those green eyes that pull me under whenever I look into them. "It's been a long time since I've had a nightmare like that." His breath shudders before he goes on. I run a hand over his skin, hoping to give him the comfort he has gone so long without. I watch as his skin shivers under my touch, smiling at the way his body reacts to mine. "It was so real." When he hesitates, I look up, giving him a reassuring smile. His eyes turn to pools of green when he looks back at me. "You are so beautiful, Ella." He cups my cheek with his hand, running his thumb over my cheek. Leaning into his touch, we stay there, looking into each other for a long moment. He smiles back, but it doesn't reach his eyes.

Sensing that he doesn't want to elaborate more, I change the subject. "So…I had a visit with Ms. Miles today." His thumb stops abruptly and he grips my chin, tilting my face up to his.

"What made you do that?" His voice is tight like he's holding back a scolding. I lift a shoulder and let it fall, the motion making my shirt slip off. Cillian's eyes flare before sweeping back to meet mine, this time I'm watching him with a smile on my face.

I tell him how I felt that maybe someone who had lived here during the twins murder might have some information that we were missing. And when that orange cat walked across the drive, it all clicked together. The air shifts when I tell him about the man who lived down the street. The man with the dog named Dolly. He shoots up in the bed, grabbing me by the shoulders so we're sitting face to face. "Ella, do you know what this means? We know who it was!" Sitting back into the bed, he runs his hands through his inky black hair. "We're the only ones who know who it was. Holy shit!" His hair sticks up in the places he's run his fingers through, places I want to spread my fingers through and pull. *God, what is it about this man that makes my mind go blank and my legs feel weak?* He laughs softly. "Now what?"

Shaking the thought from my head, I rub my hands down my face, sighing. "I have no idea. The house is gone, he's dead. I don't think he has any family, and even if he did, they aren't responsible for what he did." I lean back in the pillows and feel an odd sense of finality, but it's accompanied by an overwhelming feeling of unease. Although it feels as if we've finally figured out the mystery that surrounds the twin girls, there is nothing we can do about it.

"We have to tell someone, we have to tell the police."

I huff a laugh. *"We?"*

"Good point. *You* have to tell them."

"And say what? My ghost boyfriend is friends with the twins that were murdered in the woods by my house and they told him that the *dog man* killed them? Then I connected the dots when I talked to the grouchy old lady down the street? Yeah, that won't go over well."

There is a long pause and I feel his stare on the side of my face. I shift to look at him. "What?" His eyes roam over my face for a long time and I settle back against the pillows, doing the same. In any other situation it would be awkward—two people looking at each other with so much intensity between them. But in this moment, it's like we're basking in the light of the other, his moonlight lighting up my night.

"Nothing, you've just surprised me tonight is all." I narrow my eyes and finally he looks back to the ceiling, taking a deep breath and letting it out slowly. "I'll tell the girls tomorrow. They've been avoiding me, but I'll try again."

"Is that safe?"

He laughs uncontrollably. The bed rocks with his laughter and I slap his chest. Wiping his eyes, he rolls over to me. "What are they going to do to me, sweetheart? Kill me?"

I smack his chest again, harder. "That's not funny, Cillian!" But I can't help the laughter that slips out. After a few moments of the two of us laughing together, he settles down and rubs his hands over his face. Long fingers that have me pressing my thighs together, thoughts of how skilled he really is with his hands flooding my mind.

"Busted again, sweetheart." He nudges me to my side and pulls me close. "Let's get some sleep. Don't worry about me, I'll be fine."

My nose itches and my eyes sting. *This is the end.* I can feel it, the pieces falling into place, but it feels like I'm shattering all over again. I hug his arms tighter against my body. "I'll always worry about you," I admit, almost in a whisper.

"Promise?" It still catches me off guard, but his voice is soft as it brushes over the skin on my neck.

My promise to him slips from my lips as I drift off into a peaceful sleep.

# THIRTY-EIGHT
# PLAYING HOUSE

## CILLIAN

I HATE TO LEAVE HER. EVERY TIME I'M WITH HER I FEEL WHOLE again, like myself again. I want to hold her to me forever, mold myself around her so I never have to be apart. It's getting physically painful to walk away from her, but I know it's inevitable. That is another level of pain that I push away as I slip my arms out and tuck the covers back around her. I know what I need to do, but that doesn't make it any easier.

I reluctantly make my way out the backdoor, closing it carefully behind me so I don't wake Ella. I don't want to risk her coming out after me. If she followed me, I don't think I'd be able to confront the girls. I'd want to carry her back up to bed and pretend like we aren't living on borrowed time. Before I even make it to the tree line, the air that moments before was warm and alive with early sounds of the morning, stills. The trees before me turn chilling and unwelcome. I tuck my hands in my pockets and make my way across the grass, dew seeping into my pant legs. Dry leaves crunch under my feet as I walk across the dirt floor. When I glance behind me, the trees have swallowed any view of the house or the half done treehouse in the big oak. I'm tempted to run back, wanting nothing more in that moment than to crawl back in bed with the woman I have quickly become obsessed with.

"How can you be so happy when there is so much evil here?" Any warmth I was clinging to is washed away when the voice that is devoid of any emotion stops me in my tracks. I mask my unease with a soft smile and kneel before the girls in front of me.

"Hi, girls." I reach out to grab each of their hands in mine. One of them reaches for me, the quiet one who confided in me before.

"Emma!" The other sister snaps and all but slaps her sister's hand away. I give Emma a wink before I turn to the other who I now know is Jane. She looks at me with wide eyes like she is just now realizing she gave away their real names.

"Jane, I'm Cillian. All this time and we never really got to know each other. We just kind of fell into all of this together." I shrug as she glares back.

Her reply is simple, but bites nonetheless, "You don't know us."

"I want to, I still want us to find peace. It's just become…" I trail off, not knowing how to explain the tangle of emotions that war within me every day. Emma steps up beside Jane and puts her arm around her waist. "Jane, we can't be upset that Cillian has found some happiness. You and I, " she points back and forth between them, "we have each other. He has no one." I fight the urge to visibly cringe. She's right, but it doesn't make it sting any less. In the end, that's all I'll ever be—alone. "He has to figure all of this out on his own. We can't blame him for this situation we are in."

I see the war in Jane's eyes. They soften for the briefest moment like she is about to agree with her sister, but the pain and anger slams back in place. She shrugs out of her sister's embrace and marches towards me. It takes everything in me to not step back as she approaches. The trees seem to bend in, casting us in shadows, the hair on my arms raise.

There is so much darkness inside of her and it's pouring out around us. I look towards Emma tears have begun to stream down her face. "Jane, please don't hurt him." She falls to her knees just as Jane reaches me. The space between my shoulder blades breaks out in a cold sweat and I can't hide the shiver that racks my body.

"You. Promised. Us." She punctuates every word. I hold my head high and do my best to not wither under her stare.

"I did and I still do. We will find peace." I take a deep breath, knowing that what I say next will not be taken well. "I know what happened to you both." There is a sharp gasp from Emma. Her hands cover her mouth, tears streak her dirty cheeks. I look at Jane and her eyes flare. "I know who he was, I know it was him." I open my mouth to continue, but I'm cut off.

"Enough." Jane has gone still, her voice low and sinister. But I can't stop now, I'm close. I can feel it.

"He was your neighbor, wasn't he? Dolly was his dog." I'm about to ask how they ended up in the woods with him when I am knocked to the ground. A heavy weight sits on top of me and when I open my eyes, black ones look back at me. It's Jane's body, but there is something else inside. I suddenly feel sick, a rotten smell fills my lungs and I gag.

"I said *enough*." The voice that spews from the frail girl above me does not belong to her. It's deep, dark, terrifying. I try to move my arms to push her off of me, but without her moving her body, I feel my arms held down.

"Jane, please stop!" Emma sounds far away and I turn to find her, but the morning sun that filtered through the trees is gone as darkness swallows us. Jane simply tilts her head to the sound of her sister.

"I couldn't protect you then, but I will now."

Nine words. Nine words is all I needed to put the entire puzzle together.

As if she can see the realization in my eyes, she stands and moves towards my head, her black eyes staring into my soul. I close my eyes trying to picture Ella, my light, my ocean, *mine.* "Look at me." I try to squeeze my eyes shut, but they open on their own volition. When I meet her gaze, the pain that slams into me takes my breath away. Gasping for air, she leans down and a dark smile spreads across her pale face. "I'll help you remember what death felt like." I close my eyes to hide her terrifying face, but when they close, I'm hit with flashbacks of the night I was killed. Listening to the night around me, smiling to myself because I'd finally found direction, hopefulness at what the future held for me, confusion at the loud rumble of a car speeding around the bend.

Realization.

Terror.

Pain.

Quiet.

———

The distant sound of a hammer pounding and power tools working in the yard make me jump from my place in the dirt. Groaning when the pain surges through me, I try to move my body. But the pain is too much, so I lay there, listening. Trying to remember what happened. I'm not sure how long I lay on my back, looking up at the slivers of blue sky visible through the tops of the trees. It's not until I hear her voice and the laughter of little boys that I force my body to turn just enough that I can see her through the trunks of the trees around me. I'm engulfed in fire. My whole body thoroughly shuts down. I try to open my mouth and call for her, but nothing comes out. My body shakes on its own accord and my head throbs. Pain radiates through my body.

*I'll help you remember what death felt like.*

The words from earlier flash through my mind. Tears pour from my eyes as I lay there, watching everything I've ever wanted just out of my reach. When darkness falls and the sounds fade into the house, I'm left in a heap of exhaustion and torment. Any time I try to move, I'm hit with another wave of intense agony. Sleep overtakes me and I gladly welcome it.

# THIRTY-NINE
# WIDE OPEN SPACES

## ELLA

THIS IS THE SIXTH NIGHT I'VE CLIMBED INTO BED ALONE. EACH morning when I wake up, I roll over and pull the pillows to my chest. No lingering smell of tea tree or mint clings to them. No warm body holds me close while I slip off to sleep. The last time we were together felt like the last chapter of a really good book. You know it's coming to an end, but you also know that their story will keep going, even if you don't get to read it. I felt complete in a hollow kind of way. It makes no sense. I tire myself out, wondering if I missed any signs or indications of why Cillian hasn't crept into my bed these past few nights. I've walked through my entire house trying to find some note I may have missed or a clue that he'll be back. I can't lie to myself, I'm worried about him. We went over the pieces of the twins' story for hours and he seemed so confident that he could get them to put it all together, to finally give them answers and a way to move on.

In the moonlight, I watch my hair slip through the fingers I've been twisting it around. Over and over until my hands fall to my side and exhaustion pulls me under.

———

"Hey, cute girl." My head snaps up from the book in my lap. My hands drop the hair that I've been anxiously twirling around my index finger.

"James?" I cover my eyes and squint into the sun. It casts a heavenly glow around him as he walks towards me through a field of bright, white, wild daisies. He chuckles as he sits next to me, bracing one arm behind me and resting the other on his knee. His body leans against me and I sink into him. Home. I'm home, finally.

"Forgotten me already?" He looks at me sideways and gives me that cocky smile I've missed so much. I shake my head and turn my body towards him.

"You're a hard one to forget, but it's not like I've tried." I take a moment to look around us; I don't recognize this place. Rolling hills as far as I can see. No buildings or roads, just wide open spaces. White daisies paint little white dots across the hills, scattered with brilliant purple blossoms. It's breathtaking and so peaceful. I look back at the man next to me and soak him in. I've missed his handsome face, the way his cheeks bunch up when he smiles, the little crinkles on the edges of his eyes. He looks at me and I feel the sting of tears build up behind my eyes. I love this man. It's painful how much I love him. He reaches out and runs his thumb under my lashes, catching the tears before they fall.

"Don't you dare." It's like he's a combination of the young boy I met in high school and the grown man I lost that night. Perfect in every way.

"Where are we?" I lean into his touch. His hand slips down my face, running over my shoulder and gliding down my arm until his hand rests on top of mine.

He doesn't answer for a full minute, just staring out at the endless fields around us. "Walk with me." Standing, he grabs my hand and pulls me up beside him. We start walking, just like we've always done, side by side. We walk for a while in blissful silence, content to just be together. "I miss you. I miss Rone. God, he's so big now." When he finally speaks, I stop him and turn into his chest.

"I miss you so much, James. It's not fair. I can't do this without you. I can't raise our boy without you." I shudder at the thought of *what happened that night. "The pain you must have felt in that accident, it splits me open every time I think of you. It's like all our happy memories have been covered up in that fucking accident." He wraps his big arms around me, blocking out the memories of the cars slamming into us, horns blaring, glass breaking. He rubs his hands over my back before he brings them to my face, tilting my head back to stare into his eyes. The color of melted chocolate that I fell into back in high school has me mesmerized, instantly thrown back into the memory of the first time we met. The dark clouds in my mind part a little bit, letting the sun filter back in. Staring into his eyes, I see a series of pictures. Our entire life flashes before me: happiness, laughter, smiles, hope, peace, love. So much love. I gasp and blink up at him, a smile already sitting on his face. "How...what..." I'm lost for words.*

*He turns again, keeping an arm around me guiding me down the other side of a hill. "You can live your whole life replaying one horrific moment." He looks down at me. "Or, you can remember a lifetime of joy."*

*"It's not that easy, James." I've tried to forget that night, tried to forget waking up in the hospital and knowing, feeling, that he was gone.*

*"Nothing worthwhile is ever easy. But, if it makes you feel better, I don't remember the accident." I pull him to a stop, mouth open and eyes narrowing in question. How could he not remember? The moment that has plagued my every waking moment for the past year? "What do you mean, you don't remember?"*

*"I remember joking with you, talking about the future. I remember what happened, but I don't remember any of the pain or terror that I must have felt in the moment. The last thing I remember is holding your hand and telling you how beautiful you are." He leans down and kisses me softly. "And you're still just as beautiful." I reach up to hold him there, but he holds my elbow and runs his nose along mine. "Then it's like I fell asleep and woke up here." He gestures around us.*

*I swallow, finally building up the courage to ask the question that's been on the tip of my tongue. "And Paige?" I whisper her name, like a prayer. He tugs me closer against him.*

*"She's beautiful, Ella." Instantly, tears trickle down my face and I push my face into his chest, breathing him in. "Feisty like her mama, beautiful like her, too." He lets out a laugh, shaking his head. "When I woke up here, a woman I didn't recognize walked up to me and put this tiny little blanket in my arms. She gave me a kiss on the cheek and disappeared. I was so confused, but when I looked down at this angel in my arms, I knew. Ella, baby, I knew it was all ok. We're ok."*

*"I want to see her, can I see her?" He holds my shoulders and leans down so we're face to face. "One day, baby, but not yet. Our boy is home. Hold him for me, ok?" He pulls me into him, his lips tasting like honey. Reaching my arms around his waist, I hold on to him, trying to pull him back through my dream and into bed with me.*

---

Watching Rone play with Ty as Mike puts the finishing touches on the treehouse brings a smile to my face. My mind has been all over the place the past few days. I miss Cillian. I'm worried he's gone, for good. With no new occurrences from the twins, I'm starting to come to the realization that maybe all we needed to do was put the pieces together and then magically they'd be able to walk into whatever afterlife was waiting for them. But did that mean that Cillian left with them? I stare out the window at the boys running around. Mike has begged them to leave him alone multiple times and I think he's purposely taking time on the inside of the tree house to avoid being around the obnoxious boys any longer.

I woke from that dream in the field with James feeling tingly all over, like a leg that had fallen asleep and the blood was finally running back into it. I could still taste his honey kiss on my lips. Lately, when I think of him, which is still very often, I'm not pulled under by sadness or guilt. I feel as if I'm lucky to still be here, to witness the life before me. I get to live for James, love like James, be here as a reminder of the life that he lived. Instead of rushing by the pictures in the stairway, I take my time, reliving each memory. They make me smile. However, now it's a happy smile, not one filled with longing and heartbreak.

"I think it's pretty much done." I jump at the voice behind me, water from the glass in my hand spilling down my arm onto the floor. "Shit, Ella. I'm sorry, I didn't mean to scare you!" Mike grabs a towel from the kitchen counter and tosses it on the puddle at my feet.

"I didn't hear you come in." An embarrassed laugh spills out of me. Mike tilts his head, standing with the damp towel in his hands.

"You seem different lately." He adds on quickly, "In a good way."

This time I tilt my head at him, narrow my eyes and put my hand on my hip. "In what way?" He leans against the bookshelf, taking a moment to peek at the boys climbing up into the treehouse, living their best life in the last few weeks of summer.

"Happier, I guess. Before I always felt like you were weighed down." His head snaps up to me and he adds, "For obvious reasons, of course."

I laugh and sit back on the armrest of the couch. "Nothing can ever prepare you for losing the greatest love of your life." I gaze out the window, orange and yellow bursts of color paint the sky as the sun sinks down. "But I guess I just woke up one day realizing that I could live my whole life replaying one horrific moment. Or, I could remember a lifetime of joy." I repeat the words James spoke to me in my dream. My eyes meet Mikes again and he studies me for a brief moment.

"I lost my mom a while back." His admission makes my heart ache for him. The love you have for a parent is a different love than one you have for a spouse, but it has to hurt all the same. "I'm sorry to hear that, I didn't know." He waves his hand at me. "It's ok, she was sick for a long time—cancer. It was about the time that we had Ty. She was in the hospital, so sick she could hardly keep her eyes open. But man, did she love holding that boy." He looks out the window and shakes his head when he sees Ty and Rone jump from the treehouse door and roll on the grass like they are stunt doubles in a movie. "We rarely left the hospital towards the end. And bless Madi's heart, she let my mama hold Ty as much as she wanted. It made her so happy. I'd pay money just to see that smile on her face, just one more time."

"That's so sweet. She sounds like a special woman." I wipe my eyes. Seeing how much love Mike had for his mom gives me hope that Rone and I will be ok.

"She really was. You know what she told me before she passed?"

"I'd love to know, Mike." His eyes gloss over before he goes on.

"She said, *when I get to Heaven, I want to be the one to hold the babies*." He gives a small laugh and wipes the tears from his cheeks with a dirty hand. My hand falls to my chest, the dream replaying over again in my mind. James said a woman he didn't recognize handed him Paige. The thought of such a sweet lady holding my baby makes my eyes well up with unshed tears.

"Ah, here I go, making us both cry." His rough hand swipes at the tears falling freely down his face. "I'm a big softy."

"Nothing wrong with that, Mike. I hope that your mama got to hold my Paige for me for a little while."

"Shit, Ella. Now I'm really gonna cry." His sky blue eyes fill with a fresh set of tears and he looks up at the ceiling, taking deep breaths. I stand up and make my way over to him. He tucks me into his side and we both let the tears fall for a few more moments.

I wave as Mike and Ty make their way down the driveway in their big truck. A little tug on my heart reminds me that everything does work itself out in the end. The smell of burnt popcorn wafts through the house and I quickly shut and lock the front door before I race into the kitchen.

"Sorry, Mom!" Rone sits on a stool, nose scrunched at the smell. I open the microwave and quickly toss the smoking bag in the sink.

"It's alright, sweetheart. We can make another one. How about you get cozy on the couch and I'll bring a new bag out in a minute." With summer coming to an end, Rone and I have made a list of all the things we still need to do this summer. Movie night was highly requested and I'm more than happy to oblige.

# FORTY
# SMOKE AND FLAMES

CILLIAN

I don't know how many days have passed. My clothes are caked in dirt and mud. I've been drifting in and out of a haze. My body still aches, but it's dull enough that I can sit up without passing out. I watched Ty and Rone play in the finished treehouse for a while, trying to piece together the events of the past few days. It would have taken Mike a few days to finish it, so I know I've been out here for a while. I catch glimpses of Mike and Ella in the window overlooking the garden. She looks happy. Part of me wonders if she's missed me, how can she look so happy without me? My mind wanders with traitorous thoughts. It's not until Mike loads Ty in the truck and pulls out of sight that I push myself to my feet. The stiffness in my legs and pounding behind my eyes causes me to limp out of the trees.

I smell the burnt popcorn before I even reach the door. The window above the sink is cracked to let in the cool night breeze. I push through the backdoor and lock it behind me, the familiarity of the house bringing a sense of calm over my restless thoughts. The TV plays from the living room and I make my way through the kitchen, pausing in the doorway. I watch the two of them cuddling on the couch for a few moments. The tremors in my heart cease and I can finally breathe deeply again. She is more beautiful than I remember. It's almost as if she's stepped out of a shadow and is finally giving herself a chance to bask in the sun. I push off the doorframe and tenderly sit down on the other end of the couch. There is a brief moment where nothing happens and I wonder if maybe my presence can't even be felt. Instantly, I'm overwhelmed with the anguish of waking up to strangers in my house and not being able to talk to them. The feeling of them walking through me makes me feel cold and sick to my stomach.

"I've missed you." Her soft voice beside me jolts me back to the present.

"How did you know I was here?" My insecurity gets the best of me and the words slip out before I can stop them.

She lets out a sweet laugh. "Cillian, I can always feel you. I swear I can even see you sometimes." I sink back into the couch, letting out a lungful of air that I hadn't even realized I'd been holding. "Are you ok?" She looks down at Rone, passed out on the other end of the couch. Pushing the blanket off her lap, she scoots her body closer to me. I didn't realize how cold I was until her warmth trickles over me and buries itself in my bones. My eyes dart around her face like I'm racing to memorize every detail.

"I'm sorry. I don't know how long I was gone for. I was trying to get the girls and explain everything we found out. I didn't mean to scare you."

"And...how did they respond?" She strangles the edge blanket in her hands and I reach out to calm her. She flinches when my cold hands wrap around hers. Instead of pulling away, she tucks my hands under the blanket with hers. The comfort of her hands on me is a feeling I'm not sure I can survive without. I choose to withhold the full story and go with a half-truth instead.

"Not great...but I think in time they will come around."

She nods up and down a few times. "What can I do for you?" It's a question we all should ask those we love more often, and it takes me by surprise for a moment. I have to bite my tongue from saying what I really want to.

*Be mine. Never leave me. Choose me. Love me.*

I settle with saying, "Just let me be here with you tonight." A bright smile creeps across her face. She leans into the pillows beside me and we watch the rest of the movie. Both just happy to be in each other's presence for another moment.

Sometime throughout the night Ella and I have drifted off, the weight of her head on my shoulder bringing comfort to my racing mind. Half asleep, I move her so she's laying in my lap. The bun on top of her head leans precariously to one side, so I slip a finger under the hair band and pull it free. Her hair topples loose, pouring over my thighs. I push some strands off her face and let my fingers gently run through her hair from root to tip. The smell of her shampoo fills me and I lean into the couch, drifting off, totally surrounded in bliss.

———

*"Come on, Ian!" I look up from my tying my shoe just in time to see Mike's back disappear into the trees. Standing up, I take off after him. For years we've begged our parents to let us camp out on our own. They always told us, "When you turn fifteen, we'll let you." I'm sure they thought we'd forget by then—not a chance in hell. We'd counted down the years for this night. The bag on my back slams into me with each step so I hold the straps down tighter, moving my feet as fast as I can go. I'm giddy with excitement. We've scouted out the perfect place to set up camp. My lungs are burning by the time I catch up to Mike, who has slowed down now that we've reached the spot we've designated worthy enough for this moment. He looks at me as I come up beside*

*him, wearing his typical smile. If it got any wider, it would slip off his face. I love Mike, he's the brother I never had.*

*"Are you ready for this?" I ask, looking over at him. His excited eyes stare back and without saying anything else, we drop our packs and start to set up camp.*

*We've laid out our sleeping bags around the fire, staring up at the stars. "Dude, this is awesome." We set up a tent, but after we finished eating all the random shit we'd packed, we pulled our bags out and laid them out so we could stare up at the stars.*

*"Best night of my fucking life." We don't say much more, each too caught up in the thoughts that run through your mind as a teenager. Everything is epic shit at fifteen. You're invincible, everything is obtainable.*

---

The smell of smoke is thick in the air. *I know we put that fire out before we dragged ourselves into our tent.* My hands are tangled in something smooth and the weight in my lap drags me from my dream. Trying to orient myself and figuring out why I can still smell the fire from my dream has my head spinning. Ella stirs in my lap and I look down as she rubs her eyes and blinks up at me.

"Hey, sweetheart." I smile down at her. She is so beautiful. Even with her messy hair and lines on her face from sleeping on her hands.

"What time is it?" She taps the watch on her wrist and wrinkles her nose in disgust. "3:00 a.m., ugh. And what is that smell?" I take a deep inhale, realizing the smell was not only in my dream.

"Fire." I lift her off my lap and stand, quickly looking out the front windows. There isn't smoke in the house, that's reassuring. But the smell is so strong.

When she whispers, "Did you take Rone upstairs?" my feet skid to a stop and I turn towards Ella. Dread works its way through my blood. It's then when I look past her into the kitchen that I see the orange glow through the windows at the back of the house. Pushing past her to the backdoor, I yell over my shoulder, "Ella, call 911. *NOW!*" I don't look back, my feet moving as fast as I can make them, slamming through the back door and out into the night air.

# FORTY-ONE
# MINE

### ELLA



I can hardly hear the woman on the other end of the line. Blood is rushing in my ears, my heart is beating out of my chest, and I am trying not to throw up all over the floor. When I laid my head in Cillian's lap and fell into a peaceful sleep, I could never have imagined waking up to a missing son and a fire blazing in my backyard. My feet are glued to the doorway between the living room and kitchen. The backdoor is wide open, Cillian long gone as he raced past me into the back yard. "Hello, can you hear me? 911, what is your emergency?" As if I've come out of a tunnel, all the sound rushes back in at once. Crackling of the fire outside, Cillian yelling for Rone, and the patient woman speaking to me bring me back to reality. I turn on my heels and race up the stairs, needing to see Rone in his bed, sleeping and oblivious to the danger outside.

"Fire," I wheeze out to the dispatcher. When I reach my boy's bedroom I whisper into the phone, "And my boy is missing." I want to sink to the floor.

He's gone. The last piece I have of James. Gone.

"I have your address, fire crews are on their way. I've alerted the police, they will be there soon. Breathe for me honey, we'll take care of you..." I barely register her words as I stumble down the stairs and make my way out the backdoor. Standing on the patio, I look out over the backyard. In the distance, I can hear Cillian calling for Rone. His desperate voice does nothing to calm my panic. It's then that I feel the heat from the flames so intense that my skin starts to itch. I raise a hand to block out the blinding blaze and when I see what is at the center of the fire, I double over and throw up all over my shoes.

"Ma'am?" A large, burly man in turnout gear kneels in front of me. It's not until he puts a hand on my shoulder that I jump under his touch. He raises both hands in front of him before resting a large palm on my arm once again. "I'm Captain Morgan with the Spring Hill Fire Department. I need to talk to you about the fire if you're ready?" His name would make me laugh on any other day, but I'm still in shock. Maybe he'd get me a glass if I asked. The blanket around my shoulders does little to keep the chill away. I look over at the large oak that just hours ago held the most amazing treehouse, massive green leaves and strong branches. Now the black bark is ugly and scarred, the leaves melted and burned away. But what makes me the saddest is the shell of the design Cillian made just for Rone. I can't tear my eyes away from the horror of it all. The sickness and weight in my stomach still lingers.

*Rone. I can't find Rone.*

Fire crews and multiple police cruisers pulled up just as I was taking off across the back lawn to search for Rone. An officer wrapped a strong arm around my waist and pulled me away from the blaze, the stifling heat barely noticeable above the panic pulsing through my veins.

Looking back at the fireman before me, I stare into his kind eyes and ask the question I'm not sure I want the answer to. "Was my boy...was he in..." I can't finish my thought, tears spilling over and running down my face. He wraps both my hands in one large hand.

"No, ma'am. He wasn't. We have police and K9s in the

woods looking now." My body shakes violently as relief washes over me. *Alive, not in the fire. Alive.* "This fire didn't start on its own. Do you have any idea who would do something like this?" My mind is spinning and I shake my head no. Just as I'm about to answer him, a whistle from the trees has us both jumping to our feet.

"Rone?" I cry, slipping past the reach of Captain Morgan. On shaky legs, I sprint across the grass. A group of uniforms emerge from the trees and in one of their arms is Rone.

"Mom!" He pushes against the man's chest. Once he's placed on the ground, he runs to me and crashes into me. "I'm so sorry, Mom!" His little eyes are swollen from crying so hard. I hug him to my chest, breathing him in, memorizing how he feels tucked into me. The idea of living without him almost broke me, and now that he's in my arms, I can't let go. We rock back and forth for a while before someone wraps their arms around my shoulders and encourages us to head back into the house.

Once inside, a woman dressed in a police uniform ushers Rone and I into the kitchen.

"Can I get you anything to drink? Tea, hot chocolate?" Any other time I'd be the one asking this question, but I let her soothing voice wash over me.

I nod. "Both, please. Thank you." I gently stoke Rone's hair which is covered in dried mud. I take a second to pull him away from me and scan his body for any cuts or scrapes. He's still in the pjs I helped him change into before we fell asleep on the couch. His feet are bare and dirty. But he's here, he's safe. "Are you hurt, baby?" He nuzzles back into me and shakes his head.

Again he whispers, "I'm sorry, Mom." I hold his shoulders and look down into his sweet eyes.

"For what? You didn't do anything wrong." I notice the officer watching us as she makes our drink, no doubt listening for any details to add to her report. Rone looks up at me, wiping his dirty face with his hands. "There was a loud noise outside and it woke me up. So I went into the kitchen to see what it was and I saw them in the backyard playing in the treehouse." A cold sweat breaks out over my body and chills sweep over me. I nod my head, encouraging him to keep going. "I told them before that they couldn't play with Ty and me. So I ran outside to yell at them, but they didn't hear me. I walked over to them and when they turned around…" More tears slip down his cheeks and his body shakes as he cries. I hug him close and look over his head to the officer. She scribbles something in her notebook before placing a mug of tea in front of me and hot chocolate beside it. She reaches out and squeezes my arm, nodding at me to help Rone finish explaining what happened.

"That must have been scary. Can you tell me what happened when you walked over to them?" He's quiet for a few moments before he takes a deep inhale.

"One of the girls was crying. They looked the same, but one seemed so much meaner than the other one. The mean one looked at me and said *mine*." His whole body shakes violently, tears clouding his eyes. "Then the whole treehouse was on fire. I screamed at them to stop it and tried to run in and tell you, but they started chasing me. I didn't want them to follow me inside, so I thought I could lose them in the trees." He is talking so fast so I rub his shoulders and tell him to slow down. He takes a few deep breaths, notices his mug and takes a sip. Wiping his mouth on his sleeve he looks at me again. "But I got lost and couldn't find my way back. I could hear the sirens and I got scared. So I did what Daddy always told me to do if I was lost and sat down and waited." The officer looks up when Rone finally stops to take a breath. Another officer walks in and whispers to her, to which she nods her head and walks around the island to me.

"Ms. Carter, I've written down your son's account of this evening. I don't need anything else from you at this moment. But I'll call you later to discuss everything with you. Would you feel more comfortable if I left a patrol car out front until morning?"

It wasn't that long ago that this house felt safe. It felt like, well, home. But tonight, I've never felt so out of place. I shake my head and give her a weak smile. "That's alright. I think we'll take a trip back to Alabama to visit my parents. Thank you so much." She gives me a sympathetic smile, rubs Rone's back, and motions for the other officers lingering around the house to head out. Lights fade down the driveway and I'm left holding my boy, thinking once again how to start our lives over after something so good has fallen apart.

# FORTY-TWO

# GONE

## CILLIAN

I'VE NEVER BEEN MORE TERRIFIED IN MY ENTIRE LIFE WHEN I LOOKED past Ella and saw the fire in the backyard. The empty spot where Rone had been sleeping on the couch made my blood run cold. All I could think about was finding my boy. *My* boy. I knew I loved him, knew I'd take care of him. I even promised James I'd watch over them. But in that moment, I realized what it must feel like to be a parent. To be willing to do anything, even jump into a fire, to make sure they were safe. When I made it out the back door I ran to the treehouse, heat singeing the hair on my arms and burning my lungs. I got as close as I could, squinting through the flames and smoke, trying to make sure Rone wasn't inside. When I heard laughing from the trees, I knew this wasn't an accident. The second I heard the sirens making their way up to the house, I took off into the trees. Low tree limbs whipped against my face, slapping at my cheeks and legs. My throat burned from the smoke, but that didn't stop me from screaming Rone's name. When I wasn't yelling for him, I was rubbing my eyes, trying to ease the sting. Blinking through the spots that lingered from staring into the fire, I searched for the girls. It felt like hours, fear taking its toll on me. *Maybe I missed something. Maybe he was stuck in the treehouse and I didn't see him.* It wasn't until I heard a whistle and shouts in the distance that they had found him that I sank to the ground in relief.

That relief was short-lived. Blinding rage took its place at the terror that these two girls have inflicted upon two of the most important people in my life. The pain that Jane unleashed on my body the last time I confronted her no longer mattered to me. Until the sun bled through the trees, I walked and shouted for the girls to come out. But they didn't. I needed to get back and check on Ella and Rone. I dragged my exhausted body back through the woods and into the back yard. The sight of the once spectacular treehouse now black and smoking is almost enough to knock me to my knees again. *How could they do this? How could they be so cruel?*

I want nothing more than to walk up the stairs and crawl into bed next to Ella and Rone, holding them both and sleeping the day away. Ella makes everything better. We've been through so much these past few months, we can make it through this. But when I step through the back door, it all feels different. The house that once finally felt like home, warmth that seeped into my bones the second they crashed into my life, isn't there. It's unusually quiet. The morning routine I've come to look forward to has been disturbed—I feel it in my bones. The happiness that has quickly chipped away at my walls is slipping through my fingers. Like sand at the beach. No matter how hard you try to hold it, some always slips through the cracks. I hear muffled footsteps in the entryway.

Just as I make it through the door and into the hall, a small body barrels into me. "Ian!" I hug him so tight I worry I'll break him. Pulling him back by the shoulders I take him in, closing my eyes to hold back the tears of relief when all I see are small, dark circles under his eyes from lack of sleep. His smile is just as bright and I can't help the tear that escapes and slowly rolls down my face. Before I can wipe it away, Rone reaches out and puts his little palm on my cheek. I hold him there with my own hand and close my eyes, leaning into his touch. I never want to experience the horror of last night again. Instead I want to etch the feeling of his warm hand into my heart forever.

Ella's footsteps come down the stairs. "Rone, go get in the car please." She stops at the bottom when she sees the two of us. It's then that I notice the bags piled by the front door. Her eyes are red with hair thrown into a messy bun on her head. She looks exhausted, beautiful, and drained.

My eyes flick back to the round, chubby face before me. I kiss his palm, give his shoulders a squeeze, and gently put his arms back to his sides. "Go ahead, buddy."

"Are you coming with us to Bama?" I smile at his adorable accent, even though my stomach feels like there is lead weighing me down and my heart is shattering into oblivion.

"Not this time, but you go and tell me all about it later, ok?" I don't know if there will be a next time, but I can't help myself from throwing out the possibility. He gives me another big hug and turns towards the front door. Standing, I watch him close the door behind him before I take slow steps towards the woman in front of me. I know there is nothing I can say to fix what happened. No matter how many times I promise to keep them safe, things keep happening. I don't blame her for leaving, but fuck, I don't want her to.

"Ella..."

"Please. Don't." She cuts me off. "I can't do this anymore. I can't keep pretending that things will be ok. I have to go." I reach out and catch her elbow when she turns and starts to walk away.

"I know you do. I'm so sorry." I take a deep breath and run my hands down my face. "I don't even know what to say. I'm so fucking sorry." Dropping my hands I look into her eyes. Her usually bright blue eyes are dull and rimmed with red, unshed tears on the brink of falling. "But Ella, please, before you leave, you have to know how much you mean to me. How much you both mean to me." My chest heaves with silent sobs. She leans into me, crying into my chest. I wrap my arms around her and pull her into me. Just like I did when Rone placed his hand on my face, I memorize the way she feels in my arms, the way she smells, how her body fits into mine. I bury my face in her hair and whisper one last time, "No matter where you go, no matter where I'll be, you will always be my sweetheart. I could never forget you, never erase how I feel about you. You'll always be a part of me. You'll always be my favorite view. I promise you that."

Before I can say anything else, she moves away from me, scoops up the last couple bags, and walks out the door. I can hardly hear the car speed down the driveway over my screams and sobs. Everything closes in around me and I let myself sink into a black hole of despair. Any light that Ella brought into my fucked up existence, or lack thereof, is gone. I don't even try to get up or reason with this new reality. I curl up on the floor and beg darkness to swallow me.

# FORTY-THREE
## WRITTEN IN TIME
### ELLA

MY PARENTS GOT BACK FROM YET ANOTHER TRIP AROUND THE world. My mom called me a couple weeks ago asking about when they could come and visit our new place. Lying in bed last night, I desperately wanted to curl up next to my mom and bask in the comfort that only a mother can give their terrified child. When I packed our bags, I knew exactly where we needed to go. The drive down to my parents' house went by quickly. By the time I pulled into their driveway, I felt like I'd blinked and we were there. Rone is passed out in the backseat, his little mouth parted and sleeping peacefully. The trauma he has been through in the past couple months weighs on me. The move was supposed to be a fresh start, a chance to build a new future, just him and I. I sink back into the leather of the driver seat and bang my head back on the headrest. My life is a mess. My manuscript long forgotten due to everything that has happened. Any time I'd sit down, I couldn't concentrate, getting distracted looking up details on the death of the twins who tormented our lives or searching for that picture of Cillian. I searched for him so many times I didn't even have to enter his whole name before Google recognized my routine and pulled it up for me.

My heart squeezes at the reminder of him, the way he almost

seemed to fade away in front of me when I was holding him. He seemed so real, but just wasn't. I've lost count of how many times I've questioned my sanity over the past few months. The feelings that have grown aren't made up, they are so real. Very real. I miss his comfort, his smell, the way my body could sense him around before I even knew he was there. For the first time, I come to the realization that although I miss James more than I could ever imagine, I also miss Cillian. And that feeling twists inside me, a mixture of guilt and shame. Something I haven't felt since the first few weeks in that house. My dream house.

Looking out the windshield at the house I grew up in, my stomach is in knots. There are so many memories of James and I here and it feels wrong to make new ones without him. Before I can back out and book a hotel room, the front door opens and my parents rush out towards me. I wipe my eyes and plaster a smile on my face, opening the door to face them.

After the crews cleared out last night, I got Rone bathed and tucked in my bed. I didn't shower or even sleep. I sat in Cillian's chair under my window and watched Rone sleep. Knowing that I needed to leave, but dreading making that decision. Finally, I stood, grabbed a few bags, and packed enough clothes for a couple weeks. I called my parents once it was just early enough to not seem suspicious and asked if Rone and I could come visit. They'd just gotten back from Ireland and were desperate to see him, so here we are.

"Ella, come here, baby." My mom wraps me in her arms and I swallow down the emotion that threatens to overflow. As if she can sense it, she pulls me away, eyes narrow as she scans my face. I smile, but it doesn't reach my eyes and she notices right away. "Head inside, we'll get Rone and your bags."

"Thanks, Mom." It's all I can manage to get out before I walk up the steps to the front door. Writing in the cement catches my eye and I let out a gasp when I bend down to take a closer look. The memory washes over me and pulls me back in time.

———

"Come on, they won't be mad."

"James, I am telling you. They will know. My dad will be so pissed."

"I'm sure there are other things that he doesn't need to know about that would piss him off even more." He wiggles his eyebrows and I lunge at him. "Should I tell him how dirty his little girl is?" My mouth drops open and I stare at him, stunned he'd even say something like that out loud, just outside my front door.

"James Ronan Carter."

"Fine, I'll do it. Scaredy cat." I roll my eyes at him as he picks up a stick from the grass and walks over to the freshly poured cement on my parents' new front porch. He looks around, finally deciding on a spot, and bends down. I wince when he digs the stick into the mix and writes out a simple J & E. He beams up at me, proud of his work. Then, to my horror, he plunges the stick back in and draws the most awfully shaped heart I've ever seen.

Gasping at him I screech, "Give me that!" I snatch the stick from his hands, looking over my shoulder I make sure my parents haven't pulled into the driveway. I gently push the stick in and carefully scrap four letters into the wet cement. 4EAE. I look back at James, expecting him to be proud that I caved. Instead he stares down, eyebrows pinched together, nose scrunched, head tilted. "What does that mean?" I let out a frustrated sigh and toss the stick at his new, white Nikes. He jumps back and I laugh at him, sticking my tongue out as I walk to the garage to open the door.

"Forever and Ever, you dumbass." The way we go at each other is one of my favorite things about our relationship. It's always been so easy with James, we're best friends. He grabs his bag from the ground before chasing after me. I squeal with laughter as he effortlessly swoops me up over his shoulder and carries me through the garage into the house.

———

"You know, we didn't notice that until about five years ago." My dad's voice is soft behind me. I run my hands over the writing one more time before I stand and face him.

"Really? I thought you would be so mad if you found out. I promise, it was his idea!" I raise my hands in surrender. His hazel eyes crinkle at the edges when he laughs. His energy is effortlessly happy and I can't help but smile at the peace I feel around him.

"You both were the best kind of trouble together." He wraps his arm around my shoulders and leads me into the house.

As the sun sets I stare through the back window while Rone plays in the backyard with my parents' dog, a little, fluffy cocker spaniel they got a few years ago. He rolls on the grass laughing while she licks his face. My mom comes over to me, standing shoulder to shoulder. We are the same height and I look at her side profile. I've always thought I look more like my dad, but sometimes when I look at her, it's like I'm looking in a mirror. She turns to me, her stare makes me shift nervously. *She can totally see through me.*

"You've always done that when you're nervous." Her eyes flick down to my legs before looking back to my eyes. "Whatever it is, you can tell me." I roll my eyes and walk behind her, falling over the back of the couch. Laying on my face, I mumble into the cushions, "Where do I even begin, Mom?"

I hear her tell my dad to go outside with Rone before she walks around the couch, lifts my legs, and sits, placing my legs in her lap.

"Anywhere, but it will probably make more sense if you start at the beginning." I can feel her smile without even looking at her. I turn my head to the side before answering.

"I don't want to live in fear anymore." Tears prick at the back of my eyes and I turn my head into the couch again.

"What do you mean? What are you afraid of?"

"Everything," I mutter. She pats my legs.

"You're going to have to speak up if you want to continue

talking to the cushions like that." Then in a more serious tone she asks, "What are you afraid of, Ella?"

I push the hair out of my eyes when I roll over. I wiggle my toes in her lap, silently begging her to rub my feet like she did when I was a kid. She rolls her eyes and motions with her hand to continue.

"The list is long, so keep rubbing." She laughs and gets to work, kneading the tension out of my arches and calves. "I'm afraid of being alone. I'm afraid I can't give Rone the life he deserves without James. I'm afraid of building a future without my husband. I'm afraid of..." I trail off. It hits me out of nowhere.

There isn't a hint of judgment or shame in her voice. "Of...love?"

"I guess, yeah." I run my hands through my hair and sink back into the couch. I knew I had feelings for Cillian, but was it love? I want to laugh at the thought. How could I be in love with someone who isn't real? A shadow, a ghost. My heart thuds in my chest. If I had met Cillian on the street, real Cillian, would we have hit it off? Would I have let him take me on a date, meet Rone, be a part of my life? No matter how much I try to reason it away, the answer would always be yes. Effortlessly, yes.

"Baby, you don't have to be afraid to let yourself love again. There is no timeline for grief, no timeline for healing. If your heart is ready to let someone in again, let it." She kneads the arches of my feet for a moment before she carries on. "You are so lucky to have had the kind of love you and James did. But I don't think your luck has run out because he's gone."

I look over at her and ask the question that has plagued me for months, "But doesn't it make me a terrible person to give my heart to someone when it will always belong to James?"

Without hesitation, she says, "Absolutely not. I didn't know James like you did, but I knew him well enough to know that he would never want you to be alone, to be sad, or to ever feel afraid." I take a minute to soak in her words. I don't stop the tears that work their way slowly down my cheeks. "Honey, do you remember when you fell in love with James?"

A wet laugh breaks free. "How could I ever forget anything about that man?"

"And what about when you had Rone, held him in your arms for the first time?"

"Mama, what's your point here?" She pinches my toes and gives me a look that makes me feel like I'm thirteen again. I smile at her sheepishly and ask again, without the tone this time.

"My point is that your heart doesn't have a set amount of room. It grows to fit people into it when the time is right. Your heart grew to fit the love you had with James. And it grew again when you held that boy for the first time. It can, and will, always continue to grow."

Nodding, I settle back against the arm of the couch and let her words ping pong around in my mind for a long time. We sit in silence; me contemplating the last year and her watching my dad and Rone through the window.

"It's our anniversary tomorrow." I don't look at her when I finally speak.

"I know."

"Will you watch Rone for me for a while?"

"Of course, baby." She gives my feet one last squeeze then stands from the couch. Before she steps outside she turns back to me. "Let yourself be happy, let yourself *live*."

# FORTY-FOUR
# FUEL THE FIRE
### CILLIAN

LIGHT TRIES TO SQUEEZE BETWEEN MY EYELIDS. GROANING, I TRY TO roll away from the early morning sun spilling through the windows. *Alive.* Or as alive as I can be when I'm still dead. I cover my face with my hands and let out a defeated sigh. Watching Ella walk out the door may have hurt more than my accident. When I curled up, I honestly hoped I wouldn't wake again. But here I am, stuck in this hell between life and death. I give myself a few more minutes to feel sorry for myself and then I push up to my feet, letting the rage and anger I've pushed aside for too long inch closer to the surface. To cover up the pain and sorrow I feel of losing Ella and Rone, I dig up all the despair of the past few months and let it overtake any of the happiness or joy I felt when I was around the two of them.

I don't even notice the quiet of the house as I angrily make my way out the back door. I glance quickly at the tree, black and broken. It only fuels the fire inside me. My steps are quick and purposeful as I cross the damp grass. It's not until I reach the tree line that I stop. I'm not afraid of the girls, I'm not nervous. But I'll admit I'm hesitant. What I'm about to do may very well be the end of this whole thing. I toe the line of finally moving beyond or staying in a world where I know Ella exists, feel the way she fits so effortlessly in my arms, know how she feels, how she tastes. I close my eyes and picture the woman who has quickly stolen my heart. I picture her smile when she sees Rone happy, the way her eyes sparkle when he thinks something is funny, the way her body moves on top of mine and reacts to my touch. I dig the heels of my palms into my eyes and blink the thoughts away. The sun is hot on my back, air thick in my lungs. I'm tempted to lay down in the grass and float in the memories a while longer.

Before I can change my mind, I take that step from the grass into the dirt floored woods. As if I've crossed some imaginary line, the sun fades, chills break out over my arms, and the sounds of birds in the trees and bugs humming fade. I know the girls are here—I can feel them watching me. I'm angry, but I'm stuck contemplating how I handle this. If I react, they will, too. I don't get a chance to decide how I'll address them when I hear leaves crunching and twigs breaking to my left. I stop and turn, facing the twin girls as they walk towards me. Absent-mindedly, I rub the tattoo on my wrist. I kicked that nervous tick a long time ago, but at this moment, it's the only thing bringing me any kind of comfort. That and the fact that what I am about to do may finally bring Ella and Rone peace. I don't know if she's left for good, but I want her in my house. She deserves to live a happy, peaceful life. This house deserves to be filled with love and laughter.

"Well, look who's back. Come to beg for our forgiveness?" I want to laugh out loud at the audacity of the small, frail girl in front of me. I roll my bottom lip between my teeth instead, biting hard enough to taste the blood seep out between my teeth.

"You could have hurt that boy." I bite the words at them. I don't miss the way Emma flinches. I realize then, I need to get through to her. I kneel down, putting my weight on my heels as I get down on their level.

"He should never have been here to begin with. You should have stuck to the plan." Jane's voice is cold as ice. Her eyes have no emotion. I think back to the morning I woke up after my accident. I was confused and angry, but instead of letting the anger overtake me, I somehow managed to find joy in the space I was occupying. She's angry, tired. I can't blame her for that. I turn my attention to Emma, reaching out my hand, silently begging her to come to me. Jane's eyes flare and she snaps her head in Emma's direction when she takes her first step forward. "Emma." Her tone is sharp and Emma hesitates. I give Emma a soft smile and raise my hand to her again. She looks at her sister before walking towards me.

"Emma, I can't begin to imagine the horror you've both been through. I'm sorry I didn't do more for you. I really am. But I'm here now, let me help you both." Her tiny hand is cold and I cover it in both of mine. Her lip quivers and her head drops between her shoulders. Jane lets out an empty laugh.

"Here *now. Now* that they are gone. We won't be used by you, by anyone. Never again." She moves toward Emma, but I pull her into me. Emma gasps at the contact and Jane's eyes narrow at me. I pull Emma into me and wrap her in a hug. For a moment, she doesn't move and I'm suddenly unsure what the rest of my plan is. A second before I drop my arms, Emma lets out a sob and wraps her skinny arms around my neck. She tucks her head into my shoulder and her body shakes. I rub her back and whisper, "It will be alright," over and over again.

I risk a look over at Jane. She watches with a look of sadness over her face. I reach an arm out for her, but she doesn't move. I wrap my arms around Emma for another moment before I gently peel her off me and hold her at arm's length. I brush her hair off her face and dip my face to look into hers.

"Emma, can you tell me what happened?"

"No, she will not. You've done enough for today. We're leaving." Jane stalks forward and grabs Emma's arm. Emma looks up at me, tears streaking her dirty face and her eyes are pleading with me. She wants out just as badly as the rest of us.

"Jane, stop," she says. When Jane doesn't listen and tries to pull her away again, Emma raises her voice. "Jane! Stop!" Her sudden outburst stops her sister in her tracks. She stares at her with wide eyes.

"He hugs you and now you're on his side?" Jane goes off and all I can do is sit here and watch years of anguish and unspoken trauma billow around them. "I'm the one who takes care of you. I've done everything to protect you since that night. All he does is give you a hug and you care about him now? I can't believe you'd turn on me so quickly. Me. Your sister!" Jane is panting, her tiny body shaking with barely contained rage.

"It's not your fault." Emma's small voice cuts her sister off. It's quiet for a long moment before she speaks again. I glance over at Jane, the rage that simmered so close to the surface has dissipated so quickly she's left standing with a stunned expression on her face. "I know you carry around the weight of what happened, but it is not your fault." Tears pool in her eyes again, but she continues. "I made the choice to follow him. You did nothing wrong."

"Stop. Don't say another word. We don't need to relive that night." Jane's voice isn't angry, it's just hurt, intertwining with each word she speaks. But Emma shakes her head.

"We're not reliving it, we're moving through it. Jane, can't you see? Ever since that night, we've been here." She throws her arms out to the side, motioning to the swaying trees around us. "We've been living this nightmare, ignoring what happened to us. I'm tired of it."

"I don't want to do this." Jane turns to leave, but Emma turns back to me. She takes a deep breath. "His name was Arthur Muddle. What an awful name; we always thought it was weird. But fitting for him, he was creepy. Something always felt off about him."

"Stop, Emma." Jane admonishes, but she's stopped walking, her back still turned to us.

Emma wraps her skinny arms around her middle. "But Dolly was so adorable, everyone loved her. He never did anything to make us uncomfortable, until one day I walked Dolly home. Jane and my other friends had run off down the street. Dolly was following us so I took her back home. He answered the door and asked me to come in and give Dolly a treat. I didn't want to be rude, so I followed them inside." She swallows before she continues. "Nothing really happened that time…" She trails off and this time it's Jane who speaks up.

"He didn't have to hurt you to make you feel uncomfortable. Say it, Emma. If we're spilling secrets, then spill!" The tears have now broken free and Emma's shoulders sag. Jane waits for her to say something, but when she doesn't, she turns to me. Her eyes are cold and she practically floats towards me. *"He touched her.* Twirled her hair around his fingers and ran his sweaty hands over her arms and hips. I ran back to get her and saw the whole thing. I was standing at the door. When he tried to touch her chest, I knocked on the door. That bastard acted like nothing happened." Jane turns around, throwing her arms out to the sides. "She's always been shy, I should have been there. I would have cut his hand off if I was in the room with them. I grabbed Emma and took her away." Jane looks at Emma. "I promised you then I'd protect you, remember?" Then she flicks her gaze to me. "Happy now? You know enough. Let's go!" She turns and walks to Emma.

"No." I don't even recognize my own voice. I've always been sure of myself, comfortable speaking in front of people and make friends easily. But the tone of my voice is different than I'm used to hearing. It's commanding, strong, and demanding. I stand, my legs tingling as blood rushes back to them. "I'm not happy. I'm fucking exhausted. And I know you both are, too. I want this to end, just like you do." I look at Emma, gritting out each word. "What happened after that?"

# FORTY-FIVE
## JUST KEEP WALKING

### ELLA

I park at the bottom of the hill. Before I can change my mind, I push out of my car and walk slowly through the grass. The last time I was here was a blur, I don't remember much from that day. Lots of people I didn't recognize, sympathetic hugs, and kind words. People cried, but not me. I had no tears left and spent that day in a fog. But as if my heart is still pulled to him, I find myself stopping right in front of the stone slab.

James Ronan Carter
April 17th, 1990 - May 24th, 2024
Husband - Father - Son - Friend
John 11:25

I drop to my knees in front of it and run my hands along the smooth top. "Hi, baby. I miss you. I'm sorry I haven't been by in a while. It's been…an interesting year." I contemplate how much to speak out loud, but settle on the important details. "Rone is so big, he looks more and more like you every day. I'm in big trouble once the girls notice him." I laugh and wipe my runny nose. "It feels weird talking out loud when you're not in front of me. I know I don't need to tell you anything because you're watching it all happen." I inhale through my nose and out through my mouth. The sky is so blue, a few big fluffy clouds float across the sky. I can almost hear his voice telling me to let go, so I open my mouth and talk. The sun trails across the blue sky, I laugh, I cry, but I don't hold back. I tell him about the peace I felt when Cillian held me in the kitchen, the relief I felt when I heard him comforting Rone after his nightmare. At some point, I laid down on my back while talking to him. The grass is warm on my back and I close my eyes, imagining his arms holding me to him.

———

*"Hey, cute girl!" A shadow moves over my face and I open my eyes. The sun is bright behind him and I can only make out his outline, but I know it's him. A chubby girl in his arms looks down at me. "Mama!" James smiles at her, his long legs bending as he bounces her up and down. I know I'm dreaming, but it's so real. The grass is soft when I sink my hands into it to push me to my feet. Standing at eye level with the angel in his arms, I stick my hand out and run it over the soft skin of my baby's face. She giggles and blows raspberries against my palm. Her brown hair is up in two little pigtails that stick out behind her ears. They are uneven and I laugh as I tug on them. She giggles and leans her pudgy face further into my hand. "I'm still trying to figure out how to do her hair." James smiles a shy smile at me. I move my hand up to his face then around the back of his neck, pulling his forehead to mine. We stay like that until Paige grabs a fist full of my hair and pulls. I wince, laughing as I pry her hand out of my hair. I kiss each finger and she nuzzles into James' chest.*

*"This is so real, you both are so real." My eyes bounce back and forth between them, trying to memorize every detail of the two of them holding on to each other. My eyes fill with tears, I let out a wet laugh.*

"She looks like me!" I feel tears roll down my cheek but make no effort to wipe them away.

"Looks like it's a tie now, baby." He lays a gentle kiss on her temple, looking back at me with a smile. "Walk with me?" I look around and finally realize we aren't at the cemetery. A large building stands in the background and off in the distance I can see the track that lines the football field of our high school. He starts to walk down the sidewalk and I watch them for a few moments before he turns, looking back at me waiting. I look back at the spot in front of the building where we'd meet after school to walk home together. I force my legs to move towards the pair, waiting a few yards ahead of me. When I catch up to him, we walk together in comfortable silence. He pauses for a moment and slides the sleepy, brown haired baby girl into my arms. I hug her to me, rubbing circles on her back, stroking her hair, memorizing the weight in my arms as she slowly drifts off to sleep. James throws an arm around my shoulders and we turn the corner at the end of the street.

I look up from my daughter and stare at James' face, outlined by the sun behind him. "What do I do now, James?" He tucks his hands in his pockets. His deep, brown eyes take in the houses as we walk past. It looks just as I remember.

He doesn't answer for a minute or two, like he's trying to find the perfect explanation. "What do you mean?" We stop in the shade of a tree and stand facing each other. When I look up at him, he laughs at the confusion clearly visible on my face. "I heard everything you told me today. It sounds like you already know what you need to do."

I groan. Even though I held nothing back, it doesn't mean I'm not embarrassed that he actually heard everything I said back in the cemetery. He tosses his head back and laughs out loud. I can't help but laugh with him. "You're not upset?"

"Upset?" He drops his head back down, bending at the waist so we're eye level. "Upset that you found a way to be happy? Absolutely not. How could I ever be upset that you've found a way to live and smile again?" He reaches up and holds my chin in his hand, stroking my jaw. "Am I jealous of that fucker? Hell yes. But never upset. I like him!" He turns again, this time reaching out and holding me around *the waist. Our hips bounce against one another as we continue our walk.*

*"You…like him? You don't even know him."*

*"I don't need to meet him to know that I like him." When he looks down at me, his eyes are full of emotion. "He made you smile, he took care of my boy. That's all I need to know."*

*"He's not even real," I say flatly.*

*"Neither am I, but you still love me." I roll my eyes at him, but he just gives me a wink and that smile that will forever be ingrained in my memories. "Even if he's not real, he showed you that you are capable of living and worthy of being loved. You deserve that, baby."*

*"He'll never replace you. No one will." I lean into him, wishing that it could last longer. His arm runs up my side, squeezing my arm and pulling me further into him.*

*"He doesn't have to." Up until this moment, I felt like moving forward was moving on. But my mom's words from earlier come to mind. Maybe this doesn't have to be forgetting what I had, but walking into what I could have. We reach the corner where one way leads to his parents' house and another to mine. He reaches for Paige, but I take a step back. He gives me a timid smile, tucks his hands in his pockets, and rocks back on his heels.*

*"I don't want to leave you two," I whisper as I look down at the girl in my arms. He hooks a finger under my chin and tilts my head back so I'm looking up at him. Leaning in, he presses his lips to mine. I open my mouth to deepen the kiss and I feel him smile on my lips. He wraps his arms around me and pulls me close, his big hands sliding down to cup my ass. We kiss for a long time, tongues running against each other, teeth holding onto a lip here and there. He groans into my mouth, pushing his body into me. I run the hand that isn't holding Paige through his hair and hold the back of his head to me. When we finally break apart, our foreheads fall together and we breathe heavily for a few moments. "I'll never be far, love. I'll watch you live a life full of endless happiness. And when it's time, we'll be here waiting for you."*

*I give Paige the tightest hug I can manage without waking her and gently pass her back to James. She snuggles into him, eyes still closed.*

*He kisses her forehead before wrapping us both up in a hug. "I love you," I whisper. He gives me one last, soft kiss before he grips one of my shoulders with his free hand and turns me to face the sidewalk that leads to my childhood home. He moves behind me, his mouth meeting my neck and moving the hair from one side to the other. He bends down, kisses me softly, and whispers, "Just keep walking." I feel him turn as he walks up the sidewalk and I turn to look back at him. He turns then, too, stops, and waves before walking backwards for a few paces. I turn and look ahead of me, but this time, it isn't the sidewalk to my old house. It's the long drive that leads up to my dream home in Spring Hill, Tennessee.*

*My feet sink into the gravel as I take my time walking up the driveway. For once, I'm in no hurry. I feel light and full, like I don't have to chase happiness any longer. The tall trees drop leaves on me and the sun casts half-moon shadows on the ground. The long grass fields on either side of the drive sway in the breeze like waves in the ocean. I watch them for a while before continuing my walk. As I get closer to the house, I hear laughter from the backyard. I pause at the steps to the front door and decide to walk around the house towards the sounds coming through the garden. When I walk under the stone arch, the colors in front of me make me pause. The garden is overflowing with color; flowers in every shade of purple, orange and red and yellow. Vines grow over the walkway inside the gate and I can see bright, red strawberries ready to be picked. The smell of lavender wafts over me when I push past the bushes along the walkway. It's heaven.*

*When I round the corner to the backyard, my heart skips a beat. There in the grass is Cillian. He's lying on his stomach and on his back are two wild boys. The older one looks just like Rone, but older. The younger one looks to be about two, and from where I'm standing, looks like a miniature version of Cillian. They laugh and wrestle in the grass, their voices sending my heart into overdrive. He's adorable with them. I find myself leaning against the house just watching them. Before too long, a little girl wobbles down the steps from the back door and her tiny feet move as fast as they can over to the pile of boys. Each one of them sits up the moment they hear her and they all crouch down, trying to get her attention. I smile at the sight, but my attention is drawn to the woman who just walked out of the house.*

*I blink a few times and my knees go weak. I look back at the boys and confirm that the older boy is Rone. The woman walks towards the boys who have scooped the baby girl up and are running her around the yard. Cillian stands and grabs the woman by the hips, pulling her into him. "Ella, sweetheart." Together, they hold each other and watch the kids running wild, making their way to the big oak. My mouth falls open when I notice the treehouse they are climbing into. Beautiful and perfectly built, not a burn scar in sight. Cillian smiles down at the woman, at me, and she smiles up at him.*

———

# FORTY-SIX

# YOUR TIME ISN'T DONE

CILLIAN

"Emma, what happened?" I'm close. I can feel it. It's a pressure slowly pushing down on me. My chest heaves as I try to fill my lungs. Emma opens her mouth, but before she can speak, Jane slams her to the ground.

"No!" I scream. Jane looks up from her sister, who is crumpled on the ground. Breathing but unmoving. "What are you doing?" I make a move towards Emma, but Jane advances on me. I feel a prickle of fear as I look into her dark eyes.

"I told you, we are done talking about this."

"No, *you* are done talking about this. Can't you see she needs to talk to someone? You said you wanted to protect her, but here you are, shutting her down every time she reaches out. *You* are the one hurting her." My voice rises with each word.

"Enough." Her voice is not of this world. It's dark, haunted, possessed. But I won't stop. Something is pushing me to keep going. I know enough of the story to piece it together for myself.

"He followed you, didn't he?" That makes Jane pause, her head tilts in anger. "You told your mom you were spending the night with a friend, but you didn't make it there, did you?" Jane says nothing, but takes a step towards me. I take one in her direction, not backing down. "Arthur was here, wasn't he? He told you he couldn't find Dolly and asked you both to help him. I know you tried to get away. I know he wanted Emma, but you wouldn't leave her. You wanted to protect her."

"I couldn't!" Jane screams at me. The ground trembles with her admission, but I push on.

"Tell me!" I yell back. I drop to my knees in front of her, begging, "It's not your fault, Jane." White hot pain zaps through me and I drop my head into my hands. "Please, don't do this." I look up into her black eyes and through the pain, I reach out and grab her.

"Let me go." Each word sends another wave of pain through my body. I'm trembling and can barely hold onto her. But I grit my teeth through the agony, and wrap my arms around her, pulling her into me. She tries to pry my arms from her body, but I hold tighter.

"It's ok, Jane. I forgive you." Emma's quiet voice breaks through the darkness around us. I feel it leak out of Jane and loosen my grip just enough for her to turn towards her sister. Emma has pushed herself up on her knees, hands twisting in her lap. "It's never been your fault to start with, but I know you carry it with you. If you need forgiveness, you have it. You were always my protector, but this was bigger than both of us. I didn't feel it at the end. I just looked at you and it faded away. Then we woke up here, together." She looks up at Jane and gives her a smile. It's not sad, it's full of love.

"Emma." Jane shrugs me off and runs to her sister. They slam into each other in a heap of tangled arms. "I'm so sorry, Emma, I tried. I really tried. I didn't want to leave you." Their tears fall together, splashing in the dirt around them. I watch them, waiting to see what will happen next. They both wipe their faces and Jane stands, reaching down to pull Emma to her feet. They smile at each other before turning my way. I stand and meet them in the middle of the clearing, bending down so we're eye level. I don't ask them to go on, instead Jane gives Emma an encouraging smile and she tells me herself.

"We were on our way to spend the night at our friend's house. It was shorter to pass through the woods and over the creek. Ever since that day in his house, I stayed away from him. Jane rarely left me alone when we passed by his house. We were taking our time, picking flowers and splashing in the water. He came out of nowhere. Our clothes were wet and he kept looking at me. Jane tried to tell him we needed to leave, but he kept following us. Then he said that Dolly was missing and he was in the woods looking for her. He asked us to help him. We were hesitant, but we all loved Dolly so we walked with him for a while. We got turned around and the sun was going down, we were lost." Emma takes a deep breath, but Jane continues the story, giving her sister's hand a squeeze.

"He attacked us. He pushed me down first and tried to get Emma to…" She trails off and I reach out and grab their free hands in mine. "It's ok, you don't have to explain all the details." If he wasn't dead already, I'd walk right over there and kill him myself. The thought of his hands on these girls makes me sick. "Thank you." Jane smiles at me, a genuine smile. It throws me off. "I jumped on his back and told Emma to run, but he was too strong, too fast. He got angry, hit us, dragged us, and then it went dark. We woke up in the woods alone. It didn't take us long to figure out we'd died. We couldn't get our mom to see us, she couldn't hear us. That was the worst part." They share a sad smile.

Emma speaks up, a small smile tugs at her lips. "We found ways to stay busy, though. Arthur was never caught, but that doesn't mean we didn't make his last couple years a living hell." My eyes go wide. *A house fire. He died in a house fire.*

"You…" I motion back and forth between them. They nod, looking a little too pleased with themselves, but I can't blame them for what they did. "Wow. Good for you two." I don't know what else to say. Jane steps forward and surprises me when she rests both her palms on my cheeks, tipping my head up to look at her. For the first time since I've known her, she looks free. Her eyes are the most amazing gray color and I'm lost in them before she speaks.

"Thank you, Cillian. I didn't realize how much I needed to be forgiven."

"It was never something you needed to be forgiven for." I kneel forward and pull them both into me. "I'm sorry I wasn't there for you both. I hope that we can all find peace now." I can't explain it to them, but it feels different. I feel different. Like when you get close to the end of a book; you don't really want it to end, but you know it's coming.

"I feel at peace. For the first time in so long, I feel it." Jane wraps her arms around my waist. Emma moves in and hugs me as well. We stand like that for a few moments before Emma releases me and puts her hand out to Jane. "Come on, sister. Let's go home." Without another word, I watch them start walking off, but instead of disappearing into the shadows of the trees around us, they fade away. Almost as if they dissolve in the breeze that has floated around me.

I turn and walk back to the house. Just as I break the tree line and hit the grass, I feel the exhaustion overtake me. I take a seat in the grass and lay back, letting the midday sun beat down on me. My eyelids grow heavy and I don't resist the pull of sleep.

———

*"Come on, man." A foot nudges my boot and I grunt at the sudden intrusion.*

*I let out an irritated grumble. "Go away!" I roll to my side, determined to sleep longer. The man nudges again and this time, I swing my foot, taking down the asshole who has decided to bother me when I'm finally at peace.*

*He grunts when he hits the ground, hard. "Shit!" I smile and try to settle into my dreams again. The man mumbles some curses and I give up my attempt to fall back asleep. I take my time before I sit up. Looking over at the body laying sprawled next to me, I don't recognize him. So I look up towards the house, but it's not my house in front of me.*

*"Where am I?" I mutter quietly, more to myself. But the annoying man next to me sits up, resting his arms on his knees and answers me.*

*"We're at my house, asshole." He rubs his elbow before standing, then leans down with a grin, sticking his hand out to pull me up. My body reacts before I can stop it. I reach my hand out and he pulls me up effortlessly until I'm face to face with him. We're about the same height, but he's got at least twenty pounds of muscle on me. I stare at him for a while, not quite able to place how I know him.*

*Tipping my head to the side, I ask, "How do I know you?" His grip on my hand tightens uncomfortably before he eases up enough for me to remove my hand from his strong grip and rub my fingers. He studies me for a bit before a big smile breaks out across his face. His blonde hair falls in his face like a 90's Brad Pitt. His eyes are dancing with humor and it hits me before he even speaks. "Rone? What the hell?" I stumble backwards and he just laughs, bending over to brush the remaining dirt off his jeans.*

*"The boy does look like me, huh?" He glances up, taking in the shock lining my face. "Dude, chill." He smacks my chest with a large hand.*

*Absent-mindedly, I rub the spot on my chest where I'm sure a bruise is forming. "I'm dead, aren't I?" This really makes him laugh, a deep laugh that shakes his whole body. His laugh is infectious and his energy is something I want to reach out, take a handful, and try to absorb into myself. Standing up tall again wiping his eyes, he looks at me. "You've always been dead. Didn't quite make it all the way, but we all can't be winners, can we?" He gives me a cocky smirk.*

*Rolling my eyes I wave a hand around. "Explain."*

*He crosses his arms over his chest, eyeing me before he caves. "When we die, we either come here..." mimicking my earlier motion, he waves his hand around, "or we wait." I look at him, waiting for him to continue, but he doesn't.*

*"You're really making me work for this, aren't you, man?" I'm desperate for answers, but he just eyes me with the same big, chocolate*

eyes that I've come to grow used to every day when looking at Rone. "Waiting for what?"

"You're in love with my wife, I'll make you work for whatever I want," he deadpans. I feel the blood drain from my face. James. His lips are in a tight smile, and for a moment, I'm afraid he's going to punch me. It's been a long time since I've thrown a punch. He's clearly an athlete, built and toned. I sat at a desk and drew for a living. Maybe I deserve a punch from the husband of the girl I've fallen in love with. After a while, he throws his head back and lets out that rich, deep laugh. "No hard feelings, man. I get it, she's gorgeous." He raises his shoulders and lets them drop. "I've watched you with her and Rone. You're a good guy. I'm happy they have you." He pauses then reaches out and grabs my shoulder. "You made me a promise, though, and I'm going to hold you to it."

He knows. He knows about that day when I sat on the steps and looked through his pictures with Ella. If he knows about that, what else does he know? Images of Ella in the shower, on her bed, my head between her legs. Suddenly, I feel dizzy and nauseous. I sit down on the steps that lead up to his house and bury my head in my hands. Running my hands through my hair, I look up at him. "I broke that promise, James. I'm so sorry." He takes a seat next to me. His shoulder nudges mine before he speaks.

"What matters now is that you keep that promise moving forward." He takes in a big gulp of air before he explains more. "When I said that some of us make it here and others wait, it means that your time isn't done yet. You were left there to serve a purpose, you still had something you needed to do." I'm too stunned to speak, too confused at what is happening to be able to string a sentence together. Just then, the door behind us opens and blonde twins poke their head out. When I saw them moments ago in the trees, they looked tired, frail, lost. But now they are glowing, their blonde hair shining in the sun and big smiles resting on their faces like they've always been there.

"James?" Emma calls out to him. He turns to look up at her. "It's time." He smacks his knees with his hands and stands. I follow and he turns to me again, both his hands finding my shoulders. He gives me a *small shake and I look up at his kind, brown eyes. "Take care of them for me, please." He rests his forehead on mine and I nod my head.*

*"I promise." He nods back before giving my shoulders a tap. He bounds up the steps and scoops a baby up off a blanket I hadn't noticed in the yard. She babbles at him, gripping his cheeks with her chubby little hands. She looks just like Ella—brown hair and blue eyes that sparkle in the setting sun. When James makes it to the door, he holds it open as the twins step inside. He turns back to me one last time, gives me a nod, and smiles before he walks in the house. The door closes behind him and I'm left standing, alone on a sidewalk.*

*I start to walk. The sidewalk ends at a corner and I look up one way and down another. Turning to my right, I keep walking, hands in my pockets and mind running through everything that has happened. I stop when the ground beneath my feet suddenly shifts from concrete to gravel. I look up and almost stumble backwards. My house, her house, our house. I can just make out the back of someone walking a little ways ahead of me. Auburn hair blows gently around her shoulders, the faint smell of gardenias and roses lingers in her path.*

———

# FORTY-SEVEN
## EMPTY

### ELLA

THE DRIVE TO MY PARENTS' HOUSE FROM THE CEMETERY SHOULD only take about fifteen minutes, but I take my time. The dream is still so vivid. I can feel the heavy weight of his arms wrapped around my shoulders, my lips still tingle from our kiss, my hands still smell like my little girl. Tears run freely down my face and I drive on autopilot, playing through every detail over and over, begging my mind to remember it until the day I die. About a block away from their house, I pull over and try my best to put myself together. I know what I need to do. I'm terrified, but determined. *Just keep walking.* If I close my eyes long enough, I can feel him whisper against my neck. Taking a deep breath, I round the corner and pull into their drive.

When I walk in the house, my dad is closing the door to my old bedroom. He gives me a smile and tiptoes down the hallway, pulling me into a hug. "He just fell asleep. I'm going to head to bed, too. The energy that kid has makes me feel my age." He kisses my cheek before turning back down the hall to his room. The light in the kitchen glows and I hear my mom muttering to herself. She always talks to herself when she bakes. I stand against the wall and watch for a moment before she catches me standing there.

"I've made this recipe a million times, but unless I read this damn card, it turns out like shit." Laughing, I walk into the kitchen and sit on the bar stool. Resting my chin in my hands, I watch her a moment longer. She moves around the kitchen, opening cupboards and drawers as she goes. "There's my girl." She glances up at me, smiling. For a moment, I wonder if she's forgotten I've been here for a few minutes now.

"What?" She puts a hand on her hip and points the spoon at me. Drops of the mixture drip off the end and land with a wet splat on the counter, but she doesn't notice.

"You've been living in a shell of your past self. I've been waiting for the day you came back to us." She goes back to her bowl like she didn't just drop a bomb on me. I sit there, my mouth hanging open.

"I've got to go back to the house tomorrow. Would it be too much to ask to leave Rone here for a couple days?"

She eyes me for a moment before sticking the spoon in her mouth and licking it clean. Tossing the spoon in the sink, she rounds the island and stands beside me. She grabs my shoulders and turns me on the stool so we're face to face.

"You go and do what you need to do, baby. We'll watch him. Olivia is coming by tomorrow, maybe we'll all drive up and spend a few days with you once you're ready. How does that sound?"

My stomach flips. I'm not sure what I'm going back to, but I have to go. Something is pulling me back and I feel deep in my gut that if I don't go now, I may never find what I had while I was there. I nod my head. With a kiss to my forehead, she goes back to her baking as I slide off the stool and head to the guest room.

———

I wake before my alarm, not like I slept much, anyway. The house is quiet, so I get dressed and grab my things as quietly as I can. Ducking in Rone's room, I take in his sleeping face, brushing the hair from his face and give him a gentle kiss. Then I walk out the door and make my way back to Spring Hill. The drive goes by quickly. I do my best not to think too much about what I could walk back into. Whatever it is, it's worth it. I have to try. It's not lost on me that what I'm chasing is a literal ghost, someone who is dead, but so real and alive to me. Can I live my life not being able to have the real thing? Maybe all I need is to tell him how I feel. How much he's done for me in the past few months. Not only has he made me realize that I want love again, I want to *be loved again*. He's protected me, made me feel free, happy, alive again. The irony of someone who isn't really alive, but isn't really dead, making me feel alive again, makes me laugh out loud.

As I pull off the 396 into town, I've quickly come to fall in love with what comes into view. I make my way down the streets before finally turning into the drive. Images of my dream flash through my mind and I park my car in the middle of the driveway. Turning off the engine, I get out and make my way up the house. I look up at the trees as I walk, breathing in the air that is starting to cool now that summer is fading into fall. When I reach the bottom step, I instinctively walk up to the porch, but I stop at the front door. I turn, jog down the steps and turn down the path that leads around the side, through the garden to the backyard. The garden isn't as colorful as I remember from my dream, but it's just as I left it. I pinch a lavender bloom from the bush, rub it between my fingers, and bring it to my nose. Closing my eyes, I let my mind listen and feel the energy around me. When I got out of the car for the first time, I felt oddly at home. Even when all the incidents with the girls were happening, this place still felt like home. Unsafe and unsure at times, but still felt like it's where I needed to be. My mind drifts to the girls and I say a silent prayer that they will find the answers they need to move on. Everything feels whole, like the trees have let out a breath they've been holding for too long and the birds chirp loudly around me, as if they've been afraid to sing their songs for too long. I open my eyes, a smile on my lips, and timidly peek around the corner into the backyard.

I know deep down that I won't see Cillian wrestling with an older Rone, but my heart still sinks when all I see is the green grass and a scorched circle of dead grass around the destroyed treehouse. My phone buzzes in my pocket, no doubt a text from Madi checking in on me after word got out about the fire or my parents sending a picture of the day's outing they're on with Rone. I ignore it and take the steps up to the patio and unlock the back door. When I step inside, I let out a sigh of relief. *I'm home.* Walking around the house, I can't help but listen for footsteps, or check around for a post-it note with a message from him. I make my way up the stairway to my bedroom, my heart racing at the thought that maybe he's waiting for me, curled up in his chair under my windows, waiting for me to come back to him. The anticipation makes my feet take the stairs two at a time and I grab the door frame as I fling myself into my room. It's just as I left it with the covers thrown back and clothes strewn on the floor. The chair is empty. I sink down into it, a vague hint of mint lingers in the fabric and I fight the urge to turn into it and inhale. I don't know what I expected, but I can't push away the disappointment that this is it.

# FORTY-EIGHT
## HOME
CILLIAN

"ELLA!" I CALL HER NAME AS SHE MOVES OUT OF SIGHT. I JOG UP the driveway and stop when I reach the front of the house. She's gone, this is it. My heart is racing so fast I feel like I'm going to throw up. Sweat gathers at the base of my spine. I race up the front steps and throw the door open.

"Ella!" I call again, but the house is still. It's quiet and empty, but that doesn't stop me from making a path through the house. Coming back into the living room, I sink into the couch, memories of the last night we sat here floating back through my mind. I close my eyes and allow myself one last moment to remember her before I deflate and prepare myself to accept that this is how my life will always be. Living in a memory, a shadow, a whisper. Not quite alive, not quite dead. Just in between. As tears threaten to spill over, a creak from upstairs makes my heart stop. I hold my breath, thinking I imagined it, but then comes another. The sound is coming directly over my head in Ella's room. I stand, not sure what I'm expecting, but walk out into the entryway and turn to the stairway. I snap my head up at the sound of a sharp gasp from the top floor. Blinking away the tears in my eyes, I stare at her, drinking her in despite the streaks of tears on her face. She is breathtaking.

*"Cillian."* It's not a question, but a statement. I'm frozen in place and barely have time to register feet barreling down the stairs towards me. She flings herself off the last step and I catch her in midair, pulling her body to me. She wraps herself around me, holding me to her like I'll disappear. I wrap an arm around her waist, my other hand works its way to the back of her head, tangling in her hair. I sink my face into her neck and inhale deeply, my whole body vibrates with need for her. "It's you." She pulls back, both hands on my face, turning me from side to side.

Laughing, I look into her ocean blue eyes. "Like what you see, sweetheart?" She smiles at me, running her fingers over my face.

"I can see you." Her hands make their way down my face, ghosting over my neck and shoulders. "I can feel you. You're...*real.*" I look at my arms wrapped around her and in the corner of my eye, I notice the mirror above the entryway. I turn with Ella still wrapped around my body. In the reflection, we stare at the two of us, holding one another.

"I haven't seen my reflection in ten years, sweetheart. And I don't want to go a day without seeing your face next to mine." I can feel her heart pounding. I don't look any different than I remember. Maybe a few more lines, maybe a little more my age, but for the most part, I'm the same. I'm me, I'm *here.* Our faces are smashed together, eyes bouncing around the other's reflection. Setting her down on her feet, I hold her arms as she steadies herself. I bring both hands to her face and angle her up so I'm looking down at her. I take a moment to admire her, like I'm seeing her for the first time. Her ocean blue eyes flick back and forth from my eyes to my lips. Mere inches separate us. If I leaned in the slightest bit, I'd taste her. I freeze as the realization sets in that I haven't kissed her yet. I've felt her skin under my fingertips, let my tongue run along her skin. I've tasted her many times, but the thought of finally having my lips on hers has me hardening in my jeans. I want to kiss her. Every ounce of my body is begging me to close the gap between us and kiss her. My mouth is dry and I suddenly feel like it's the first time all over again.

She smiles up at me and I know she's thinking the same thing. Her tongue swipes along her bottom lip and I pull mine between my teeth, watching as she slowly wets her lips. I groan and drop my forehead to hers. The tension between us turns into a buzz and all I can hear is the sound of my blood pumping in my ears. There is so much we need to talk about, so much we need to figure out. But I can't even begin to try and string two words together, not when I have her in my arms, looking at me like she wants me. Her hands run down my sides before slipping beneath my shirt. Her fingertips are smooth and my muscles tighten at her touch. She drags her nails against my skin, the sensation plowing through me as I groan in anticipation.

"Kiss me." The demand is so quiet I'm not sure if I've heard right. Letting my eyes focus on her again, I let my eyes roam over her body. Her chest rises and falls with her quick breaths and I can see her pulse beating rapidly just beneath the skin on her neck. Closing the distance between us, she pushes herself up on her toes and her lips brush against mine. The touch is so soft, but it makes me feel lightheaded. I can't breathe. Every thought, every fear slips away and all that's left is the woman before me. She stays there, her mouth ever so silently begging me for more. I feel her body begin to move away and she starts to sink back down to her feet. I slide my hands around her ass and roughly haul her up on my hips. We're both at the same level now and I can't help but smile against her skin. She lets out a breathy gasp and that little sound is my downfall. Spinning us, I walk us across the space and roughly push her up against the wall. My hands hold her ass and I dig my fingers into her soft skin. Pushing myself between her legs, I step into her, leaving no room between us with my length flat against her. She moans, her head falling back and hitting the wall with a hard thud. I kiss up her neck, savoring in the way she tastes like sunshine after a cloudy day. Like the promise of something more. I open my mouth, biting and sucking my way along her shoulder and neck. She rewards me with a tremble that I can feel run from her head to her toes. Her body instinctively rubs up against me, silently asking for more. I run my hot tongue along her jaw and when I reach her mouth, I don't hesitate. I bite her chin, pulling her back down to me and take what I've wanted to have for so long.

Our lips melt together. *"Fuuck, Ella."* It's all I manage to get out before she runs her fingers through my hair, scrapping my scalp and pulling me back to her mouth. Slow, passionate kisses pass between us, a longing for one another like I've never felt before. My tongue slips out and runs along hers. She opens her mouth and lets me in. We are a mess of scraping tongues and desperate hands. We slam into each other rough and hard, making up for all the times before. She grinds into me, shifting her hips the best she can while I still have her pinned against the wall. I drop her down onto my thigh and I can feel how hot and wet she is through my pant leg. I feel like I've run a marathon in five minutes. My heart is beating so hard against my chest I'm in physical pain. My mind is lagging, trying to catch up to what the fuck is happening.

The only sound in the quiet house is our heavy breathing. I look up to meet her stare, her lips are wet and swollen from our kisses, her cheeks flushed in the most adorable way. She brings her hands up to cup my face. Closing my eyes, I let myself settle into her touch, feeling her seep into all the cracks that have broken me apart over the last decade. Her fingernails scratch at the scruff on my face and I dig my fingers into her ass. My palms drag over her body, settling on her hips and slowly moving her against me again.

She drops her head into my chest, breathing fast. "This is crazy." She fists my shirt in her hands and drags me to her. I move my hands to her face and bring our foreheads together again. I can't not be touching her. After all this time in and out of reality, I don't want to waste another minute not holding her against me. "What do we do now?" Her hands run over my chest. "You're here…you're so real."

I run my nose along hers and whisper, "I'm real, sweetheart. And I want to be here with you. Ella, I…" I pause. The urge to tell her how I really feel pushes against the surface, but it suddenly feels too heavy. *What if she doesn't want me?* It's a fleeting thought, gone in a heartbeat because this woman shifts against my thigh. Any thought of her not wanting me packs up and walks right out the door. My voice is breathy, full of lust and need. "I want you." I slam my mouth back on hers, pushing my way inside and drinking her in. "God, I fucking want you."

The smile I've missed so much the past couple days creeps across her face. "Take me, Cillian." Her smile turns devilish. I can sense that she wants to say something else, but she swallows it down. I'll wait as long as she wants me to, as long as she promises to be mine. Her throat bobs before she mumbles, "Maybe we can talk about all of this…after we…" she trails off, but her eyes glint when she looks into mine. I wrap my arms around her again, pushing us off the wall. Her legs hold tightly to my hips as I walk us down the hall towards the kitchen.

"I think that is a great plan," I say, setting her on the island.

She looks around the kitchen, confusion written across her face. "What are you doing?"

Giving her a feral grin, I wink at her. "I'm going to show you why I made this island so big." Pushing her legs apart, I step between them. Her eyes go big with recognition, then she settles back on her elbows, letting her knees spread wider.

# FORTY-NINE
## CALL ME THAT AGAIN

ELLA

*Fuck. Me.*

When he walked in the front door and yelled my name, I thought I had imagined it. I sat in his chair, praying for him to somehow be real. To defy everything I know to be true and just be *real*. Seeing him at the bottom of the stairs took my breath away. I'm pretty sure my heart stopped. Before my mind could catch up, I was throwing myself down the stairs and into his arms. *Real. So real.* The feel of his body, his hair, the way he smells. I can't stop touching him. I want him, I need him. I've always been drawn to him, like the waves to the shore, but at this moment, I *crave* him. The desperation that I feel for him is consuming. If I don't taste him right this second, I might die.

His hands push my knees apart and he runs them down my legs. Stepping back, he just looks at me, soaking in every inch of me like he's seeing me for the first time. I shift so I'm sitting back on my elbows and we watch each other. Chests heaving, our breaths are ragged and I feel like all the oxygen has been sucked out of my lungs. He is stunning. Even in that simple, white t-shirt, stretching across his broad shoulders. Through the fabric I can tell his chest is defined. I have flashbacks to the night in my room where I could see him lying beneath me. But this time, *this time* I know he is here for good. The feeling is concrete. Somewhere deep inside, I just know he won't fade away. My eyes travel down his strong arms laced with veins to his hands clenched at his side like he's holding himself back. But *fucking hell, his hands.* Seeing them is a new experience. I want to feel them again. Large palms and long fingers. I move to squeeze my thighs together at the sudden rush of need between my legs, but his hands snap out to hold them apart. I've felt those hands and fingers before and I lick my lips in anticipation. He follows my movement, and through the sun pouring in from the windows against the wall, I can make out small flecks of gold, as if someone took a paintbrush and splattered it across the green of his eyes.

Suddenly feeling more alive under his stare, I lean forward and reach to the hem of my sweater. In one quick step, he's in front of me again, his fingers circle my wrists. "Not yet, sweetheart." His voice is low and husky, tumbling over me as a soft moan escapes me. He smiles against my lips before licking them, making my eyes roll. He moves my hands to the side and replaces them with his own. Slowly, torturously slow, he pulls it over my head and arms, tossing it across the room. Groaning at the sight of me in my lace bra, he reaches behind me and in one quick motion, the lace falls off my skin. I watch as his eyes widen with lust and he bends down, taking one nipple in his mouth. His tongue circles the tip, hot, and wet, and so fucking sexy. My hands sink through his inky hair and when he growls against me, I pull. Not able to get my fill of seeing him before me, I reach over his head, running my hand down his spine. My fingers curl around the soft fabric and I pull it up his body. He releases my nipple with a pop, just long enough to pull the shirt off before latching on to the other one. I hiss as his teeth graze the sensitive skin. He sucks and tugs, making my head fall back. I lean into him, relishing in the feel of him.

Cillian runs his hands over my bare skin, up and down each side, slowly working their way to the dip between my breasts. "I told you once before that I would worship your body. And I promise to worship it every day for as long as you'll let me." He licks the skin between my breasts and teases the peaks with his fingers. Moaning, I rub shamelessly against him.

"Take these off." I tug at the waist of his jeans. "I've waited too long to see all of you." With a cocky smile, he slowly undoes the button, the sound of the zipper sliding down each of the teeth lights a fire inside me. I wiggle against the granite countertop, a shiver running through me. I remember how he felt in my mouth, smooth and hard. The memory of holding him in my hand has me biting my lip in excitement. Now that it's in front of me in the light, I try and fail to hide my excitement. When I break my gaze away from his hands and look at his face, he stares hungrily back at me. Then he winks at me, the man *fucking winks*. I quirk an eyebrow at him and he gives me the sexiest grin I've ever seen. I lean forward, licking the smile on his face, capturing one lip between my teeth and holding him there. I swat his hands away from his waistband and finish the job for him. I reach in and free him, holding it in one hand. My fingers barely touch around him, but I run my hand up and down, twisting as I go.

"Fuck me," he mutters. I release his lip and whisper, "I plan to." He sets a new record of pulling my leggings and underwear off, just about pulling me off the counter in the process. They drop to the floor with a slap.

Running his palms up my thighs, he dips a finger between my legs. Dropping his head back, he murmurs a string of curses before dropping his face back to me. "So wet for me, sweetheart." I arch into his touch, but he drags his hands back down my inner thighs. He smirks when I pout at him. "What do you want first, my fingers or my mouth?" My eyelids flutter and my blood heats, pumping through my body so fiercely I feel like I'll combust. I shake my head, unable to get the words out. Looking down between us, I give him a tug, urging him closer to me. "Greedy for me, aren't you?"

A shiver runs over my skin. "I've had your fingers and mouth already, I want *all of you* now." He wraps a large hand around mine and guides himself to me, rubbing his head against me. His other hand grips my hip, holding me from pushing into him. For a moment, we're still. His eyes lock with mine and inch by inch, he pushes inside of me. I let out a satisfied moan. I'm stretched so full, I doubt I can fit any more of him. But looking between us, my eyes widen when I see that he's not even half way in. He lets out a little chuckle and lifts my chin, bringing my eyes back to his.

"You can take it." I whimper at the rasp in his voice. "And you will look at me until I feel you come so hard you see stars." All I can do is nod in response. I've gone too long feeling his gaze on me, but never being able to look into those mossy eyes. I sure as hell don't plan to look away now. He moves in so slowly it hurts. When he bottoms out, he stays there, letting me adjust. I lean in and take his mouth in mine. His kisses match the pace of his hips thrusting between my legs, pulling out and slowly pushing back in as I move with him. Meeting him each time, my skin is slick with sweat. I feel the heat pool deep inside me, feel the spring inside me wind tight as he moves against me. His pelvis rubs against my sensitive skin while he swells inside of me. My ass slips against the countertop and I almost slide off the edge until his broad hands catch me and hold me in place. I tilt my head back as the pleasure builds, but he wraps his fingers in my hair and holds my head forward. "We're so good together, you're made for me. Look at me when you come. Milk my cock, sweetheart."

*Holy shit.* I feel him all around me, hand in my hair while the other moves my hips to meet his every thrust. Pressing my breasts against him, his soft dusting of chest hair rubs against my hard nipples. "Cillian, I'm..." Hurdling off the cliff into the deep end, floating, lost at sea. His thrusts come faster as he chases his high while I run right after him. Stars. I see stars, just like he said I would. He stills inside me before collapsing on top of me. "Fuck, sweetheart." His breath is hot against my neck, the cold counter feeling heavenly against my overheated skin. I run my hands down his back, feeling his skin under my fingertips. I feel him slip out of me and he moves around the kitchen, grabbing a towel and running it under the faucet. I don't move. My body is spent and for the first time in a long time, my mind is quiet. I turn my head and watch him walk back towards me, blinking a few times to make sure the man before me is real. He pauses in front of me, eyes making their way over my naked flesh. I feel the heat in his gaze and watch as he carefully cleans me up. When his hands touch the oversensitive skin on my inner thighs, I hiss at the contact. His eyes snap to mine. His pupils dilate and I feel the heat of his stare sink into my skin, shivering at the thought of having him again.

He lets out a feral growl, throwing the towel across the kitchen into the sink. In a quick movement, he places both of his palms on either side of me and hauls himself onto the island, hovering over me. Sex permeates the air and I suffocate on the heaviness of how I feel about this man. I crawl backwards, slipping over the surface of the countertop. Slipping one arm around me, he effortlessly flips us over and I find myself kneeling over his torso. His eyes are full of mischief and desire, the way he's looking at me has my heart fumbling for grip. He palms my ass, pulling me closer to his face. Dropping my hands on either side of his gorgeous face, I stop him. "Ian, what..." His fingers dig into my fleshy cheeks. Eyes closed, he runs a hand through his disheveled hair before those green, gold eyes flare open. "Call me that again, sweetheart."

Leaning down closer to him, I trace the shell of his ear with my tongue. "Ian," I drawl, planting kisses all down his neck and pulling his skin between my teeth. His body tenses and then he yanks me up and over his mouth. "Let me eat." Three words and a split second later, I'm gasping at the fresh wave of ecstasy that washes over me as his mouth latches onto my clit. He runs his tongue between me. "Mmm, we taste so good together." My eyes roll back and I give into the sensation that works its way over my body, happy to be consumed, figuratively and literally, by the solid mass of man between my legs. I tug at his hair, clawing at his hands on my thighs, begging for more. He delivers over and over again until I'm shaking, barely able to hold myself up. His abs flex beneath me when he sits up and pulls me into him. Burying his face in between my breasts, he mumbles something I can't quite make out.

I pull his head back an inch. "Talk to me." He smiles up at me and my fragile heart quakes at the image of him. "All this time I've been waiting to go to Heaven." He lets out a soft laugh and kisses the spot above my heart. "But all along, I've just been waiting for you."

# FIFTY
# OUR ROOM
CILLIAN

HER BODY RELAXES AGAINST ME AND SHE NUZZLES INTO THE SPACE between my neck and shoulder. Her soft kisses send my emotions into a frenzy. I hold her tightly to me, too afraid to let go. Ella's head falls back and she lets out a laugh when I slide us off the counter and make my way towards the stairs. That sound, *God*, that sound is something I will chase for the rest of my life. Her hold around my neck tightens when I start up the stairs.

"Where are you taking me?" I take in each picture as we pass them. James smiles back at us, his words playing over in my mind. *Take care of them for me, please.* I dip my chin as I make it up to the hallway.

I lean down and whisper against her ear, "To our room." *Our* room. It sounds so natural, it feels so right. I slow at the landing, looking down to her. "This may come as a shock to you, but you need to tell me right now if this isn't what you want. I'm yours, Ella. Every piece of me. You're my ocean, pulling me in when I thought I needed to run away. And unless you tell me that you want me gone, I am all in." Continuing through the doorway, I set her on the edge of the bed. She's still naked before me, so I reach out and grab the throw blanket at the foot of the bed and wrap it around her. I kneel naked between her legs, reaching my arms around her waist as I wrap my arms around her and pull her into me. I rest my chin just above her breasts and tilt my head up to look at her. I can feel my eyes cloud over with emotion. She gives me a soft smile and reaches out, her small palms holding my face. Leaning into her touch, I close my eyes and say what I have wanted to admit for what feels like a very long time, "I love you, Ella." My admission takes her off guard and I hear her take a sharp breath. I quickly push forward. "You don't have to say it back, but I love you so fucking much. I promised you I would be whatever you needed me to be and I still will. But honestly, if you don't want me, I don't know what I'll do. Living with the thought that one day I would wake up and this all would be a dream shattered my fucking heart. But somehow, every day I woke up and got to live in a weird alternative reality with you. And that was fine with me. I would have been happy if that was my path, because it meant I got to have you."

"Cillian, I…" I kiss her palm and keep going. The words are stuck in my throat and I swallow hard to push the emotion away. If I don't get all of this out in the air between us, I'll suffocate.

"I thought I was lost before, but when you and Rone walked out that door…" I shudder at the memory of watching them walk away and the sound of her car driving down the drive. "That image is one I never want to see again. You gave me another chance at life, Ella. I don't know how or why, but I never want to live a life that doesn't have the two of you in it."

Her thumbs scrape over the rough stubble on my face. She closes her eyes and swallows before she speaks. "Cillian, I was lost when I came here, broken beyond repair. You picked up every piece that fell as I walked around numb to everything. You held on to those pieces until I was ready to be put back together again." She wipes unshed tears from her eyes. "I need you in my life.." She lets out a sob and throws her arms around my neck, leaning back on the bed and pulling me with her. "I love you, Cillian. Never leave us, *please.*"

My heart threatens to break through my chest and my eyes fill with tears. I would have waited a lifetime to hear her say those words, but hearing them now and feeling how deeply she feels the same is almost too much to comprehend. "Never, sweetheart. I promise." Her body shakes and I roll so I'm on top of her. Holding my weight up with one arm, I brush the hair from her face and kiss her. Gentle and slow, like I want to live wrapped up in her for the rest of my life. I pull back and stare into her blue eyes, getting lost in them like I have since the second she stepped out of her car that first day. The woman who was so broken is long gone. The woman before me is full of life. A life I want to be a part of.

"Where do we go from here?" She strokes my freckles across my cheek, over my nose, and across the other side. "How do we explain all of this?" I move to rest against the headboard and she climbs between my legs. I pull her back against me and revel in the feel of her skin against mine. Her hair tickles my nose when I nestle my face into her neck. I take my time responding, too caught up in the woman in my arms. I breathe her in, her familiar smell filling me. I sink back into the pillows, running a hand through my hair. My mind races, trying to think of how we could ever explain this when it doesn't even make sense to me.

"All I care about is being here with you, building the life I've waited so long to have. We'll walk through whatever comes our way. Together."

"Promise?" She squeezes my arms tighter around her and tilts her head back to look up at me. Her eyes stare into mine, blue waves pulling me in and pulling me under. Nothing else matters; not the hows, whys, or what ifs.

"Promise." I smile down at her, wrapping one hand around her neck and stroking her cheek with my thumb. I pull her into me, kissing her again and again.

# FIFTY-ONE
## THREE YEARS LATER

## CILLIAN

"Holy shit!" I spin around at the voice behind me. Mike, my childhood best friend, strolls across the grass. His long legs close the distance between us quickly. Reaching me, he throws an arm around my shoulder, shaking me slightly. Together, we look up at the sweeping oak tree, its bark showing the faintest scars from the fire three years ago. The branches have grown back stronger, giving a more solid base for the new treehouse we've just finished building. The smell of fresh cut wood and lacquer lingers in the air. For a while, the two of us stand there, admiring what we've made. The silence is broken by the thunder of little feet rushing out the backdoor and down the patio steps. Four pairs of feet come to a skidding stop next to us. I look down into chocolate brown eyes. Somehow in the past few years, Rone has grown up, now reaching just above my waist. He gazes up, taking in the large windows, tall ladder, and tire swing hanging to the side.

"Holy shit!" him and Ty say in unison. Mike and I reach down and flick their ears. Rubbing their red ears, they look up at us, "Ouch!" Rone says, I nod my head next to him and he looks down at his little brother. "Sorry, Sammy." His two-year-old brother holds the small hand of Mike's little girl, Rae. Sammy puts his other hand over his eyes, pushing black hair like mine out of the way, shielding him from the afternoon sun. "Hoy sit," Sammy says, giggling as the four of them take off to the tree, the older boys scrambling up the ladder as fast as they can. I eye Mike. "They get that shit from you." Laughing, we turn at the sound of laughter coming out of the house. The air gets stuck in my lungs and Mike smacks my back a few times as I cough and sputter.

Ella stares back at me, smile wide and blue eyes shining back at me. Even after three years of holding her every night and waking up next to her every morning, she still takes my breath away. She leans down and places the little feet of the girl she is holding in her arms into the soft grass. Grace wobbles for a moment and then takes tentative steps towards me. I rush over to her, falling to my knees a few feet in front of her. "Come on, Gracie sweetheart, you got this." Her big, green eyes look up from under deep, auburn hair. She stumbles into my arms and claps her chubby hands together.

"Wow, that is…" Ella looks up at the massive treehouse built into the oak tree. "Holy shit. I don't even know what to say, it's amazing!" Mike tucks Madi under his arm, one hand over his mouth trying to cover his smile, he throws me a wink as the two of them walk over to the tree.

"I told you I was good with my hands," I whisper into the soft curve of her neck. She trembles beneath my lips and I smile against her skin. We walk over to the blanket on the grass and together, we sit and watch the life we built together play out around us. Her in my arms, my kids running wild, my house glowing in the background. I look up at the sky as white, puffy clouds float on by and I drink in the life that I get to live. A second chance at the life I was always chasing.

———

# ELLA

I watch Cillian as he stares up at the sky, taking in every line that has taken up a permanent spot on his skin over the past three years. Every line is well deserved, earned, and cherished. I settle back against his chest, watching the boys play in the treehouse and the two little girls teeter around the trunk of the tree. A phone buzzing beside me draws my attention and I grin at the sound of Cillian's deep voice when he answers.

"This is Ian." He gives my shoulders a squeeze as he stands and heads inside to the office to take his call. Three years ago, we laid in our bed, making promises to each other and planning out how we'd ever explain the impossible. He grew up here, people knew him, the town planned his *funeral*. We stayed up all night tossing ideas around, everything from moving to a different country, which was ruled out because he was Cillian Rose, *deceased*, Cillian Rose. To boarding up the windows and never leaving, which we quickly decided wasn't possible. As the early sun worked its way over the trees and through the window, we settled on the story we've been spewing to anyone who questions us. No matter how hard we sell the lie that Ian is a distant relative, a love child of late Martha Rose's husband William, we still get the double takes and curious glances from people in town. Cillian agreed to keep his signature long hair trimmed shorter to play into our lie a bit more. Ian is a structural engineer who designs buildings on the *side*. Mike was quick to hire him to his construction firm to help us solidify the details.

Mike and Madi, on the other hand, were not so easy to fool. They took one look at Cillian and both burst into tears. When we tried to convince them that Ian had shown up one day looking to reconnect with a lost family member and somehow we fell in love, Madi grabbed Cillian's wrist, held it up in the air, and pointed to the tattoo. The whole story went to shit. We spent the entire day sitting with them, retelling every detail of the summer over and over. Madi swears she knew something was up when I told her someone named *Ian* had made Rone pancakes that one morning. If it's affected them negatively in any way, they haven't let on. Mike and Cillian fell right back into where they left off, as if no time had passed.

My parents and Olivia adore him, borderline obsessing over him. I see how they look at him, like they can't put into words how happy it makes them that I found someone to give another piece of my heart to. As if I can feel him making his way back to me, I glance at the patio door just as a head of black as night hair and bright emerald eyes emerge through it. He stops when he notices me staring and gives me a devilish grin. God, I pray that even in the next life, my heart still skips a beat when he looks at me like that.

———

## RONE

Leaning on the railing of the treehouse, I watch my mom stare at Ian as he walks across the grass. His bare feet trek through the long grass before he settles himself behind her, pulling her against his chest and laying a kiss on her forehead. They are so in love it's gross. They kiss way too much and I have to leave the room when they whisper and giggle to each other. I gag and tell them to get a room, to which they always howl with laughter.

I still have vague memories of my real dad, James. When I look in the mirror, I see him staring back at me. I miss him, I really do, but Ian just…fits. There is a piece of our life that will always be missing; my dad and baby sister in heaven. But I never questioned why Ian just showed up one day in my kitchen and made the most amazing pancakes I've ever tasted. My mom's tears became less and she smiled more. He felt safe and I never had to worry about being alone. He showed up and never left.

I remember pulling up the drive after my grandparents

brought me back home after our trip to Bama. The house came into view and there he was, sitting with my mom on the front steps. There was a happiness that washed over me, like waiting for something to finally happen and when it does, you can breathe deep again.

As if he can feel me looking at them, Ian looks up into the tree, his eyes landing on me. He grins up at me and I can't help the smile I give him back. Then he does what he's always done, what I remember my other dad doing.

He winks.

———

# ACKNOWLEDGMENTS

This book has been a journey. To be honest I still don't feel worthy enough to call myself an "author". When this story came to mind I pushed it off for days, I didn't tell anyone about it until I'd finished my first draft. It's not easy putting something so personal out there to the world. Being vulnerable and willing to take constructive feedback is vital, yet, hard to do. I met SO many incredible people while creating "Promise". To each and every one of you that I've met along the way, THANK YOU!

To my husband. Thank you for hearing this crazy idea and never once making me feel like I was incapable of making something amazing. You cried, laughed, and rolled your eyes. I adore you, you are the *ultimate* book boyfriend.

To my boys. If you've made it this far I'm going to assume you read this book. Don't ever tell me, let me believe that you think I'm innocent and naive. But if you did, I hope you learned that love is not a one size fits all. Your heart never stops growing. Stay wild, I love you.

To my sister Hannah, you never cease to amaze me. You are determined and fierce. I am proud of the woman you are, I love you.

To the Smut Society, y'all are the best friend group I could ever ask for. You all have shown me how to embrace every part of myself. I love each of you for this wonderfully chaotic book club.

To Hannah, my editor. GIRL!! You are the ultimate hype woman. From the moment we met, I knew you were special.

Thank you for making me feel like this was possible. You are incredible at what you do. Now go eat some frozen Jr. Mints.

Ashley, I am so proud of you. I am so happy and blessed that we met on this wild ride of publishing our first book. If you haven't read a book by Ashley Vargas yet. Get to it!

Sharon, Kat and the whole Inkspire team, thank you for taking a chance on this book. Your time, support, and encouragement means the world to me.

And last but most importantly, to you, the reader! Thank you for picking up this book written by a nobody, 30 something, working mom from Utah. Supporting independent authors and helping us accomplish something as amazing as publishing a book goes beyond a simple thank you.

# ABOUT THE AUTHOR

Leigh Morgan is an emerging author of contemporary romance. She lives in UT with her husband and three wild boys. When she isn't writing or reading, Leigh works part time in the music industry. She's a windows down music turned up loud kind of woman.

This is Leigh's first book, and hopefully not her last. Take a look at what's to come on her social media accounts.

Instagram: @leigh_morgan_author
TikTok: @leigh_morgan_author

xo

Leigh

instagram.com/leigh_morgan_author
tiktok.com/@leigh_morgan_author

www.ingramcontent.com/pod-product-compliance
Lightning Source LLC
Chambersburg PA
CBHW032355310726
48973CB00007B/2022